RICH
AND
PRETTY

RICH
AND
PRETTY

RUMAAN ALAM

An Imprint of HarperCollins*Publishers*

HarperCollins books may be purchased for educational, business, or sales promotional use. For information please e-mail the Special Markets Department at SPsales@harpercollins.com.

FIRST EDITION

Designed by Ashley Tucker

Library of Congress Cataloging-in-Publication Data has been applied for.

ISBN 978-0-06-242993-3

16 17 18 19 20   OV/RRD   10 9 8 7 6 5 4 3 2 1

for David, for Simon, for Xavier

RICH
AND
PRETTY

Sarah talks too loud. It's a problem.

Usually, Lauren tries to correct for the pitch of Sarah's voice by whispering. It never works. This has been going on for years.

"I mean, when is the last time I even saw you?" Sarah gestures around the restaurant, wineglass in hand like a scepter in a queen's. The Gewürztraminer sloshes close to the rim of the paper-thin glass but doesn't spill.

"I saw you . . ." Lauren can't remember. Two weeks, maybe three? Maybe twenty days. Possibly a month. A month doesn't seem so long. A lot happens in a month. They're busy, they're adults, it is what it is. She shrugs.

"Anyway." Sarah puts the glass down. She leans forward across the table, like they're about to start conspiring. "How are you?" She reaches a hand out, as though to take Lauren's.

Lauren pulls her hand back, a reflex. She sips her own drink, vodka, soda. The ice tinkles prettily: There's no more inviting sound to her, it's sophistication, like a British accent or that call-and-response of high-heeled shoes on tile. "I'm fine."

What sort of question is this, and is it even truly a question? She's the same. They're both the same.

"How are you?" There's no other way to answer the question than by asking it back. This is the point. It's catechism, not conversation.

Sarah clears her throat. There's a smile at the corner of her mouth, but there almost always is; she's almost always happy, she has very little reason not to be. She's charmed, her life is charmed. "Well," she says.

Of course, there's a reason they're here, this unremarkable bistro, poor lighting, potted plants, chalkboard menus. Sarah has news, and news is something she believes should be delivered in person. She should have gone into a field where you're often charged with having life-altering conversations: oncology, the Nobel Prize committee. As it is, she has no field in particular, and her news is rarely life altering, to anyone but herself. They are best friends.

The thing that's galling, or irritating, or whatever the word is, is that though it's Sarah who always wants to make plans, Sarah is always so, so busy. She's at the store twice a week, sometimes more often, it's a shifting schedule. She has a standing dinner engagement with her parents, Sunday nights: the three of them, cozy in their big house, roast chicken off those handmade ceramic plates her mom bought in Sausalito forty years ago. Always a roast chicken; potatoes, soaked for hours so they bake up crispy, with rosemary; chardonnay from old jam jars. Sometimes a fourth guest, one of her dad's acolytes, or one of Sarah's friends. Lauren has been that fourth, many times, and now, presumably, there's Dan, too, placid, efficient Dan. She can picture the orange and yellow plates perfectly. Other nights, it's a movie with this friend, the theater with that friend, this person is reading at that bookstore downtown, this person is giving a lecture, there's that dance performance at the theater space on whose board Sarah's mother has sat for decades, or she's with Dan, reliable Dan whose face Lauren can barely stand, but whatever, they're in love. Yet it's Sarah who calls, Sarah who sends text messages and e-mails, *Hey, I never see you, where are you, why can't I see you, how about a week from next Wednesday?* Lauren puts it off, and puts it off. She likes the frisson of improvisation. Fun cannot be scheduled. Fun simply occurs.

"This is fun," Lauren says, for no reason.

"I'm getting married," Sarah says.

She holds up her hand, but there's no ring on it. Lauren would have noticed. She's a thirty-two-year-old woman. She sees every ring, whether she wants to or not.

Sarah waves her hand about again. "The ring is being sized. It was his grandmother's. I don't know why I'm holding my hand up like this."

"You're getting married!" Lauren lifts her glass in salute. She's probably supposed to scream. To feel tears stinging the corners of her eyes. Unsure what to do next, she grins like a maniac.

"I'm getting married!" Sarah, louder even than before, but no one cares; even bystanders are excited about marriage.

"To Dan?"

Sarah looks at her. Her smile doesn't fade, exactly. It doesn't diminish, not really. But something else slips into it, or over it. It changes somehow. "Yes," she says. "Of course."

"Of course!" Lauren yells.

Huck and Lulu throw parties. It's their thing. The second act of their American lives. Huck does other things, too: teaches those sought-after seminars colleges trumpet in their promotional materials, gives talks at the Council on Foreign Relations, takes the shuttle to D.C. to meet think-tank people to do think-tank things, writes querulous letters to the editors of policy journals, shuffles to his office on the fourth floor of the house to produce op-eds or the introductions to books his friends and students have written. Henry "Huck" Thomas (CNN's chyron usually includes the quotation marks; the nickname's origins are forgotten): not a maker of history, but present at its conception. Confidant to presidents (some of them, anyway), an ambassador to the world on behalf of what he's always believed to be its greatest nation. Huck is hardworking, sure, but it's possible to view his rise as evidence of something else—luck; right time, right place; the indomitable spirit of a certain kind of white man. Arriving at the State Department just as one presidency was collapsing, then proving himself invaluable as the subsequent officeholder tried to find his feet.

That brief American presidency had birthed Huck's long and successful career. He knew enough about the game to get his wife's assets out of Venezuela by 1979, and, from there, into all the right places. They've been millionaires for at least that long. That is his specialty: being a step ahead of things.

Huck's office has dormer windows from which you can see the backs of all the houses on the next block over. Lauren and Sarah used to smoke cigarettes in there, fanning the smoke out of the open window, even though no one would have smelled it because at the time Huck himself went through half a pack a day, the Kents burning away to nothing in the ashtray as he typed furiously about what Johnson got wrong in Vietnam or the welfare state's inherent evils. They were idiots as teenagers.

Lulu is retired. Her one album—a couple of traditional corridos, a Chilean tune closely associated with Joan Baez, a few folky pop songs—remains a cult favorite, had a bit of a renaissance when one of her originals was used over the opening titles of what turned out to be a blockbuster holiday film. Royalties: one way the rich get richer. The voice is not entirely gone, though it's changed, deepened, grown slack, as female voices do with age. She'd never seriously made a go of it, had ended up married while only twenty-four, which was how it was done at the time. She'd followed the rest of the script: decamping to New Haven and making lunches and dinners for Huck, as though he were her child, tagging along to Washington and dressing to impress for various, boring parties, giving birth, going out to dinner, decorating the Connecticut house, hosting fund-raisers for this and that. It's time-consuming, being a part of this family. Lauren never knew three busier people. It's remarkable that none of them actually have jobs.

They're throwing a party tonight. Something to do with a book, maybe, she can't remember, but Sarah has insisted that she come, has reminded her about it with weekly e-mails for two months now, as well as helpful voice-mail messages:

Hey Lolo, it's me, don't forget, Thursday night, my parents' place, you promised promised promised, wear something amazing, be your usual beautiful self, but don't be late, I'm going to have no one to talk to because Dan can't make it because who cares OK, I'll see you the day after tomorrow.

Lauren's office is freezing. You could keep butter on the desk. You could perform surgery. Every woman in the office—they're all women—keeps a cashmere sweater on the back of her chair. They sit, hands outstretched over computer keyboards like a bum's over a flaming garbage can. The usual office noises: typing, telephones, people using indoor voices, the double ding of an elevator going down. For some reason, the double ding of the elevator going down is louder than the single ding of the elevator going up. There's a metaphor in there, waiting to be untangled. They make cookbooks, these women. There's no food, just stacks of paper and editorial assistants in glasses. She's worked here for four years. It's fine.

Today is different because today there's a guy, an actual dude, in the office with them, not a photographer or stylist popping by for a meeting, as does happen: He's a temp, because Kristen is having a baby and her doctor put her on bed rest. Lauren isn't totally clear on what Kristen does, but now there's a dude doing it. He's wearing a button-down shirt and jeans, and loafers, not sneakers, which implies a certain maturity. Lauren's been trying to get him to notice her all day. She's the second-prettiest woman in the office, so it isn't hard. Hannah, the prettiest, has a vacant quality about her. She's not stupid, exactly—in fact, she's very competent—but she doesn't have spark. She's not interesting, just thin and blond, with heavy eyeglasses and a photograph of her French bulldog on her computer screen.

Lauren has it all planned out. She'll walk past his desk a couple of times, which isn't suspicious because his desk isn't far from the kitchen, and the kitchen is where the coffee is, and by the third time, he'll follow her in there, and she'll make a wisecrack about the coffee, and he'll say it's not so bad, and they'll talk, and exchange phone numbers, e-mail addresses, whatever, and then later they'll leave the office at the same time, ride down together in the elevator and not talk because they both understand that the social contract dictates that sane people do not talk in elevators, and then he'll let her go through the revolving door first, even though she's pretty sure that etiquette has it that men precede women through revolving doors, and then they'll both be standing on Broadway, and there will be traffic and that vague smell of charred, ethnic meat from the guy with the lunch cart on the corner, and he'll suggest they get a drink, and she'll say sure, and they'll go to the Irish pub on Fifty-Fifth Street, because there's nowhere else to go, and after two drinks they'll be starving, and he'll suggest they get dinner, but there's nowhere to eat in this part of town, so they'll take the train to Union Square and realize there's nowhere to eat there either, and they'll walk down into the East Village and find something, maybe ramen, or that Moroccan-y place that she always forgets she likes, and they'll eat, and they'll start touching each other, casually but deliberately, carefully, and the check will come and she'll say let's split it, and he'll say no let me, even though he's a temp and can't make that much money, right? Then they'll be drunk, so taking a cab seems wise and they'll make out in the backseat, but just a little bit, and kind of laugh about it, too: stop to check their phones, or admire the view, or so he can explain that he lives with a roommate or a dog, or so she can tell him some stupid story about work that won't mean anything to him anyway because it's only his first day and he doesn't know anyone's name, let alone their personality quirks and the complexities of the office's political and social ecosystem.

Then he'll pay the driver, because they'll go to his place—she doesn't want to bring the temp back to her place—and it'll be nice, or fine, or ugly, and he'll open beers because all he has are beers, and she'll pretend to drink hers even though she's had enough, and he'll excuse himself for a minute to go to the bathroom, but really it's to brush his teeth, piss, maybe rub some wet toilet paper around his ass and under his balls. This is something Gabe had told her, years ago, that men do this, or at least, that he did. Unerotic, but somehow touching. Then the temp will come sit next to her on the couch, please let it be a couch and not a futon, and he'll play with her hair a little before he kisses her, his mouth minty, hers beery. He'll be out of his shirt, then, and he's hard and hairy, but also a little soft at the belly, which she likes. She once slept with this guy Sean, whose torso, hairless and lean, freaked her out. It was like having sex with a female mannequin. The temp will push or pull her into his bedroom, just the right balance of aggression and respect, and the room will be fine, or ugly, and the bedsheets will be navy, as men's bedsheets always are, and there will be venetian blinds, and lots of books on the nightstand because he's temping at a publishing company so he must love to read. She'll tug her shirt over her head, and he'll pull at her bra, and they'll be naked, and he'll fumble around for a condom, and his dick will be long but not, crucially, thick, and it will be good, and then it will be over. They'll laugh about how this whole thing is against the company's sexual harassment policy. She'll try to cover herself with the sheet, and he'll do the same, suddenly embarrassed by his smaller, slightly sticky dick. When he's out of the room, to get a beer, to piss, whatever, she'll get dressed. He'll call her a car service, because there are no yellow cabs wherever he lives. They'll both spend the part of the night right before they fall asleep trying to figure out how to act around each other in the office tomorrow.

Or maybe not that. Maybe she'll find a way to go up to him and say, what, exactly, *Hey, do you like parties? Do you want to go to a party . . . tonight? No, the jeans and tie are fine. It's not fancy. A party. A good party. Good open bar, for sure. Probably canapés, what are canapés exactly, whatever they are, there will probably be some. Last party, there were these balls of cornbread and shrimp, like deep fried, holy shit they were great. That was last year, I think. Anyway, there might be celebrities there. There will definitely be celebrities there. I once saw Bill Clinton at one of these parties. He's skinnier than you'd think. Anyway, think about it, it'll be a time, and by the way, I'm Lauren, I'm an associate editor here and you are?* She can picture this conversation, the words coming to her so easily, as they do in fantasy but never in reality. They call it meeting cute, in movies, but it only happens in movies.

People start leaving the office around five thirty. It's summer, still light and lovely outside. Some of her coworkers say good-bye and good night to everyone, stop to check in about one another's plans for the evening. She prefers to bolt. Sunglasses on, checks her bag four times for phone, phone charger, keys—she once forgot her keys, had to come all the way back, it was fucking horrible. She does this now, throws everything into the bag, checks for the keys, opens her wallet and frowns into it—thirty-seven dollars, enough for a cab home, but not enough for a cab to. She'll walk. Abrupt wave to Dallie (Dallie, yes, that's her name), a nod to Hannah, a "Good-bye!" from Antonia across the office, and she's out into the lobby, then scanning her ID card on the little white pad to get in the door on the other side, which opens to the offices of the imprint they share the floor with (serious nonfiction about wars and maritime disasters) and the ladies' room. Ladies' room, what an idiotic phrase. When she and Sarah lived together, that first terrible apartment in the East Village, the summer after graduation, she tried for a time referring to the bathroom as the Shit House, which Sarah did not care for.

The lighting is not good. There are no windows. Lauren washes her face, but maddeningly the faucet is the kind that you press and water comes out for about twelve seconds then shuts off so you have to keep pressing it again and again. She brushes her teeth, checks her armpits, which are fine; she hasn't sweat since her walk from the subway to the office. She pulls her hair away from her face; it still gets a little wet but it doesn't matter. Her hair looks great, it always does: It's thick, falls in this subtle wave that's natural and not studied, and that some girl in college once told her she was lucky to have and ever since then she's been proud of it. She doesn't wear jewelry, not even a watch. She's got on a sort of hippie dress that she found somewhere, vaguely Mexican. It's prettier than she normally wears to the office, and under the belted sweater she keeps stashed on the back of her chair, and with the heels she's just slipped on, it looks like a real I'm-going-to-a-party outfit. A bit of color on the lips, something on the lashes. She hurries, she doesn't want anyone to see her in the bathroom and think she's primping for a date like some kind of loser.

She takes the bus east on Fifty-Seventh Street and waits eight minutes for another going down Second Avenue, but grows impatient and decides to just walk. Even when she sweats she's not very smelly. It should be fine. She takes her place among confused tourists, the occasional jogger, dog walker, little old lady, coworkers and friends drinking cold wine at sidewalk cafés; al fresco dining in Manhattan, she's never understood that, the whole thing smells like exhaust and urine.

Huck and Lulu's house is covered in ivy. The window boxes—Lulu's handiwork—look bountiful. The parlor windows are open, and Lauren can hear those party sounds drifting out: polite chatter, the occasional decorous laugh, ahems and footfalls on parquet, the cell phones of rude guests. Though it's still light out, in her mind she sees the house theatrically illuminated, light spilling onto the stoop, onto the sidewalk, the windows offering a glimpse of something, another way of life, like the dioramas at a museum, the vignettes in a department store. The house was always lit up as though for a party, life with Huck and Lulu and Sarah is always a party.

You don't ring the doorbell at this sort of party, and anyway, it's been years since she used this particular doorbell. She comes and goes with impunity, or she did, once upon a time. She walks in, and there are people in the parlor, attended by a pretty girl in a black polo shirt and black pants, cherry red apron around her waist, passing a tray of something that looks tasty even from far away. The men are wearing jackets and ties; these parties are attended exclusively by the kinds of men who wear jackets and ties everywhere, possibly even to bed. There are women, too, of course, and somewhere in the distance she can hear Lulu, because you always can hear her, that big laugh from deep in the throat, the mix of tongues in which she speaks, her native Spanish, her never-wholly-Americanized English, a touch of French, when warranted, for emphasis. Lauren can picture her; she'll be standing in profile, head tilted back a bit, kind of like the woman in that Sargent portrait that so scandalized the public he had to revise it, adding a dress strap. That's how Lulu always stands; she thinks it shows to best advantage her "good side." In her cotton dress, Lauren's underdressed, but her relative youth makes up for this. She's not one of the powerful matrons in geometric, collarless blazers, not a Ph.D. in a pencil skirt. She's just some girl. She doesn't see Huck anywhere. She climbs the staircase.

Sarah's room shares the top floor with Huck's office. The second floor is divided between her parents' room and a guest room, frequently occupied. Lauren strolls past the line of women—it's always women, these lines—waiting outside of the second-floor powder room, past the door to Huck and Lulu's inner sanctum, which now as ever has a little folk art painting, a portrait of a girl, strung on a silk ribbon, hanging from a nail on the door, because Lulu, in her enthusiastic collecting, long ago used up all the available wall space. The stairs creak horribly. There's an unspoken consensus among the party guests that it's fair to wander to the second floor, queue up there for the bathroom, but anything farther than that is an intrusion, so there are raised eyebrows as Lauren continues past the scrum and ascends to the top floor. She tries to look proprietary.

On the walls: frames, a collage of photographs, hundreds of them. Photographs are meant to be forever, but they're not. The quality of light, the once-fashionable haircuts and colors of clothing: You can tell these are old from afar, so old they might as well be cave paintings. Everything's done tastefully, under plastic, but the way the pictures are mounted seems somehow passé, a relic. Lauren doesn't need to look closely, doesn't need to scan the pictures to pick out her own face: there beside Sarah's, girlish attempts at makeup and comic grimaces instead of smiles, on their way out, something to do with boys, she can't recall now. Or there, hair pulled back into a ponytail that snaked (could it be?) through the gap in the back of a corduroy, suede-brimmed baseball cap. That day, class field trip to a farm, or Storm King, or the Noguchi Museum, something of that order. And Sarah, of course: here, proudly atop a horse, because she had been one of those girls, a horse girl, until the age of thirteen, when it started seeming babyish, like Barbie, Archie comics, drawing with crayons. Sarah as a toddler, utterly recognizable (long nose, wild hair), studying one of her dad's fat books, a mocking frown on her face, modeling his glasses to boot. Sarah, in overalls, buried in necklaces, because she'd had that phase of making necklaces, stringing beads onto cord and calling it her art. Lauren still has one of those necklaces.

Lauren thinks of her own parents, their suburban split-level with a far less architecturally interesting stairwell, which is also hung with pictures of the children, though only three, one of each of them. Her parents don't decorate in quite the same way as Lulu; they prefer the store-bought to the timeworn. The door is closed. She knocks.

"You hiding?"

"Just a minute!"

"I said, you hiding?" Lauren jiggles the knob, which catches. Locked. "It's me."

The door opens. "Shit. You scared me." Sarah, fanning away smoke, guilty. "Come in here."

Lauren closes the door behind her quickly, absurdly afraid of being caught at something. She can't help it. On the top floor of this house everything she does seems somehow girlish. Sarah drops onto the bed. She's wearing a navy dress, a little conservative, something that blouses and gathers at the waist in a way that implies the early stages of pregnancy or one's fifth decade. It's not a great color for her, but she's always drawn to strong, declarative shades—blue, black, red—that don't flatter her skin. She's somehow not mindful of how she looks in them. Lauren has always been a little jealous of Sarah's obliviousness to certain things.

There are two beds, matching headboards, matching upholstered benches at their feet. The bench at the foot of the left bed, that's where Lauren dropped her overnight bag, nights she came to stay. The bench at the foot of the right bed, that's where Sarah discarded sweaters and shirts, the ones she'd rejected that morning, with the labels Lauren loved, Benetton this, Gap that, Ralph Lauren this, Donna Karan that, the last less hand-me-down than a pilfered-from courtesy of Lulu, cashmere as perfect as a baby's skin. The housekeeper would come up in the afternoons, put everything away.

"Fuck me, it's like a museum in here." Lauren sits on the edge of the bed, her bed. She seems to swear more under this roof, shades of her adolescent self.

Sarah laughs. "A museum to the excellence that is me." She's got a pipe in her hand, glass, emblazoned with colorful daisies. "Exhibit A."

"Exhibit A is trials, not museums."

"Do you want to get stoned or not?"

"Where did you even find that thing?" Lauren recognizes it, vaguely, studies it with revulsion but also fondness, like a hideous sweater that once made you feel beautiful.

"The jewelry box, in the little drawer, next to earrings you shoplifted from Bloomingdale's, I think?"

Lauren knows just which earrings Sarah is referring to. "You had pot hidden in here, too?"

Sarah hands her the glass pipe and a tiny, lime-green lighter. She shakes her head. "That, believe it or not, is from the personal collection of Mr. Henry 'Huck' Thomas."

Lauren is holding her breath, feeling the smoke build in her lungs and then it's in her nose, as if by magic, and her mouth. She opens it, and it escapes—mere wisps. She'd imagined more. "You're fucking kidding me," she says with a cough.

"I'm fucking not, my dear." Sarah has taken off her shoes, folds her feet up under her body so she's in a sitting position but still looks very attentive. "Arthritis. Doctor's orders."

"Oh?" Lauren is coughing more. It's been a long time since she got high.

"Too much hand shaking maybe?" Sarah smiles. "Poor Papa. A decade plus on I'm still dipping into his stash."

"Kents, that was his brand, right?" Lauren remembers: Sarah, in the other room, distracting him with some nonsense about their school day while Lauren searched the blazer, hung on the back of a dining chair, helped herself to two or three. She passes the pipe and the lighter back to Sarah.

"You were good, Lolo. Nerves of steel. Unafraid of shopgirls at Bloomingdale's, unintimidated by the man of this house."

"They say everyone is good at something," Lauren says. She wants to take her shoes off, but also doesn't want to. She doesn't want to get too comfortable in this room. The poster of the Van Gogh at MoMA, the jumble of madras belts on a peg on the back of the door; it's too familiar and too foreign, a country she visited once, but doesn't want to go back to. She's outgrown this.

The little flame flickers out of the lighter, rising higher as Sarah inhales in one, two, three gulps. She sets the glass pipe onto the piece of glass that Lulu had cut to protect the antique nightstand from rings from the diet soda the girls drank religiously at age fourteen. "Fuck, actually, I'm pretty stoned."

"I'll open the window," Lauren says. She's feeling stifled. She pushes aside the curtains, trimmed in a pale green grosgrain that complements the headboards, slides the window up.

"That helps," Sarah says. She's risen from her bed, stands behind Lauren, rests her chin on her shoulder. Muscle memory: the two of them joined, if not at the hip, then physically, always—

hands held, hot mouths at ears trading confidences, knees pushed together in the backseats of taxicabs. Like infant twins, happily entwined in their crib, they could never stand to be apart. While Sarah showered, Lauren would sit on the floor of the bathroom and talk to her, though the splash of the water on tile made it hard to hear.

They breathe in the hot city air. It is better, somehow. Sarah sits back on the bed, idly fiddling with her skirt, which pools up around her waist like a deflated life preserver. Lauren sits on the bed opposite, almost knee to knee.

"So what's new?"

"Nothing's new," Lauren says. "What's new with you? What made you decide to sneak away from your parents' party to get stoned alone on a Thursday night?"

"You said it, my parents' party," Sarah says. "That's reason enough. I mean, Dan's not here, and I knew you were coming and was sort of in the mood for a trip down memory lane."

"Cool," Lauren says.

"Cool?" Sarah says, teasing.

"Shit, trip is right." Lauren shakes her head, which feels fuzzy, thick.

"It's that medicinal shit," Sarah says. She starts to giggle. She has a very charming laugh, Sarah does, a girlish giggle that can grow into a very big guffaw. She alone could record a laugh track for a sitcom. Her laugh is that varied, that infectious. "You didn't call me back."

"I didn't?" She is not good with the calling back, Lauren knows this about herself. Isn't it enough to hear the message, to think about the person calling? She knows it is not.

"Sorry." Lauren is not good at apologizing. She is not being insincere though. This is the kind of thing that bothers Sarah.

"I'm used to it."

"It's just. I'm here! I came. Sorry." Now, annoyance: Sarah gives in to injury so easily.

"I know, you come through," Sarah says. "Even if you're too busy to call back. I know how it goes with you. It's always something. Or, you know, someone."

"No someone." This, another peeve of Sarah's: the suggestion that she's been supplanted, that sex outranks her. And a peeve of Lauren's: this dance around. Just ask, she thinks. Sarah wouldn't though; conversationally, she bobs, she weaves, she suggests, she retreats. This is recent, recent-ish, Sarah's way of talking to Lauren, as blunt and transparent as using simple grammar and a too-loud voice when speaking to cabdrivers or waiters for whom you assume English is a second language.

"No someone?"

"No someone." Lauren fidgets with the rubber band that's around her wrist. The office of the future and she always ends up with rubber bands around her wrist. "I would tell you if there was a someone."

"I was so sure. When you're hard to get on the phone I just assume it's because your attention is elsewhere."

And there it is: Sarah's real fear. "First off, bros before hos, as always," Lauren says. "Second off, there is no one my attention has been on. Well, almost no one." Lauren never has been able to keep much from Sarah, at least, not the stuff she secretly wants her to know.

"Aha." Sarah, triumphant, and more interested.

"Nothing yet," Lauren says. "I mean, he's just, well, he doesn't know he's someone yet, but maybe he'll get promoted to someone. But there's a complication. We work together."

"Not your boss, just tell me he's not your boss." Sarah's tone contains something: an accusation, but also titillation.

"My bosses are women, obviously. No man has ever been a boss at a cookbook publisher. He's a *temp*," she says, whispering it, not like it's a swear word, like it's a bad one: *cancer*, or *holocaust*.

"That's a no-no, right?" Sarah says, suddenly herself.

"I don't know," Lauren says. "I think office romance sounds so 1960s. Kissing secretaries and all that. He seems nice."

"Then what's the problem, precisely?"

"I don't know if fucking the temp is the way to climb the ladder, exactly." Lauren coughs.

"If he's a temp, stupid, that means temporary. It's not for life. You're an editor, not a justice of the Supreme Court."

"I just have to time this right, I guess," Lauren says, grateful for Sarah's omission of her titular "associate." "You know how terrible I am at keeping a secret."

"Well, I don't know, I don't think you've ever kept one from me. But maybe you have and you're secretly great at it? Anyway, just try a little discretion. Poker faces. Speaking of the Supreme Court, one of them is here tonight."

"Which one?"

"Not one of the good ones."

"Oh." Lauren has long since learned there's little point talking politics under this roof. It's discussed, of course, but you don't talk, you listen. Huck's conservatism is so deeply felt he's only ever bemused by dissent, and bemusement is the most infuriating response in any kind of conversation. He's an asshole. "Forget I said anything. It's nothing. He's no one. He's a temp." Lauren's temporarily forgotten what is real and what she imagined. She's stoned. "I was distracted. Sorry for not calling. I was coming. I came. I'm here. Should we go downstairs?"

"Probably," Sarah says.

In the distressingly pink—toilet, shower, tiles—bathroom, they find a toothbrush, reason it must be Sarah's, and take turns with it, using a very old tube of Aquafresh that must be prodded and coaxed back into pliability but they figure is probably not poisonous. Sarah wets the corner of a towel, dabs at her eyes, then has to reapply her eye makeup. Lauren sniffs at the dozens of perfume bottles, almost every scent a memory. There's a cologne they'd stolen from Huck, they thought it so outré to wear a man's fragrance, something amber, in a bottle shaped like a lozenge, or a stone from a riverbed. She sprays a bit on her wrist, rubs the one against the other, dabs it in the general direction of her armpits, and behind her ears. Mint on her breath, musk on her breasts, she feels ready for the party. Forget the temp: Maybe she'll meet a man, some ambitious, not-too-sycophantic sort with a very specific goal in life, like to be, say, the secretary of agriculture. You meet that sort of person at the kind of parties Huck and Lulu throw. She wouldn't mind. She would be happy to be spared having to do anything herself. She could be a trophy wife, or she could have been. At thirty-two you're not a trophy wife. You're a plaque wife, a certificate-of-participation wife.

Sarah has freshened her breath but mangled her eyes. She's got her shoes back on, adding three inches—in shoes her taste is unassailable. They're sexy: pointed, aerodynamic, gleaming, expensive. They are shoes that make a commanding clack on the floor, shoes to be reckoned with, less shoes than an actual stage on which you can strut and preen and act the role of a woman who must be taken seriously.

"Did you see Mom and Papa yet?"

Lauren shakes her head. Sarah is gripping her arm as they walk down to the party. There's no line for the second-floor powder room anymore. There's music coming up from downstairs, and voices, and because it's summer, the party will have spilled into the basement kitchen and out into the garden. Lulu likes a party where the guests gather in the kitchen; she doesn't mind them seeing the hired waiters and the chef and only engages caterers who don't mind being looked at, wielding skewers of satay while prestigious personages squeeze past, behind the stove and around the island and out the French doors. To Lulu, the effect is magic—it's showmanship.

"God, you smell fantastic," Sarah says, and they are in the foyer, and there's Huck, grinning his grin, comfortable, knowing, holding his drink, and calling them girls, my girls, and they are that for a minute, girls again.

Huck is not very tall but seems massive; Huck is not fat but seems so. Huck's natural tone of voice is loud, but because when he speaks, everyone else stops speaking to hear what he's going to say, it seems he's always shouting. That's probably why he's so successful, his ability to shut other people up simply by speaking.

"This is Lauren," Huck declares. "She grew up with my Sarah. An honorary member of the family, this one. They were girls only days ago. I don't understand!"

Someone says "Nice to meet you," and Lauren realizes, too late, that this has been an introduction. She smiles. There's no need to speak, since Huck has the floor.

"You know my Sarah, of course, the only real work I've ever done. Lead line in my obituary. There it is. Tell that to Lehmann at the *Times*, I mean it." General laughter. "And if you can believe this, she's getting married. Betrothed. 'Thou art sad. Get thee a wife!' Is that *Much Ado?* The Venetian Merchant? Never mind. Promised to a wonderful young man. Sarah, Dan's not here to-night, is he?" Sarah shakes her head. "A doctor. But not one of the saps making rounds, stethoscope at the ready. *How are we feeling, Mrs. Johnson?* Jesus no. Ten bucks a pop for that shit, though the socialists would have it like the sanitation department. Free for all! A doctor drops by for your vaccinations, Mondays, Wednesdays, Saturdays. Thursdays, they'll pick up the recyclables and send the gynecologist." More laughter. Four more minutes of this and he's leading an honest-to-God toast to Sarah, right there in the foyer, a clutch of guests raising highball glasses to the future health and happiness of Doctor Dan and Huck's little girl.

Lauren escapes his grasp—it's physical, he's had an arm around her waist all this time, right up through the raising of glasses, but unlike Sarah's touch, Huck's doesn't kindle fond memories—and steps backward slowly the way you're supposed to leave the presence of the Queen of England. She's in the living room, she's free, no one has noticed. Huck is talking about monetary policy now.

The living room is not that crowded, but the walls are covered with Lulu's collection of folk portraits so it seems full of life.

A trio of women with identical haircuts are having a serious conversation near the fireplace. Lauren sits on the sofa, which is covered with pillows. She's never understood that, lots of pillows on a sofa; how are you supposed to sit with all that comfort? It's aggressive. She takes one cushion from behind her, leans back into the couch, and places it on her lap. She wishes she had a drink, but doesn't want to move. She wants to check her watch but doesn't wear one. Forty minutes. She can leave in forty minutes. A wave of loud laughter from the back garden: Something funny has happened. She feels no curiosity at all about it.

"Don't hide." Sarah sits on the couch. "It's not ladylike."

Lauren studies her. There's a bit of pink in Sarah's eyes but she's feigning sobriety pretty well. "I don't want to get up," Lauren says. "I'm comfortable."

"It's a party," Sarah says. She stands, grabs her by the hand.

Lauren lets the velveteen pillow fall on the floor. She doesn't pick it up.

They cut through the dining room and down the back staircase without having to go past Huck in the foyer. The basement stairwell is bright, white, the only bare walls in the place, because Lulu figured it's best to create the impression of light and space where there isn't any. Lulu could have been a decorator. She likes to bring this up in conversation.

There's a table in the kitchen, plates of grapes and strawberries and something wrapped in some kind of very thinly sliced meat, and sweating bottles of white wine and sparkling water. Lauren grabs the glasses, Sarah pours both full, takes a healthy sip from one glass, tops it off. Lauren tastes the wine. It's too sweet, but never mind. Sarah is pulling on her arm still, and they squeeze through the scrum toward the back doors, and out onto the blue-stone slabs of the garden.

There is Lulu, in just the pose Lauren imagines when she imagines her—head turned to the left as if someone's only just called her name, cocked just a bit as if there's some music she's straining to hear, mouth communicating a smile without actually smiling. There are lanterns in the trees, and the light from neighboring houses, and the ambient glow of the city, and anyway it's not late so there are traces of sun, and the effect is theatrical. Retired or not, Lulu is a star.

She can be loud, is maybe the only person in the world who can be louder than Huck, but she's most effective when silent. She sees them, she sees all, and beckons urgently, waving enthusiastically but also commandingly. Gripping wineglasses and holding hands, they trip across the stones, weave past partygoers, Lauren's arm brushing right up against the back of the honorable associate justice. Lulu is standing on the stone, too, but seems somehow to be onstage. She grabs them both, one hand on each girl's arm.

"There you are" is all she says.

"Hi, Mom," says Sarah.

"Hi, Lulu," says Lauren.

"Hi nothing." She squeezes Lauren's arm. "You never come anymore. You came."

"I came," Lauren says. "I come sometimes."

"You came!" She relinquishes their forearms and claps her hands together, once, twice, three times. "I'm so happy. Oh, you've made me so happy, but darling, where's Dan; Dan's not here tonight?"

"Dan's not here tonight," says Sarah, in a tone that implies she's already explained this to her mother.

"Never mind, never mind; oh God, Lauren, you're so beautiful, look at her, Sarah, isn't she beautiful, it's preposterous."

"Preposterous," Sarah agrees.

"You never come," says Lulu again. Another squeeze, something between affection and punishment.

Lauren considers the things she might say in response. *I find you ridiculous. Your husband is a warmonger. Your daughter is marrying a fat man. I have not lived up to my potential.* She smiles. "I always love coming here," she says, and it is the right thing to say.

"Everyone always loves being at our home," Lulu says. She sparkles, Lulu does; it's not makeup and not beauty, it's some sort of natural incandescence. She nods her head like the matter is settled. "Everyone loves being at our home. Don't go away. Stay out here with me. Meet our friends. Your fiancé isn't here but you can still show off that ring. Lauren, have you seen the ring? It was in his family."

"I think you can see it from space," Lauren says. She has seen the ring. Sarah sent her a picture, when it came back from being resized—a diamond like an almond.

Lulu laughs loudly. Once again, the right thing to say. "Do not go, stay, stay, drink more, but sit, stay, stay with me," she commands. It has been forty minutes, surely, it has been forty years, it has been forever, and Lauren is still here. She takes Sarah's hand. They are here together.

Lauren's apartment smells of something—fried oil, a suggestion of an herb—her neighbors have cooked. Sarah is paranoid about smells clinging to her. Once, years ago, dinner with friends, then a party at the home of some guys someone knew from law school, she'd struck up a conversation with a handsome-ish Brian or Ryan. After hellos and how-do-you-knows, Brian or Ryan said, "Thai food?" Not accusatory, but yes: They had gone out for Thai. Sarah had blushed. She had stopped talking. The most insidious thing about smells is how you can be immune to your own. She hopes this fried scent won't stay with her, though this does remind her that she needs to drop off the dry cleaning.

Sarah strokes the sofa, a chocolate brown corduroy relic of the '70s that showed up in the store collection one day. It had sat in the unused maid's room of a Park Avenue apartment for forty-two years until the old lady died and her kids shipped everything to the store to be disposed of—raising some cash for AIDS patients in the bargain. Sarah had known Lauren would love it, in fact, she herself loved it, but Lauren was the one in the market for cheap furniture, had made Sarah promise to be on the lookout for her. Sarah paid for it, held it at the store, and eventually Lauren hired some guy with a van from the Internet to pick it up and deliver it. She can't remember if Lauren ever paid her back for the sofa. Four hundred dollars. Lauren's apartment is stylish in a way that is so unforced. Sarah admires that.

Though daylight savings hasn't ended yet, it's clear fall has arrived. This is how it goes, always: Labor Day is hot and sunny, then that Tuesday the morning air feels chilly, the evening sky looks so different, and the fashionable girls start wearing their boots. Though it was only days ago, summer feels like something forgotten, something that barely happened. Those ten days on the Vineyard, her skin changing from whole milk to almond milk, maybe, vanilla to French vanilla—faded now, the holiday forgotten. Fall is wonderful, but brief. Winter is a betrayal. Tonight they're going out; *just the two of us* is the phrase they kept using in e-mails and text messages, *just the two of us,* a promise and maybe a lament.

This has become their way: Sarah asks, Lauren demurs. For a long time they were inseparable; for almost as long a time now they've been separate, and it's mostly Sarah's doing that they still see each other. Mostly, but not always. Sarah doesn't mind it. She's good at making reservations, coordinating schedules, developing a plan. Tonight, it's to go back to a restaurant they went to a few months ago, a place not far from Lauren's apartment, the kind of restaurant that's become popular in recent years, pledging no fealty to any particular nationality, just cooking whatever strikes their fancy, sometimes in incomprehensible combinations,

and often featuring ingredients you need to ask the server to identify even if you think you know them—the way you can know a
word but not quite articulate its meaning, hesitate before using it
in a sentence—things like salsify, or chicory, or epazote. That last
time, Lauren had greeted the bartender with a familiar "Hey," the
hostess with a kiss on the cheek, so Sarah had gleaned that she was
something of a regular and suggested it once more. Maybe it can
be their place.

Sarah is on time, always is; in fact, she's early, and after eleven
minutes on the bench in front of the restaurant, she decides to
walk to Lauren's building and wait in the apartment with her
while she finishes doing whatever she is doing. Sarah's building
has a Realtor's office in its storefront level, its windows containing
an elaborate display of picture frames suspended from the ceiling
by wires, within each frame another portrait of another charming apartment. The apartments in this neighborhood are all lovely,
and expensive. Lauren's is lovely and inexpensive, a quirk. It's
very small, but delightful for its smallness, like a dollhouse. The
floors aren't level, the windowsills are black with soot, one of the
living room windows' top panes doesn't sit right, sinks down an
inch, and Lauren's propped it in place with a broomstick. Door,
living room, closet, fireplace that doesn't work, two windows over
the street, kitchen, fridge that hums too loudly, hallway that's four
steps long, bathroom too close to the kitchen, bedroom with ex-
posed brick wall. It is, though, one specific kind of idea about a
city apartment, done perfectly, even down to the mice that appear
every summer. Sarah sits on the sofa and waits. Lauren would
never ask her if she wanted water or a drink, would never play

hostess, not for Sarah; she's able to get her own drink of whatever is inside Lauren's fridge.

The étagère near the sofa is stuffed with books. It was another find at the store. That one Lauren came to pick up herself, with Gabe, whose younger brother lived in Brooklyn and had a van because he was in a band. They drove into the city, loaded it into little brother's van, and were gone. That might have been the last time Sarah saw Gabe. She always liked Gabe, whose work has to do with historical preservation, not manually but academically, of important buildings. In fact, Gabe was her responsibility, her doing. She'd met him first. She has a good instinct for matchmaking. He has nice eyes and a very hairy chest, the hair always peeking out of the collars of his shirts. He is a bookish guy but strong, had lifted the bookcase; well, it wasn't all that heavy, but she remembers how he maneuvered it into the back of the van so capably, remembers the veins standing out along his forearms. She misses Gabe, wishes he was still around, imagines the four of them at dinner, the four of them at drinks, the four of them on vacation. That had seemed, for a time, to be the promise. That had seemed inevitable. The étagère looks nice, shiny brass against the dark wood floor.

"How was work?" Sarah barely has to raise her voice, knows Lauren can hear her from the bathroom, would have been able to even if she'd closed the door behind her, which she has not done.

"Work was work," Lauren says, mouth full of toothpaste. "The coauthor on this book had a family tragedy, so that was my day. Looking for someone to replace her."

"Family tragedy?"

"I assume dead mother, but don't want to ask." Lauren spits.

"Dead mothers," Sarah says. "So inconvenient."

"I'm not trying to be heartless." Lauren comes into the room, pulling a sweater over her arms. "Too soon for this?"

Sarah shakes her head. "No, probably not, actually."

"I'm always cold anyway," Lauren says. "How was your thing?"

"My thing was a bit of a disaster," she says. She doesn't want to get into it now. She pictured this conversation transpiring in the restaurant: a chorus of background noise, the comfort of a cabernet. "I'm totally behind, Lolo. At least, according to Claudia Quinn at the Chelsea Terrace."

"What does that even mean?" Lauren sits on the floor, looks up at her.

"Evidently, if I am getting married next April, I should have started planning on my fourteenth birthday."

"No room at the inn?" Lauren asks.

"You should have seen the look she gave me when I told her April," Sarah says. "It was like she was personally insulted as well as embarrassed on my behalf."

"Well, screw her," Lauren says.

"True, but still. She has a point. I wasted the whole summer when I should have been making lists and booking a venue and a photographer and all that shit." She felt like an idiot, that afternoon, with Claudia Quinn, feels like an idiot still. She prides herself on being prepared, on competently dealing with complex situations.

"It'll be fine," Lauren says, standing. "Let's go eat. And drink. And forget about it."

The restaurant is crowded but not so crowded they have to wait, and after the single kiss on the cheek (more than one is affected) the hostess, whom Lauren introduces as Meg, her second time introducing them now, shows them to a table, and the restaurant is small enough that no one table is any better than the rest. The menu is just a slip of butcher paper left atop the table.

"What's celeriac?" Lauren frowns. "I can't remember."

"It's gross," Sarah says. "You know what being in your place reminded me of, just now? Gabe."

"Gabe?" Lauren looks at her.

"Yeah. I'm not sure why. Actually, I am. It was the bookcase."

"Gabe." She exhales. "God, that seems like so long ago."

"Not so long," says Sarah. "You sound positively elderly when you say it like that."

"Almost two years," Lauren says. "That's a while. A full sixteenth of my life. I forgot about the bookcase. We borrowed that van from his brother. Do you remember his band? We went to see them once."

Sarah remembers. Three guys, skinny as teenagers, posing prettily with their instruments on a stage in some bar somewhere. "I recall that."

"They actually ended up kind of making it," Lauren says. "Some song of theirs was in a commercial, a good commercial, for Apple, or maybe a credit card. Anyway, yeah, no idea about Gabe, we haven't kept in touch."

"But it was amicable. It was *we'll be friends*."

"That's a thing people say," Lauren says.

"I didn't think it was a thing you'd say," she says. "I liked Gabe. You liked Gabe. I'm just wondering."

"We're not all Sarah and Dan, you know," Lauren says. She gestures for the waiter, but when he arrives, they realize they both intend to order the fish. They negotiate, retract, urge, then settle (fish for Sarah, steak for Lauren). The waiter brings their wine.

"I realize you and Gabe are not me and Dan," Sarah says. She's not done with this conversation. She's not good at broaching conversational topics subtly. She knows this about herself. Huck raised her with a rhetorical style that brooks no disagreement. She's a pundit. That's her heritage.

"This is ancient history, Sarah." Lauren sips her wine. "You liked Gabe. You think I shouldn't be alone. I get it. I don't know." She shakes her head.

"I'm only saying I liked your ex-boyfriend. Jesus."

"Thanks, Mom," Lauren says.

"Could we not, please?" Sarah says at last. That terrible sting that precedes tears. "I've had a shitty day."

"Because of that woman?" Lauren's cheeks are flushed. She smiles, no longer irritated. They can do this, move easily between annoyance and affection.

"She had a point." Sarah swirls her glass aimlessly, like a connoisseur, which she is not. "I told myself I'd just take the summer. Work as usual. But otherwise relax. We went on one lousy vacation, to the Vineyard, not even, like, something extravagant. The wedding will wait, I thought. But now I feel like I messed up, like it's one of those dreams where you've got the final for a class you don't remember enrolling in, and you haven't done the reading and have no idea what anyone is talking about."

"Maybe this is your excuse then," Lauren says. "Just bail. City hall. Brunch afterward. Done and done."

"Lulu keeps buying me wedding magazines, but they all look the same, so she keeps buying the same ones over and over." On her bedside: a stack, some of them the size of telephone directories, fragrant with those perfume ads you're meant to unfold and rub onto your skin. "She's got plans."

"Are big white dresses still in this season?"

"Do you think I should wear white? My mom is worried about what it implies about my virginity." That had been abandoned at seventeen, their last year in high school, to a boy named Alex Heard, whose middle name was, incredibly, Elvis. He had a baby face and greasy hair and fat fingers and a stupid, halting laugh, but he was not stupid and was not a terrible guy, either. He'd gone to Princeton, moved to California, did something in tech, that's what people do out in California, that or make movies. It happened during a party at Hannah Cho's apartment, a Friday night, October 12, actually; Sarah remembers the date, why wouldn't she. She'd told her mother about it the next day.

"She's not serious." Lauren knows that Sarah told Lulu about it. Fifteen years later still can't quite believe it. "I can't believe that people still think like that."

"Lulu's old-fashioned. But for God's sake, I've been sleeping with Dan for a decade." Sarah finishes her wine. "Hey, how are your parents?" She hasn't seen Lauren's parents in—she can't think how long. Indeed, she sometimes forgets their very existence. It's as though her parents live far away, in New Mexico, instead of across the river, in South Orange. Lauren's mother had introduced herself first, those years ago, as Mrs. Brooks. Sarah had grown up calling grown-ups by their first names, but tripped over that "Isabella." She could tell that it was an affront of some sort. Anyway, Sarah's always thought of her as Bella—that's how Lauren had referred to her, teenage disdain distilled into two bitten-off syllables. *Bella says I can't wear lipstick. Bella says call by nine. Bella says it's not healthy to be a vegetarian.* She was nice, though, Bella, with kind, tired eyes, and a reassuring way of speaking. Sarah can't picture Lauren's dad, Mike, quite as clearly, but that's the way it is with most dads, her own excepted, of course.

"My parents?" Lauren, elbows on the table, tears into the piece of butcher paper that's meant to serve as her placemat. It makes a small but satisfying sound. "I don't know. But speaking of parents—can't you just outsource? Lulu knows how to throw a party."

"My wedding is too small for Lulu," Sarah says. "She should be planning an inauguration. A coronation."

Lauren shakes her head. "Maybe she's the one who should wear white." They both laugh.

"So here's the thing," Sarah says. Again: Huck's way of doing things. You need something, you make a call, you ask, though asking and telling are not so far apart. "I'm going to need your help."

Lauren shrugs. "I'll help. I'm helpful. First things first, are we going dress shopping and can I try one on, too, or will the salesgirl find this suspicious?"

"You're the maid of honor; you tell me," she says. "Anyway, we can pretend it's a double wedding. We can pretend to be Mormon sisters."

"I'm not married, are you sure it's maid? God, that's such a gay term."

"Yeah. *Maid* is unmarried, I think. *Matron* is married."

"Shit, you get married and suddenly you turn into a matron?" Lauren frowns.

"Sexy, don't you think?"

35

"That's almost reason enough for me to get married before you do. So I can be a matron of honor. *This is my friend Lauren, she's my matron of honor.*"

"So you're okay with this, right? Your maidly duties?"

"Don't be dumb," Lauren says. "You can count on me, I'm equal to the task, whatever. Licking envelopes. Filling bags with rice? Tying cans to your car?"

"I'm just making sure," Sarah says. "We talked about this but then we never really got into it and now it's fall already. And you can't do rice anymore. It doesn't actually make birds explode, but people think it does, and it's a bummer to end a wedding with visions of bursting pigeons."

"Wait, are you trying to tell me I am a bad matron of honor?" Lauren reaches across the table as though to take Sarah's hand, but doesn't. "Is this an intervention? Do you not want me as matron?"

"Don't be an asshole," she says.

"You're being the asshole. Just tell me what to do. I don't know about matrimonial custom. Everything I know about weddings comes from sitcoms."

Sarah remembers the years they lived together in the city. Sarah would handle the bills, and Lauren, in a gesture that approached, but did not achieve, the apologetic, would come home with hundreds of dollars of groceries—repayment not quite in kind. She's not irresponsible, not exactly, she just has her way of doing these things, and it's not Sarah's way. She's going to have to guide Lauren through this, which is fine, because Sarah wants only help, not to cede all responsibility. "Fine." It comes out more meanly than she wants it to, so she says it again. "Fine. I guess to start, we should make a list. There's the dress. There's a party.

Something bachelorettey, but not too, I guess. There's the hair and makeup. The flowers, the cake. Photographer."

"I didn't realize this was going to be such a traditional wedding."

"I don't think it's the worst thing in the world to want some pretty flowers around the day I get married."

"I'm going to help, relax," Lauren says, suddenly a little nicer. "We'll find a dress that's not too poufy but still implies that your hymen is intact."

The food arrives. Sarah doesn't say anything to the waiter. Lauren says something, a thank-you maybe, it's not clear. Sarah picks up her fork, assesses the plate. She's not hungry, she wants to leave but wants another glass of wine, too. She had a feeling that Lauren might make her feel this way about the wedding, a wedding done in a way that Lauren would never do things.

When the check comes, Lauren pays. Sarah doesn't care. When they leave, they kiss on the cheeks, in a way that's somehow different from the way Lauren kissed the hostess when they arrived at the restaurant. There is a taxi outside, so Sarah doesn't walk Lauren home, as she normally might.

The building Sarah and Dan live in was built in the 1980s and has a corporate feel that she's never much liked, but the apartment is a good one: both bedrooms roughly the same size, a closet in the foyer that's big enough to hold a bike, a kitchen with real walls and a window so when he cooks (it's mostly Dan who cooks), the whole apartment won't smell like puttanesca or stir-fry. He's got a pretty small repertoire. They order in a lot.

There's a doorman, which makes life easier with things like dry cleaning and UPS, and there's a rooftop garden, though they rarely take advantage of that amenity. When she saw the apartment, she fell in love with its straight solid floors; its modern, hefty windows; how you could see but not hear the traffic below. Her parents' house is so rickety, so idiosyncratic, by contrast. Windows swollen by rain and impossible to open more than an inch; in her father's study, the chair, on casters, forever sliding across the crooked floor. Who needs character? She wanted comfort. So they bought the place, two years ago. They agreed they wanted two bedrooms, said it was for out-of-town guests, but in truth it was because eventually they'd have a baby, though they never said as much out loud, which seemed bad form, or tempting fate.

Dan is on the couch. The television is on, but he's not paying attention. He's looking at his phone, but also has his computer on his lap, and the newspaper crumpled up on the couch beside him. He's a multitasker. It's how his mind works—quickly, enthusiastically. His general knowledge of the universe always surprises her. He can talk to almost anyone about almost anything. The only thing people talk about anymore is what they do for a living, but he's comfortable talking about people's careers no matter what they do: doctors, real estate agents, financial analysts, computer people, journalists, publicists, cabdrivers, people who do things with art. A polymath, maybe that's the word. He skipped the tenth grade.

"You're home," he says. He doesn't get up.

"I'm home." There's a chair by the door where Sarah always puts her bag when she comes in. There's mail on the table: junk, and a magazine she's not interested in reading. "Did you have dinner?"

"Bethany ordered from that Korean place. I just got home."

"Late night." She slips out of her shoes, shoves the newspaper aside, and sits, their bodies barely touching.

"Hi." He looks away from his phone, kisses her on the cheek. "Do you believe this thing with this congressman?"

She hasn't been following the story. Staying on top of the news is her father's job, one she's never wanted for herself. She makes a noncommittal *mm hmm*. The way spouses communicate. They are as good as married already. It's been a long time.

"Our exhibitionist representative is distracting me from my work." He puts the phone down and turns his attention back to the computer. The television is showing a commercial for Boeing. The music is stirring. "You can turn that down."

He knows she doesn't like the television to be as loud as he does. She wonders sometimes if he's a little bit deaf. She turns it down.

"Where were you again?" He's typing as he talks.

"Dinner with Lauren. That place near her place, you know the one she likes?"

"Something ampersand something? That place is pretty good. I liked whatever I ate that time we went there. Skate, I think? Purple potatoes. I remember purple potatoes." He has an amazing memory. She loves that he is brilliant, that it's true brilliance because it's so effortless. He could never set out to impress someone because it would not be his nature. He impresses simply by being. Women like being on the arm of a beautiful man, but she prefers being on the arm of an impressive man. Dan is the kind of man you would want to have near you at a party.

"What's happening at work?"

"Same as usual," he says. He's not unhappy. Dan never seems to find his work especially stressful. "Everything had to happen yesterday. It's almost the weekend, people are going to be away. No one can handle anything except Bethany and me. It would be funny if it weren't always the way these things happen."

Sarah is not the kind of woman to be jealous of his reliance on another woman and is proud of that fact. Besides which, it would never occur to Dan to cheat on her. He's too busy.

Dan went to Penn with her friend Meredith's brother Ben.
The computer of whoever decides these things selected them to be
roommates and did a good job of it: They are great friends still, as
she is still good friends with Meredith, whom she's known since
the sixth grade, when Meredith, Ben, and their parents moved to
the city from suburban Maryland. Ten years ago, she and Meredith
had to drop by a bar in the West Village to leave her keys with
her brother, in town for the night and crashing at her place. He
was out having drinks with his college roommate, Dan. It wasn't a
setup, an elaborate ruse, though in retrospect it could have seemed
like one, and the fact that Meredith was responsible for her knowing Dan at all has forever colored Sarah's opinion of her friend.

Sarah has a lot of friends. She knows a lot of people. It is
important to her to always know and understand precisely how
she feels about everyone in her orbit. She maintains a complex ranking system, tracking the last time she's seen someone,
the last time they've spoken, the conversation they had, how
they felt about each other, how long she's known someone generally, whether they are similar enough to talk politics, whether
she likes their spouse, whether their job or marriage or whatever
has changed who they are, fundamentally. This is how she thinks.
If she knows someone, if someone is a friend, she has a sense of
what that friendship is like, what it's been historically, what it is
now. This helps her understand who other people are. It helps her
understand who she is.

She sighs without realizing it.

"What's tomorrow?" Dan asks.

"Tomorrow, um, Friday. Oh, tomorrow there's a meeting of
that group that Carol is trying to get off the ground."

"Which one is that?"

"Which group or which Carol?"

"No, Carol Abbott, right, Lulu's friend? That I remember, but tell me what the group does?"

"Doesn't do. Will do. Math literacy. Early childhood. Fostering a love of numbers. Minorities, girls particularly."

"Worthy." He nods. "Definitely worthy."

"It's early stages still; I think it's just Carol and a partner and maybe an intern, someone at Columbia? Her husband teaches there. I think that's right. Anyway, it's about the money at the moment. She thinks I might be able to help her with some of the grant writing."

"Of course you can," Dan says. "You're brilliant."

"I'm not brilliant." She yawns. "Should we have a drink?"

"I'd have a drink," he says.

There's a bottle of wine in the door of the fridge, stopped up with one of those rubberized corks. It's so cold it doesn't actually taste like anything, but it's the sensation of cold, the comfort of holding a glass and curling up next to Dan, also holding a glass, that she wants now, more than the taste of wine on her tongue.

———·———

Friday, Sarah wakes early. There's a spin class at the gym down the block—the gym down the block is one of the reasons she chose the apartment in the ugly 1980s building—so she does that, then walks home, eats yogurt and frozen blueberries while half watching the morning talk shows, a segment on the season's new beauty trends, an interview with an actress who's adopted a baby from Burundi. She checks her e-mail: a message from Willa, a wedding planner who's come highly recommended by a friend of Lulu's; a reminder from the store about a staff meeting next week; an invitation from her friend Lexi for brunch Sunday at her new place out in Brooklyn.

She showers. Her hair is a disaster after the class so she has to shampoo it, so then she has to blow it dry, because if she doesn't it'll be fine as long as it's wet, but once it no longer is it'll dry into a preposterous tangle that's neither curl nor not curl. Her hair must be tamed. So she does that, dries and brushes it into submission. Better. She brushes her teeth, reminds herself to make a dentist's appointment, because she's been wondering about whitening. She fumbles about with lipstick and cream and perfume and a little bit of color on the lids of her eyes. She has to make the effort. It's part of being an adult.

She puts on a suit and feels ridiculous, changes into jeans and feels less so, but keeps the blazer: happy medium. The buttons on the blazer hit in the wrong places: She buttons, unbuttons, rebuttons—office harlot or Orthodox Jew. She decides devout is better. She puts on her watch, puts on a necklace, then another, one a hammered silver pendant with an S on it, the other a simple piece of turquoise, unpolished, a gift from Lulu. She puts on shoes, they're too high, so she puts on another pair. She considers herself in the mirror screwed into the back of the bathroom door. Fine.

The meeting is at Carol's apartment uptown. She shouldn't have taken her time with her e-mail. It's not that she's late, she's just not early, and she dislikes this feeling that the commute can only take as long as it normally takes, that there's no cushion, to account for the unplanned-for ambulance, the impromptu stop at Starbucks. Sarah checks her phone in the cab, more e-mails, reminders about this or that. She has a mechanical pencil and a little notebook and makes more notes. She remembers the things she needs to do better when she writes them down. She needs to e-mail her friend Stephanie, an art director at a big luxury goods maker, about a letterpress that she's used, because she needs to get save-the-date cards and invitations. Someone told her you can order custom stamps from the post office now, printed with anything you want. There's a picture of her and Dan from their trip to Istanbul that she's always loved and thought would be a cute stamp, but she needs to see what the dimensions of the stamp are to be sure.

The meeting is somewhat productive. Carol is joined by an unpleasant graduate student named Eliza who has a meandering, exhausting way of speaking without ever making a point. They drink tea and talk about some of the city's existing educational enrichment programs, most of which Sarah researched a few nights before, computer on her lap, on the couch next to Dan, computer on his lap. Sarah mentions a few organizations she thinks might be helpful, or that she thinks are good at what they do.

"See," Carol says. "I knew you'd know. I knew she'd know. You're a wonder."

They talk for ninety minutes, eventually ignoring Eliza's long-winded tangents, then Carol has to leave for a meeting at her son's school, and Sarah has to leave for lunch with Fiona. She's known Fiona since college, though Fiona had transferred away to finish her education at Parsons. Now she's a jewelry designer, which is unsurprising, as she looks like the kind of woman who makes a living designing jewelry: aquiline in the very truest sense, with that nose and arms somehow very like wings, blond hair at once bedraggled and tidy, a penchant for dramatic dresses and statement fashion—a turban, a fur shrug, rings of every color on every single finger. Fiona works for a gigantic apparel maker, designing complicated multicolored beaded necklaces, faux-pearl and feather adornments for the hair. All one size fits all, assembled in Bangladesh then shipped to stores in this country where they sell for $98. Sarah wants to ask her to make their wedding bands.

Fiona has chosen a restaurant that's not far from her office—she can only spare an hour, an actual hour, it's that kind of office—and, when Sarah arrives, is perched on a bench in front of the restaurant. She wears a simple white button-down, but the buttons all hit in just the right place, the top one undone, so she looks like Katharine Hepburn instead of a woman trying to appear sexy. She stands, and Sarah is surprised again at how tall she is, how lovely.

Fiona somehow looks English, which she is. "Sarah," she says. Her accent is wonderful.

"Hi!" Sarah reaches up, deposits a kiss on each cheek.

Lunch is a departure—normally, when she sees Fiona, it's at a party. Fiona is a woman who's reliably invited to a certain kind of party and remembers to extend that invitation to Sarah, at least a few times a year. A post–fashion show celebration for a mutual friend, also from college, now well known enough that her initials are embroidered on the tags inside asymmetrical dresses sold at Barneys; a genteel fund-raiser for an organization that plants trees in Costa Rica. Sarah relishes these invitations. Sometimes it's fun to do something so frivolous, so glamorous, and Fiona moves through such parties with an ease that makes Sarah, too, feel at home. With Fiona, she feels like a different version of herself. She knows it's silly, and knows it's pretend, but she enjoys it.

There's small talk about the men in their lives, about the rigors of work, but the clock is ticking—that hour, Fiona was clear about that hour—so Sarah broaches the subject of the wedding bands with her usual forthrightness.

No sooner are the words out of her mouth than Fiona claps, actually claps, once, twice, three times. "Of course, my God, what an honor, I can't believe you'd ask," she says.

"Really?" Relief. "I was worried you'd be insulted."

"Insulted, don't be silly."

"Obviously, I'll pay you, for your time, for the materials, for everything. I would just love to have something special, something unique."

Fiona waves this away. "I know just what to do. Rose gold for you, a simple silver for Dan. Or platinum? Maybe platinum." Fiona produces a small tape measure from her bag, wraps it around Sarah's finger.

"I can't tell you what this means to me," Sarah says.

"We're going to make you something beautiful," Fiona says.

Because Fiona's office is not far from her parents' place Sarah decides to stop there. Papa's gone but her mother is sure to be there, and there's a lot they need to talk about, not to mention that if she hears that Sarah had lunch nearby and didn't come over there will be a whole discussion, one that's easier to avoid. She walks Fiona back to the office, they kiss their good-byes and say their let's do it again soons.

Downstairs from her office is an outpost of the chain for which Fiona works. Sarah goes in, browses. The music is just the right volume, the salesgirls just the right amount of pushy. There's a table of simple cashmere sweaters in several colors that feel like fall—burnt orange, saffron, chocolate, moss. She chooses two; they're the perfect, simple weight, and they're cheaper if you buy two, actually. She hates taking a big paper shopping bag. She always carries a little cotton tote, folded up into nothing, in her bag, so she takes this out and the salesgirl deposits her sweaters, wrapped in tissue paper, sealed with a sticker, into it. The bag weighs nothing because the sweaters weigh nothing.

It's warm now but she can tell it won't be all day, that in a couple of hours, wherever she is, probably walking back to the apartment, she'll be glad she has the blazer on. At the moment, though, she feels damp. She's heard about people injecting something into the armpits, that this can control your perspiration. Her legs are a bit sore from the morning's class. She doesn't get to class as often as she means to. She's a little out of practice.

Sarah walks east. The sun is bright. She worries her sunglasses might be leaving a tan line on her face. In only a few weeks, though, she'll be yearning for the sun. She hates the winter. She's been thinking of a getaway before the wedding, her and some friends— Amina, Fiona, Meredith, Lauren, of course. Florida, Mexico, maybe even into the Bahamas, somewhere that's the right blend of tacky (tropical drinks in comically sized glasses, dance contests) and luxurious (a proper restaurant, somewhere to get a massage). She meant to mention this to Lauren last night, had thought Lauren might actually know just the right destination. She reads a lot of magazines. They had not, in the end, talked about the wedding as much as she'd hoped to. Their conversations lately do not seem to go the way that she imagines they will go.

Lauren, whom she has always known and understood so well, suddenly seems a mystery. Things change, in life—of course they do. People grow up, become interested in new things, new people. Our way of being in the world is probably a lot less fixed than most people think. But Lauren is a part of her world, and she's a part of Lauren's. She knows this. The circumstances have changed over the years, of course—but that fact has remained. They've fought. They've grown apart. Those first few years, after living as roommates, it had been Lauren who wanted a place of her own and seemed to begrudge every dinner invitation (there was always some guy). Then, there had been Gabe, whom Lauren had put at the very center of her life. Sarah had been jealous, but that had passed. She continues to tender the invitations, to make the telephone calls, and Lauren continues to answer them. They have a good time together, and they need each other.

She worries that on some level Lauren is jealous, and there is no way to ask her that, no way to suggest the possibility, nor is there anything that Sarah can do to undo it if that is the case. Thinking of Lauren makes her think of being a kid. It is a wonderful thing, to have a friend who knew you as a kid. It is the closest of course that she has to a sibling, a thought she doesn't like to spend too much time on, because it reminds her that she had one, a sibling, once, a long time ago, but he is dead.

She'd have to get over it, or through it, somehow. She'll buy Lauren a gift, or take her out for another dinner, and reassure her that the wedding is going to be cool, is going to be their thing, not Lulu's thing. Not white dresses and ornate flower arrangements, not guys in tuxedos and a string quartet. She hates that kind of wedding. She wants to have fun, and good food, and people she likes around her, and she wants them all to be happy. She knows that she can make Lauren understand this, and she knows that Lauren can help her make the wedding this way. It's important, it's imperative, really, because the only way to get Lulu to realize it's not her party is to show her that it's theirs.

Sarah is excited to get married and annoyed that it seems that Lauren is embarrassed by her excitement about this. She feels embarrassed herself, like someone has caught her wearing something out of fashion, like she's admitted to liking a movie everyone hates. She thought this was what people wanted: a happy ending. Do people not want happy endings after all?

Lauren would be better off with a man. It sounds a stupidly unfeminist thing to say, but it's what she thinks, not because she thinks a woman needs a man to be happy, not because she thinks a person who is single can't be as happy as a person in a romantic relationship, but because she knows Lauren. She's known her since she was a kid, she's known her with boyfriends and without boyfriends and she knows which is the better Lauren. She knew her with Gabe, and the Lauren with Gabe was the best Lauren she's known in the twenty years she's known her. The Lauren with Gabe smiled, and laughed, and was never in any hurry, and always seemed so satisfied to be doing whatever she was doing. The Lauren with Gabe was a beat slower, almost like she was stoned—perhaps she was stoned, come to think of it. But he had a way of looking at her and Lauren had a way of being looked at by him: Sarah liked it. She liked him. Lauren pretends now that the whole thing meant less than it did, but Sarah is not fooled by this. She wants Lauren to be happy, and she wants her to be happy for her. She wants them to be happy at the same time.

The blocks are long. She prefers to walk on quieter ones, away from the avenues, away from the buses. A nanny on a cell phone pushes a stroller past, the baby sound asleep. An old woman with terrible posture is waiting on the corner, an envelope in her hands. A man unloads a van, shouting companionably at a man from the corner grocery to which he is delivering whatever it is he has in those cardboard boxes. There's a siren, somewhere, and a car alarm, and a helicopter, and a jackhammer, and from somewhere, some music she can only barely hear. She steps around a puddle. She stops to wait for the light.

Getting things done makes Sarah so happy. She's accomplished a lot: meeting with Carol, lunch with Fiona, picking up some sweaters, and now, stopping to see her mom. She's solved what to do about the wedding bands and still has time this afternoon to send more e-mails, figure out what to do about dinner, maybe surprise Dan with mushroom risotto, the only thing she truly knows how to cook. A specialty of sorts. Just reviewing this list, these to-dos and dones, her pace quickens; she feels lighter, she feels smarter, she feels in control, she feels alive. She thinks about Dan, in his suit, in his office, somewhere blocks from where she is now, and smiles. She'll call him in a bit, when she leaves her parents' place.

A section of the street on this block is cordoned off with yellow tape. Some men are milling about, repairing or rejiggering something, it's not clear what. They're from the gas company, she can tell by their uniforms. It takes a million people to make life run the way it should run. Everyone has their own part to play in it. This is what she loves about being in the city, living in the city—seeing this all unfold around her. She likes to know the part she plays in the whole system, in the whole universe.

Her parents' house is just here, on the left. Sarah climbs the steps, her keys are already out and in her hand, one of those actions your body performs before your brain even asks it to. She unlocks the door, gives it a shove, it's a heavy door, prone to sticking. The door falls shut behind her, and the sounds, the alarm, the helicopter, the siren, the bus, they vanish. The house is quiet, though not silent. Footsteps from above.

"My darling." Her mother walks down the steps, head held like a queen's, smiling. She has been expecting her. There's a lot to be done.

His name is Rob. Lauren figures it out pretty quickly—the office isn't big, she's not an idiot—but she pretends, still, that she's not a hundred percent clear on who he is when Antonia mentions him.

"You could ask Rob to pitch in on this one," Antonia says, helpfully, she's always very helpful. She's not the boss, so she's careful to never sound too bossy. Women learn this at an early age.

"Rob?" Lauren makes a face that's vaguely unpleasant, a little confused, like Antonia has lapsed into a foreign tongue.

"The temp," Antonia says. "He should have some time. And he's got a lot of writing experience, so it shouldn't take him long. You should divide the list and then edit each other, don't you think?" Phrasing it as a question turns what is a command into something else.

"Rob?" She says his name aloud to him like she has no idea if it's his name.

He swivels around in his seat. He's smiling. He stands. "I'm Rob. We haven't had a chance to meet." He proffers his hand.

"Lauren." She shakes his hand firmly. She hates weak hand-shakes. A lot of women give pathetically weak handshakes, but she doesn't believe there's a correlation between gender and the strength of one's hand. She thinks women are taught to fake this.

"Nice to meet you finally," he says. "Of course, I've seen you around."

"It's a small office." She nods. They've been nodding hello for weeks, but she's avoided being alone with him in the kitchen or the elevator or at the printer, embarrassed by the depth and specificity of her initial fantasy about him, a fantasy so vivid in its mundane detail she can almost picture the holes in his socks. Thus far, they've only been together among crowds, and an introduction seemed beside the point. Maybe she doesn't want to fuck him, after all; maybe she only wants to pretend. It's hard to tell the difference sometimes.

"Antonia said you might have some time to help me on this project?"

He sits back in his swiveling chair, a posture of insouciance. "Sure, no problem," he says.

"Great. It's simple, you know they're doing this site redesign, and we were thinking it's a good time to update all the bios of all the authors." She's lapsing into the first person plural for reasons that are unclear.

"Cool." He seems amenable. He'd do anything she asked. He's that sort of guy.

"So just, like, update with new projects and new books or whatever they've been up to," she says. It sounds idiotic, this explanation, but she can't stop herself. "I can give you the actual update info, or e-mail addresses or whatever so you can kind of figure that out from them."

"Not a problem."

"Well, there are thirty-eight bios, so we can just split it in half. I'll do the first nineteen? That sound good?" Maybe she should be doing what Antonia does, saying things more nicely so it sounds more like a suggestion than a command.

"That sounds good," he says.

She feels odd standing when he is sitting down. "Good."

"Good."

"I'll e-mail you the details."

He picks up a pen, writes his address on the back of one of Kristen's business cards. "This is me," he says.

She takes the card from his hand. "Awesome," she says, overly enthusiastically.

———·———

Everything makes Lauren think of something else. That morning, the weather, which was so perfect she'd gotten off at Thirty-Fourth Street, two stops early, eager to enjoy it before spending another day confined to the computer, made her think of California, that one trip to San Francisco, the shock of the clarity of the air, which she noticed the second she stepped out of the airport's sliding glass doors. You couldn't not notice. A work trip, that one, a rarity she wishes were not. She took her place in the steady flow of commuters in the knot of tunnels issuing from Penn Station, which she knew well enough to navigate without thinking, or while thinking about other matters, like the delicious liberty of San Francisco, working while away from the office she'd arrive at in a little less than half an hour, and the fact that, despite what she thinks has been her best effort, the working day still takes place there and there alone. She had imagined better: shared confidences with her bosses, invitations into important meetings in the glass-walled conference room, the chime of the computer reminding her about another lunch or conference call, being asked her opinion, being thanked in the acknowledgments by grateful authors. She used the exit on Thirty-Seventh Street, as she always did, and thoughts of California had given way to thoughts of Thanksgiving, of cranberry sauce, of awkward silence. How did this happen, she wondered, trying to retrace her thoughts, how did her mind leap from one thing to the other, and did this happen to everyone? Maybe it was the autumnal note in the air.

Thanksgiving has always been at home, the place she still thinks of as home, though it hasn't been that for years, her room transformed, anonymized, the perfect place for guests. She's never been able to bring herself to spend a night there, sipping coffee after dinner, then proclaiming her own alertness, rushing out to catch the train. The pale purple carpet, which she'd chosen, had loved as a girl then loathed as a teen, had been ripped up, replaced by that wood flooring you buy at the hardware store then snap together like a child's toy, her dad, who had always been handy, doing the work with her younger brother Adam over the course of one weekend. The twin bed had been replaced by a full, flanked now by matching nightstands with a box of tissues and a coaster: all the comforts. There was a framed poster, from when all those Monets came to the Met. She and her mom had played hooky, gone into the city to see them, a jaunt that seems out of character, now that she thinks about it.

Thanksgiving is a Brooks family specialty. Her mother cooks amiably and ably, checking measurements against handwritten notes decades old. Her dad was a chemistry teacher, once upon a time, so he does the baking. "Baking is science," he says. He wears an apron, though he doesn't need one: He works with a scientist's precision and doesn't spill. Thanksgiving, he does pies, both pumpkin and pecan, and bread, a beautiful, warm thing, perfectly shaped and very soft inside. The day's rites haven't changed much over the course of her life; there are no grandparents left, so there are no longer grandparents in attendance; instead there's Alexis, Ben's girlfriend, but otherwise, it's the same as it ever was. Lauren finds Alexis uninteresting. A little too pushy, a little too proprietary inside the house—it might not be Lauren's house anymore, but she doesn't want to think of it as Alexis's. And at the previous Thanksgiving, Alexis had made a fuss about Lauren's bag.

"Ba-len-ci-ag-a." The enunciation was meant to be indicate awe. "That must have cost a fortune."

"It was on sale," Lauren lied. It had most certainly not been on sale, but she didn't want to defend having spent fourteen hundred dollars on a bag to Alexis, and discussing having spent fourteen hundred dollars on a bag at the holiday table was as unthinkable as discussing anal sex or Israeli settlements. The Lauren who goes home to South Orange is not the same Lauren who shops at Barneys. The Lauren who goes home to South Orange is her parents' only daughter, the smart one, the one with drive, the one off in the city living the sort of grown-up life parents want for their children.

Since Lauren's never entirely been certain what her parents' image of that life entails, she glosses over most of the details. She's shaved a third off her rent, in the telling, and her parents still think it an astronomical sum. Still, they never appeal to her to move to Jersey City or Hoboken. That would be a concession of some sort, they realize. That would be losing at whatever game it is their daughter is playing, and at least she's in the game—better than poor Adam, with his deep voice and an adolescent reluctance to make eye contact, despite the fact that he's fast approaching thirty. Adam's bedroom decor has changed, too, but unfortunately, he's still occupying the place. Anyway, her mother hasn't mentioned law school in at least three years, which is a relief.

Lauren pulls her chair closer to her desk, frowns at her computer, can't remember what she was working on. She checks her e-mail. That's what work is, that's all work is, anymore, discussing the work to be done. She does the work, thinks about something else. She can do that: She's been in this job long enough, unexpectedly long, if she's being honest. She'd studied English with some vague idea that she'd work at a magazine, but began her career at a website, where a fellow alumna was a highly placed editor. After a year and a half of picking up her boss's prescriptions and writing the occasional eighty-word movie review, she'd moved into book publishing, first as an assistant, later a junior editor, at one of the conglomerate's more literary houses. Now: cookbooks. At least this imprint is profitable; a measure of job security.

She's got a piece of paper stuck inside her book and takes it out. It's her running list. She has to return the bedsheets that she bought online because she buys everything online, but they feel terrible, and so she stuffed them back into the box they'd come in, borrowed the tape gun from one of the guys at the messenger center, and sealed it up, and the box is sitting under her desk, a persistent reminder that she's out eighty-nine dollars until she can stomach standing in line at the post office with the local sociopaths. That's been on the list for a few days now. There was a problem with her taxes last year, damn the inexpensive Chinatown accountant she'd made the mistake of trusting, and there was a letter that she ignored, then another letter that seemed slightly more serious, then there was a bill for more than a thousand dollars, which just didn't seem possible, seemed like a mistake, so she ignored that, then there was another, and another, and then there was something that said Warrant on it, which she knows is serious but still doesn't want to deal with so there's that, folded up carefully in its envelope back in her apartment waiting for her like a poltergeist. It's her parents' wedding anniversary next week, so there's a reminder to *buy a card!* And she's supposed to see Sarah; there's a note to remind her to e-mail her to schedule a time, a drink—it's been specified that this is a meeting that is to happen over a drink. Sarah wants to talk wedding strategy. For a crazy moment, Lauren considers taking the red pen from her black metal mesh cup of pens, the one with the red top that slides off so smoothly, a thick wet tip like a child's marker. She'll write *Fuck Rob* in tiny, neat print on her to-do list. She doesn't do it, of course, but it's returned, her initial sense that the man in their midst might be an enjoyable fuck. There's just something in his unhesitant eye contact that appeals to her.

———·———

It's a week before Lauren deals with the package under the desk and the anniversary card for her parents. Writing these things down sometimes makes her feel that she's done them, the downside of the to-do list. Finally, she lugs the cardboard box home and leaves it at a little office supply place down the street where you can ship boxes, make copies, send faxes on those rare occasions faxes must be sent, and where she also finds an acceptable greeting card (the Brooklyn Bridge, rendered in ink) and leaves with the satisfaction of having patronized a mom-and-pop joint, when so many of the local ones have been supplanted by pet boutiques and fussy grocery stores and the sort of charmless, middle-of-the-road chain retailers (ugly handbags, cellular telephones) that can afford the newly astronomical rent.

Stepping back on the street she hears someone calling, and her instinct is to ignore it. *Hey lady, miss, excuse me*—no good ever comes of all this: scams, pleas for directions, hassles about caring for our animals or ensuring our rights to abort our fetuses.

"Lauren. Lauren Brooks."

"Oh." She says it, too, like it's a word, not a sound; like it's a greeting. She's staring. The neurons are firing but nothing is happening, it's a terrible moment. She went to high school in the city and a college upstate that excels at producing the next generation of publishing and art world talent, so of course, she's run into old classmates from time to time. She finds it baffling. Melissa Reid had frozen for her at seventeen; to see her, as she had a year or so ago, in her mannish blazer, stabbing away at a phone, looking a little thick around the waist—it was hard to make sense of. It isn't that Lauren has a bad recall, it's just that she can only recall what she knows. She had been able to recall the Melissa Reid with the hot older brother, the Melissa Reid whose parents divorced in such spectacular fashion that she ended up with two cars on her sixteenth birthday, the Melissa Reid who was alleged to have sucked Dylan Berk's dick in the backseat of a bus en route to a field trip at Fallingwater. Melissa Reid, securities trader—she was someone Lauren never knew.

"God, how are you?" the girl says, unhelpfully. She has high cheekbones and short hair, like a fashion model from the nineties, like a girlish lesbian, like a little French boy. She leans forward, toward Lauren, doing this thing with her neck that is so unflattering Lauren almost wants to tell her to stop before remembering that she's trying to figure out who she is; the tips on comportment can come later.

Lauren can't tell what's warranted: handshake, half hug, kiss, sincere embrace. She tugs her tote bag over her shoulder and sort of hides behind it, protectively. "Hey!"

"God, you look beautiful, look at you!" The girl puts a hand on Lauren's arm, a gesture that is clue enough—the implication of an intimacy now passed—and as their skins come into contact, Lauren remembers. Maybe it's hormonal, animal, some secretion by which we can identify others of our species. Jill Hansen. Fraternal twin brother, Riley (fat, pale, much less pretty than Jill), elderly dad, and much-younger mother, from whom Jill had, fortunately, inherited a perfect, perfect nose, and of course, those cheekbones. Jill Hansen. Lauren hasn't had occasion to imagine Jill Hansen in the past decade and a half, but they were friends, once. Lauren's default attitude to these old acquaintances encountered on the street is usually disdain, so she's surprised to discover she still feels warmly toward Jill Hansen.

"Jill. Wow!"

"It's great to see you." Jill Hansen's eyes widen. She's turned out to be one of those people who look better at thirty-two than at thirteen.

"You look amazing!" This is what you say, but Jill does.

"I don't." A dismissive wave. "But I'll take it. I need to hear it. I just had our second, I feel like a corpse."

"Your second!" Lauren's at the age now where she's required to affect enthusiasm about other people's fecundity. She likes babies well enough but feels the false note in her own words.

"Yeah, do you have kids?" An excited edge in Jill's voice: visions of playdates, the kids squirming in front of a movie, the husbands discussing whatever heterosexual men discuss with one another.

"Me? No, no kids." She has a strange urge to proffer her hand, show there's no wedding band there. How hetero-normative someone like Jill—an early adopter of veganism, who refused to wear leather shoes and organized a schoolwide letter-writing campaign in support of Mumia Abu-Jamal—would probably find that. "You have two!" Changing the subject.

"Leo, he's four, and Audie, she's two months." She says it proudly, but doesn't produce photographs.

"Two months. God, you do look amazing." Lauren means it more now that she better knows the context. It's hard to believe that Jill's body, only eight weeks or so prior, produced the body of another human being.

Another dismissive wave. "So what are you up to?"

"Oh, I live around here," Lauren says, answering a question different from the one that's been asked.

"So do we! God, what a small world. We just bought over on Degraw; where are you?"

The conversation Lauren likes less than the conversation about children is the conversation about career and the conversation she likes still less than that is the conversation about real estate: original details, the expense of boiler repair, the logistics of adding a powder room on the parlor floor, the state of the local public schools and whether, a couple of years from now, they'll have improved enough to be a viable option. If Jill Hansen's cheekbones are her mother's contribution, the three-million-dollar house on Degraw is probably her father's doing. "Oh, over there," Lauren gestures vaguely over her shoulder. "Have you been in the city all this time? All these years? And we've never seen each other even once?"

"I was out west for college. And that kind of stuck. But, we lost our dad, and Riley's here, you remember my brother?"

"I do, of course." Now it's weird that she's holding the tote bag to her torso like it was an infirm dog, and weird that they haven't hugged. They were friends, once.

"He and his husband are here, too. We wanted to raise our kids close to each other."

Lauren makes a somber face. "I'm sorry about your dad." Condolences, though it was hardly a tragedy. She remembers more: Jill Hansen's father was a doctor who had invented a mechanical device that fit into broken bodies to do the work of some piece of failed flesh. The family were zillionaires, not uncommon at school—a town house somewhere in the Seventies, an honest-to-God compound on the ocean out on Long Island, where her mother had been a party planner Doctor Hansen picked up at (where else?) a party. Jill had two half brothers who had to have been in their sixties by now.

"I appreciate that, thanks. Anyway, Portland was great, but we just wanted to be here. And we are loving Brooklyn!"

This last: like it's Disney World.

"What about you? Do you still see anyone from school? You must still be friends with Sarah."

"I am still friends with Sarah."

"God, how is she?" A touch of awe, customary when discussing Sarah.

"She's great! She's getting married, actually." Wonderful. Let's talk about Sarah then.

"Amazing! You'll have to tell her I said hello. And congratulations and all that. Wait, are you married?"

"Uh, no." Lauren shakes her head, smiling to communicate that this isn't a bad thing; her being unmarried is simply a thing. She needs another subject to change to, quickly. "You know, we should all get together some time."

"I would love that," Jill says, so enthusiastically it's clear she's misread the sincerity.

"Me too," Lauren says and feels, suddenly, that she would, in fact, love it. Jill Hansen, maybe she's been missing a Jill Hansen in her life. Lauren is not lonely, exactly, though she is often alone. She has Sarah to tell things to, yes, but no one to whom she might tell things about Sarah. She doesn't actually believe Jill Hansen will fill this role—Jill Hansen will presumably be too busy caring for her offspring, though now that she thinks about it, where are those offspring, and why is Jill Hansen, a new mother, roaming the streets unencumbered?—but there is something unexpectedly appealing about the idea of the three of them, Sarah, Lauren, Jill, "getting together," even as Lauren knows it will never happen.

Her mother's dress is out of the question. Lulu and Huck married in 1970. Lulu, stick thin, twenty-four, gigantic eyes rimmed in mascara, an earlier marriage (an impulsive four-day union to a middling Mexican musician) annulled. Lulu, then as now, looked incredible. The pictures capture it vividly: chiffon, ruched and belted at the waist, an embellished collar up the neck, her long arms bare but for a gold cuff, the dress trailing to the floor but light enough that it's drifting, seems to be moving even in the picture for which they posed. Huck's suit, basic black and not altogether that dated, though the jacket was cut long, and the big tortoiseshell glasses feel very much a relic of the time, as do his sideburns. The picture has hung in the kitchen for Sarah's entire life.

The dress must be somewhere: Lulu is sentimental. Nevertheless, it's not for Sarah. The truth, unspoken but many times mulled over, is that she looks nothing like Lulu. An irony, that one, a missed opportunity: the great beauty whose genes turn out to be recessive. It doesn't make Sarah laugh, even now, nor, though, does it make her cry. There's little point in that. She's her father's daughter: as tall as him, the very same posture, the exact chin, the echoing laugh, the same way of holding a fork—that weird specificity of DNA. She's learned Lulu: the cock of the head, the purposeful stride, the girlish tendency to touch her own hair, self-taught comportment, a secret project of Sarah's when she was twelve. Of course, she'd known, much earlier than that, even, how genetics disappoint. Lulu's hair, just like the hair on that disembodied bust of Barbie, a birthday present on which she was meant to practice the feminine arts, could be pinned up prettily, pulled over her shoulder casually, or folded into a lush, delicious chignon. Lulu wore it to her waist, once upon a time, a much younger woman, though now, in her sixties, it's mannishly cropped, which has the effect of making her face appear even finer. Those drugstore elastics never seemed to do anything to Sarah's hair but choke it, like a too-tight bandage that makes your finger swell.

Then the yearned-for breasts, they simply kept growing, adolescence as horror story (isn't it always?), the areolae spreading like a bruise, Sarah looking on in private shock, shielding herself with a rough towel in the postswim shower. They stopped, eventually, of course, though they hurt her back, sometimes. Those breasts are two of the many reasons she could never wear her mother's gown down an aisle. There's also her shoulders (those are Huck's, too), broad and powerful, not an altogether bad thing, but the effect would be more pleasant if her waist tapered, as her mother's does, even after childbirth twice over, Lulu in her pleated skirts like a paper doll. Lulu's means of sustaining herself: occasional bites from a plate piled high, while she darts around the room, making conversation, before scraping the thing into the garbage disposal. She doesn't need more than a few cubes of cantaloupe in the morning, a cup of tea with honey and lemon in the afternoon, a half of an English muffin, some desultory bites of a salad, the drumstick from the chicken, gnawed with a precision that's somehow more like a lady than a rodent. Sarah requires more than this to survive, and she has learned to ignore, or not ignore, make peace with, or not wage war against, the excess. That excess, it sits comfortably on her body, everywhere: the slope of chin into neck, that bit from elbow to armpit, that swell just above the waist, with the humorous puckered punctuation of her navel. It's there, from the back of the knees up: more cushion than she'd like, and it's stubborn, this stuff, whatever she should call it. She goes to the gym. Nothing changes.

So, absent a hand-me-down dress, time to go shopping. This is no store; it is an atelier. The entrance unmarked like a therefore more sought-after bar or restaurant, the buzzer admitting her immediately. The far too beautiful Korean girl brandished a clipboard authoritatively, led Sarah to the sunny, well-appointed room, lined with rolling racks. Here, a clutch of overly complicated confections of chiffon and lace, for the bride young enough to still fancy herself a princess. There, a quintet of slinky silks wilting on velvet-lined hangers, too sexy by far, the sort of thing a movie star might navigate the red carpet in, the supplicant television correspondent demanding to know the designer's name.

The Korean girl bats her lashes—such lashes, they have to be fake—and tells Sarah she has a face from the past. Neither insult nor compliment; oracular pronouncement. She leads Sarah to the rack she feels is right for her: dresses Jackie Bouvier might have worn. They are pretty, have a certain geometric propriety, a festive dignity, these flawless satins or cottons, in shades of cream and cloud so pure it seems they've never been touched, but of course, they were, lovingly worked over by the hands of unknown seamstresses somewhere far off. Even on their hangers they have a certain presence, that's how powerful the very idea of the wedding dress is. Sarah selects two, and the Korean girl ferries them off to the dressing area, one at a time, the hook of the hanger held high in one hand, the excess of the dress draped lovingly over the crook of her other arm.

Putting on a dress this complex is a rite unto itself: unzipping and unhooking, slithering and draping, buttoning and fastening. This is a task for four hands, really, but she's damned if she's going to undress in front of that girl. She steps out of her flats, the ones that leave that terrible crimp across the top of her feet, and kicks off her jeans, not bothering to drape them over the back of the chair presumably provided for that purpose. She pulls her shirt off inelegantly—there's no other way to do this—and catches herself, near naked, in the wood-framed mirror, for only a second. The dress hangs from a hook on the wall. Sarah struggles with preparing it for her body, understanding the architecture of the thing, locating its secret latches and recesses. She lifts it overhead, and lets it fall; it's heavy with some unnoticed embellishment, with the solidity of its own expensive fabric, and slides down her body with a muffled but very satisfying sound. She considers herself again. The room is softly lit. The dress looks mostly like a white void, like a shroud. Her face looks rather as it always does. She's disappointed.

It's not the dress's fault. The dress is lovely. It's not right, though. She's scared to take it off, scared to snag it, stain it, bruise it. Sarah shimmies out of it carefully, is fleetingly grateful that, with the garment over her face, she can't see her body's response to this improvised dance. She guides the thing back onto its hanger, tries the other one. This one is plainer, simpler, more straightforward, but the transformation is astonishing. If she looks past the red feet, the stubble on her legs, the interaction between the dress and her breasts (she'll need a better bra, for sure), it's actually quite—well, she looks like a bride, anyway. At last, a contender. This is her fourth time trying on dresses.

She tries standing this way and then that, shifting the weight from hip to hip like those kouroi discovered beneath the Aegean. She turns her back to the mirror, looks over her shoulder, not coy but calculating. It's bare on the back but only a bit—just enough. It's nice, or maybe she simply wants it to be nice. She has lost perspective. Shopping for a wedding dress is like swimming in that regard: Even if you're truly expert, it's something best not done alone. She should have brought Lauren with her. She could overlook the ever-present rejoinder of Lauren's easy prettiness for her valuable candor. Lauren would know if the dress was nice or not, and Lauren would tell her.

Sarah tells the girl that she's interested in that second dress, and the girl makes a note for her, in her file—they keep a file here, as in a doctor's office. The girl gives Sarah a bottle of water and a sincere thank you, and then she's in a taxi, on her way to the store. This was a lunchtime errand. They're very particular about lunches at the store. Sarah is not that interested in lunch, or trying not to be, visions of herself in a wedding dress and all, so she fills that mandated hour with errands. It's a job, not volunteerism, though there are many volunteers associated with the store. She has to follow the rules, so she does, thus she accepts the wage, though it's a nominal amount, one almost certainly exceeded by the sum she's spent at the store, over time. She thinks it's important, like the ceremonial dollar the billionaire CEO might pay himself. It sends a message, even if she and Dan are the only ones getting that message. The message is: This is her work. And it is. She had aspirations, once, of an MBA, maybe law school, the nonprofit world. It's hard to say now what happened to those. It wasn't a conscious choice that kept her from filling out the applications, from soliciting the letters of recommendation. It's like when that restaurant that you always heard about closes—you meant to go there, and never did. How strange. A chance missed. A door closed. On to the next.

Sarah tries to think of herself as a consultant. That is the thing to be, in this modern world, Papa tells her, and she knows he is right. The board that runs the store and the umbrella charitable organization seem surprised when she comes to the meetings, though all are welcome to attend them. She makes suggestions and knows when she's being humored. The board is a dozen people, the most powerful a hostile interior designer who is a terrible name-dropper. He hates her. She knows that her hopes for her role at the organization have been circumscribed by his dislike for her. She tries to focus on what's important: serving New Yorkers suffering with AIDS.

What Sarah says, when asked, at parties, in passing, by Dan's or Papa's colleagues: *There have been so many advances in how we think about AIDS, and how we treat it. Our understanding of the disease shifts almost annually; shouldn't our organizational infrastructure similarly shift to accommodate new ways of combating the disease?* It sounds impressive, or at least, it sounds right. She shows up, she puts on the name tag and sits behind the desk, she wanders the floor, trying to put that once-loved vase into a setting that shows its loveliness to greater advantage. She is not going to let a power struggle undermine her commitment. There are board members who are noticeably nicer to her now than when she first showed up. It's been two years. This is vindicating.

The taxi is taking too long. The driver is hesitant. He seems irritatingly uncertain. Though she's lived here all her life, except the sojourn of college, she can't direct him. She's never paid attention, not to the way the roads unfold. She can drive from the garage where her parents keep their beat-up old car to their house in Connecticut without thinking, but she can't remember which avenues run uptown and which down. She says nothing. She looks at her phone. She looks out the window. There's been a study, recently, about how often parents look at their phones, about the phones representing some kind of competition to the children, about how addicted we all are to being connected to each other, to being able to access the sum of human knowledge whenever we need it. She's trying to look at her phone less, since reading that, but it's true that the things are addictive.

She finds the container of cashews in her bag, chews one thoughtfully. This trying on of dresses: hard to square with her principles, but it makes her want to eat less. She wants to look beautiful. People will remember them as they were on their wedding day, and she wants to be remembered as having looked perfect. It matters, and if it's stupid that it matters, well, then so be it.

Sarah thinks again of that photograph, Lulu in her gown, less beatific than stunned. They'd dressed the part but in fact, they'd eloped, the two of them, visited a federal judge of Huck's acquaintance. Was Lulu sad, Sarah wonders, marrying a man her parents had never met, thousands of miles from home? Does it matter how you get married or only that you do? She hasn't thought yet about who will actually pronounce them husband and wife, who will represent the state, the only god she and Dan actually believe in. She's been to those weddings where a friend of the couple did the thing, earning his credentials online, which surely illustrated something important about religion. Their love is important, but she can't think of anything that approaches the sacred in her life, the sort of spirit that inspired great cathedrals, mass hallucinations, civil wars. Their wedding, however it will be, it feels smaller than God. A church is out of the question.

She actually shakes her head as though to dispel the thoughts of the divine. There doesn't seem to be time for that now. It's probably an intellectual response to the sheer stupidity of shopping, a sad state because for a long time shopping was all she ever wanted to do. She and Lauren, nosing around the boutiques near Washington Square Park, which were for college kids and therefore irresistible, considering a nose piercing, a pair of thick-soled boots, glittery nail polish, or she and Lauren, uptown at the sort of store Lulu liked, considering a miniature leather backpack, a flowery cotton dress by Betsey Johnson, that sexy unisex perfume in the smooth glass flask. The trying on of dresses, even then, was no fun, not if they were both trying the same thing, because it was clear on whom it would look better. But the Longchamp bag, the dangly earrings, the perfume—with those, it didn't matter who looked better, and Sarah was the one with the allowance, and later, the credit card. Lauren had saved for that Kate Spade wallet, but she just had less to keep inside it.

Sarah needs that Lauren, the old Lauren. They held each other in mutual thrall. Everything was exciting. Now, so little seems to be, or at least, so little seems to be to Lauren. Sarah doesn't want this to be true of herself; she doesn't want to be a cynic. She fiddles with the button to open the window. A bit more breeze might be nice. Yes, the dress thing, it's humiliating, but she's going to have to find a way to get excited about it. She's hungry, but the fresh, bracing air on her face might waken her, stir her, change her. She looks at her phone.

The celebrity chef is crying into the telephone. These are her plaints: computer trouble, moving to a new office, the death of her dog, the firing of an embezzling assistant. This is above Lauren's pay grade. This calls for more than she, with that "associate" lodged firmly before her title, is able to affect, to mitigate. What can she say to this but "There, there." She's no confessor. She cannot prescribe. She can only listen, listen as the litany turns to tirade. The celebrity chef, she is angry: disappointed by technology, dismayed by the relocation, betrayed by the pettiness of thievery and the grim fact of death itself.

"That's terrible" is what Lauren manages. This is what it's come to. She has ideas, chefs she'd love to work with, writers whose work she admires, themes that might be interesting books, events that might actually generate some press attention, but here she is, cooing to a stranger over the telephone.

The woman continues, her impeccable Cuban accent cracking, a coarse edge peeking through, a frayed hem, a shame. It makes Lauren like her better. It makes her remember their impolitic teasing, as kids, about Sarah's being Latina. It's there, lodged at the very heart of her name—Sarah Rojas Thomas, corruption or compromise of Venezuelan convention, Lulu's maiden name as her middle name—and she and their other friends, idiots every one of them, had thought it hilarious, at certain moments, to imply that Sarah was the maid. They lacked the imagination to think of other occupations for a woman named Rojas.

The upshot is: The book is going to be late. Lauren knows this the second she spies the 305 area code on the telephone's caller ID. This is Miranda's territory, but Miranda is not here, and the celebrity chef is afraid of Miranda anyway. She knows Miranda outranks Lauren, she knows there's nothing Lauren can do to her, so it's Lauren she's decided to tell. She's canny, you don't get to be a celebrity without being canny.

Lauren nods and fiddles on the computer and wills her mind away from her body, wills herself away from this conversation. It ends, eventually, as conversations must. The celebrity chef a little less unhappy, barely disguising her relief at having jettisoned at least one of her many responsibilities—the contractual obligation to deliver a manuscript by the end of the following month. She has gotten her way, as she no doubt knew she would.

The shadow of this conversation stretches across the rest of the day. It gives Lauren that dry feeling in her mouth, that quickening of the breath that makes her feel she's somehow been at fault, when of course she's not. This is true power, she thinks, walking home, exorcising the negative thoughts in the bracing air, breathing in the cool, exhaling the stress, to take your problem and make it someone else's, to slip out of the bonds of your promise, your responsibility, and—nothing. No consequence. This is celebrity. She has known celebrity, in her work, of course; this chef, she's not the only one. But beyond work, there was that guy from college, a year younger, but they knew him pretty well, who won an Oscar shortly after graduation. Her high school had been lousy with the children of celebrities, and some of them are celebrated now, for owning art galleries on the Lower East Side or throwing charity events or being beautiful and out and about. And of course, there are Huck and Lulu, not celebrities the way some of their fellow students' parents had been—not models or television stars, rock musicians or English actors who appeared on Broadway—but Huck and Lulu were known. If not celebrities, celebrated. They had nothing to do with what was happening currently in the culture, were not a momentary apparition, the ingénue who graces one magazine cover then vanishes. They endured. Huck endured, anyway, and Lulu sat by his side and was mentioned in the same breath, always with the same parentheticals, the same formulation: "his wife, Lulu, the well-regarded singer." *Well-regarded*, to be regarded at all: the American dream.

Huck has never been a celebrity to Lauren; she met him at eleven, and few children that age are conversant in international diplomacy. She remembers very well that first visit to that house—the photographs of Huck, at every age but always, puzzlingly, the same: glasses, hair of varying degrees of thickness and grayness, cigarettes, jackets with strangely wide lapels, smiling comfortably, gripping the hands of Ford and Mrs. Ford, Reagan and the wisp of Mrs. Reagan, Bush and Mrs. Bush, then another Bush and another Mrs. Bush, and Tony Blair, and Mitterrand, and Thatcher, and Powell, and Rumsfeld, and Cheney, that whole lot. Who was this man, her friend from school's father? It had never before occurred to her that a friend from school's father could be a subject worthy of further thought.

Lauren doesn't normally consider Huck a role model but she has to admit: He'd never miss a deadline, would never call and badger an associate editor into accepting the fact that his promised manuscript would be arriving late, and, well, too bad. True, it can't take much effort to turn out the garbage he writes, which is less artful than a charming anecdote about and instructions for a beloved *ropa vieja*. No matter. Real power never apologizes. The celebrity chef is not sorry about her deadline any more than Huck is about Iraq.

It's that country—the skirmish, the quagmire, any noun seems more appropriate than war—that showed her who Huck really is. She'd known, all along, that he was important, but they'd been insulated by their youth and unbothered by whatever it was Sarah's papa was writing up in his fourth-floor office. The summer after graduation, at a smallish gathering at Huck and Lulu's (twenty guests instead of a hundred, sitting around the dining table instead of milling about with plates), Lauren met the man who'd run Iraq on behalf of—well, whom, exactly was not quite clear. Everyone knew, of course, about the looting, the disbanding of the army, the banishment of the political class, the missing millions: It had all, every last bit of it, been a disaster, though if you'd happened in, helped yourself to some of the spinach samosas, which were delicious, you'd never have known it. Handshakes and warm embraces, smiles and Hermès ties, updates on the kids, in law school, at Goldman, and promises to meet up in the Vineyard later that summer.

Her parents had voted for Reagan once upon a time, but her father was vocal on the many children who had, in fact, been left behind. Talk of the war was everywhere, that year they finished school. The subject had come up, to her great dismay, at Poughkeepsie's best restaurant, reservations secured two months in advance, the whole clan gathered to celebrate graduation. Her mother had insisted Lauren invite Sarah, who remained focused on her pappardelle while her dad railed against the administration. They did not know—or if they did, they did not learn it from Lauren—the extent of Huck's reach in the world. And Lauren had learned, from watching Sarah, that it was best to simply pretend that current events had nothing to do with real life.

That was, in essence, the takeaway from her expensive education: You are either the sort of person who shapes society, or the sort of person whose life is affected by the shape of society. She wonders if that's what her parents had hoped for when they decided to ship Lauren off to school in the city. The idea came from the Doctors Khan (Mohammad and Anjali) whose combined practice her mother had been managing for almost two decades now. The Doctors Khan represented the very highest standard of being in her family's household: as hardworking as they were well educated, sensible despite their financial security (they drove to work together, a Toyota station wagon, used), and savvy in the ways of a culture to which they hadn't even been born. It was Anjali Khan who had explained to a dumbfounded Bella Brooks that enough parents were willing and able to pay the full near-thirty-thousand-dollar tuition that ample money was left over to ease the burden for those parents who couldn't swing it. Bella, Dr. Khan thought, owed it to herself and her children to look into this.

Mike and Bella Brooks deemed the small indignities of life as a scholarship parent worth what was gained in exchange: visions of impressive extracurriculars (an archaeological dig over spring break!), college acceptances, graduate degrees, financial liberty. Before the sixth grade, Lauren had delivered straight As across the board, a matter more of competence than brilliance, though no one would figure that out for many years. So she went to the school, the special school, the well-endowed school, the sought-after school, and came out six years later as much a stranger to her parents as Grace Chang was to her Fujianese fishmonger father and seamstress mother. Grace had gone off to Harvard, naturally, then on to Columbia, and worked in the city government. Lauren has seen her on television.

The cumulative effect of the cool air and a longer-than-necessary walk: She's cold. It's one of those nights Lauren wishes she could take her brain from her skull and rinse it off. The day—its complaints, the celebrity chef—sticks to her, and there's the attendant guilt—if this job is so silly, so meaningless, how can she let it affect her this deeply? What did her own mother do, when she was Lauren's age, with a toddler and newborn at home? Did she sigh this same kind of sigh, did her shoulders slump in precisely this manner? Lauren looks like her mother, and they share mannerisms, as happens in families; she's recognized it, the way they say hello on the telephone, the way they cross their legs, the way they rub the backs of their heads when they're tired, and there's probably more. It's hard to observe yourself. She showers, the warmth returns slowly to her body, and she tries to picture her mother, imagine what she's doing at that very moment, Wednesday, a little after 7:30, October well on its way, the air cool and dry.

Is she in the house, reheating something for dinner? Is she at the Khans' office, catching up on paperwork? Is she stuck in traffic, is she auditioning for the next show at the community theater, is she volunteering and delivering meals to shut-ins, is she grocery shopping, is she taking the car in to be serviced, is she on her way to the dentist, did she stop at the library after work, is she meeting Lauren's dad for an early movie? Lauren has no idea.

———·———

Karen is Lauren's only work friend. The rest of them are fine. Antonia is sweet, if odd, forever bringing up subjects unrelated to anything being discussed (her mother's foot surgery, the city council elections, the new security guard in the lobby). Dallie talks too much, but generally means well. Hannah is not much younger but somehow of a wholly different generation, and Lauren can never relate to the things she talks about (late nights out, social media, bands Lauren's never heard of). Kristen has a strange habit of speaking too often in question form, not a terrible character flaw but one Lauren finds very irritating, though she's inclined now to think charitably about Kristen because it's her absence that has made possible Rob's presence. Mary-Beth and Miranda are her bosses, and therefore can't be considered friends, though she's fond of them both. Mary-Beth is unglamorous in a way that's almost glamorous: She wears black and navy blue together, walks around with a pencil behind her ear, has hair streaked with silver. Her not caring makes Mary-Beth seem somehow chic. The office, like every sample group of humanity, breaks into its smaller components. The art directors are friendly with the photo department. The bosses go out to lunches together.

Lauren and Karen are stuck firmly in the middle of this to-gether, a marriage of convenience, though as luck has it, she quite likes Karen and the feeling is mutual. Karen is two years younger than Lauren but acts a decade older. She evinces weariness with the world, vocally dismissing whatever annoys her: the foibles of the bosses, the fawnings of their underlings. Lauren is aware that she's two years too old to be in the middle of this totem pole—too old for that "Associate"—and that the same weariness, coming from her, feels sometimes like bitterness.

She works at keeping that bitterness at bay. She never wanted this particular turn in her career, so she can't begrudge not having climbed higher. It would be dishonest. She's still planning, still plotting, still keeping her options open, though to what end she's not entirely sure, not yet anyway. She has options but she also has insurance, and the occasional Balenciaga bag.

"This is good, but this isn't a meal." Karen is quite expert with her chopsticks. A new restaurant, an all-dumpling menu, and she's not wrong: The food is fine but unsatisfying.

Lauren knows it's small of her but she doesn't like going to a restaurant alone. She supposes this is a measure of her failure as a human being, a certain kind of human being, an evolved hu-man being. How can you claim comfort with yourself if you can't sit and read *The New Yorker* while dunking something into a tiny plastic cup of inky soy sauce? You can't. Maybe she can't. But don't we all have those memories of hesitating, plastic tray in hands, while scanning the cafeteria for a friendly face, and aren't friendly faces hard to come by when you're eleven? She's always needed a friend. At eleven, at the new school, she was panicked. Who wouldn't be? The teachers didn't make her stand up in front of the class and say something about herself, nothing like that, teachers don't actually do that, do they? But eleven is old enough to understand a lot more than some might think, and Lauren understood, eyeing the queue of taxis and town cars that morning, that things were going to be different.

Her mother had held her hand, then it was her mother who let go of it, her mother who understood she needed to not risk coloring her classmates' perceptions of her daughter. There were other parents in evidence, fathers and mothers who similarly sensed that they should play it cool for the good of their child's social capital. But there were unattended children as well: They'd gone to this school for six years together, this was not a first day, merely a return. Lauren took her place among them: They lined up, as they'd been taught to for half their lives, and disappeared inside the school's actually-ivied walls and Lauren said nothing, not even to the chubby girl who pointed out they had the same model backpack. She would need to make friends, but she would need to be discriminating. She saw the desperation on that girl's face and was not going to let it pull her into its orbit.

It is not clear to either Lauren or Sarah why they spoke. They can't recall who approached whom. But they met, almost right away; on that, there's consensus. Sarah nice enough, but still as fierce as her compatriots; no one is more fierce than an eleven-year-old girl. Even Lauren, eager, nervous, was defended—her need guarded, and because it was hidden, it was vanquished by lunchtime. They were friends by noon. That first moment, conversation, exchange lost to time, but twenty-one years later here they are still.

Sarah introduced her—introduced her! Explained who was who and everything, though certainly there couldn't have been hands shaken?—to the other girls she deemed worth knowing. At her old school, Lauren had known the other kids her whole life. You learned who people were quickly, learned them alphabetically. Three weeks later, she was going to Sarah's house after school. By fall break, she was with her at their house in Connecticut—a whole other house, meant only for the weekends and days off, something she'd never considered. Her mother had made her send a thank-you card, and she'd been mortified when she went back to Sarah's house and the thank-you card in question was pinned to the corkboard by the kitchen telephone.

Lauren's mother used to lament Sarah's being an only child, feeling that explained some of the girls' incredible, instantaneous closeness. Of course, she wasn't truly an only child, but Bella never came to know Lulu well enough to learn any of this. Lauren didn't see Sarah's condition as solitude. She was envious: no big brother, burping in her face then laughing hysterically, none of that rank, powerful smell of teenage boys, the one that she understood much later has to do with the discovery of masturbation. At any rate, Sarah was never alone, so she couldn't have been lonely. She was always in a group, always a group of girls. Sarah had authority, she had presence. She was a leader, born to it. She had a kind of stardom, one that had nothing to do with who her parents were or how much money they had—everyone's parents were someone, except Lauren's, and they all had money, except for Lauren's—but it was something that came naturally, like the way her hair kinked when the air was steamy.

Seven years later, another first meal in another strange cafeteria; Lauren had never been so relieved to see Lulu's daffy face, Huck's dignified head. She didn't care if their classmates would denounce him, later, as a war criminal. She just sat and watched Lulu poke her fork at a salad, exclaim over the fact that the salad bar had lentils, watched Huck eat a grilled cheese sandwich, which seemed at once incongruous and wholly fitting. He loved America so, et cetera. Sarah's glow was diminished, a bit, in this unfamiliar setting, a grand columned building that had suffered an institutional adaptation, stripping away its character, mostly by means of harsh fluorescent lighting, which is better for the planet. Maybe it had to do with Huck and Lulu. Her own mother and father had dropped her off, said their good-byes, and Lauren feigned sorrow though her chest was breaking open with excitement. The liberation of adulthood. She watched them disappear out of the parking lot in the maroon station wagon, and a burden lifted off her shoulders, flew away into the late summer afternoon. She had spent her entire life waiting for the next thing; this was the first moment she'd actually experienced that thing. It seems impossible and hilarious to her now that this was fourteen years ago.

There had followed four years of meals together. Breakfast, which Sarah loved and Lauren did not, only coffee for her. Lunch, when their schedules allowed. Dinner, most nights. There was a fourth meal—they were college students, they stayed up late and thought nothing of a plate of Tater Tots at 11:00 P.M. while discussing *Middlemarch*, a book everyone resented reading but would get much mileage, years thence, for having read. Once it seemed if not inconceivable then certainly odd that she and Sarah wouldn't dine together; now it seemed noteworthy that they had. Life, life is funny.

Karen has reddish hair and a sardonic laugh. She has a sardonic everything. She grew up in Ohio and has a strange way of pronouncing everything. Her wryness has an accuracy to it. One of the first times they had lunch together—Karen had tendered the invitation, "Hey, let's have lunch," and it seemed so logical Lauren naturally said yes, though it wouldn't have occurred to her to make the same offer, not ever—Karen had entertained her with her observations about their bosses. She pointed out that one of Mary-Beth's legs is shorter than the other, by a significant margin; you can tell it by the way she walks. Lauren had been there two years before Karen showed up, had never noticed. She wasn't that attentive, in the end, to the small details of other people's lives. Karen mimicked Mary-Beth's gait—not cruelly, more imitatively—and Lauren was astonished. Karen was perceptive. Maybe in the end being perceptive is better than being smart.

"So what's the deal with the temp?" Karen, nonchalant.

"The deal?" She can't look elegant with chopsticks. She's using a fork.

"He's cute." Karen has a boyfriend, named Evan. He's an illustrator, which doesn't seem like a proper job, but he makes a living. He's nice, but he has a goatee. The three of them had a drink once, after work, last summer. Evan hadn't been wearing enough deodorant.

"Yeah, he's cute," Lauren says, like they're discussing the weather.

"Oh fuck off like you haven't noticed." This is another thing about Karen: She's foulmouthed.

"I've noticed," Lauren says.

As a kid, Sarah hated Sundays, felt itchy from first thing in the morning, not because of church, Huck and Lulu weren't church people, but from that awareness of the looming Monday, that quiet sadness of the city on a Sunday, though it was worse, worse by far, to spend the Sunday in Connecticut, as they sometimes did, and she'd lobby to leave the house by lunchtime so she could be home, safe, ready for something, some nameless thing that was gathering, that she could sense. She still doesn't love Sundays.

They wake early. Dan gets the coffee, she gets the paper, which the doorman has dropped in front of their door, pointlessly wrapped in its blue plastic bag. They don't lie around in bed, which she makes up the minute they're up because she hates an unmade bed, but they don't rush to dress either, and Dan will turn on one of those soft news Sunday-morning programs, folksy and upbeat, and do four, five things at once, drink coffee, watch television, check e-mail, read the paper, make notes, look at his phone.

Sunday nights are, it's understood, dinner as a family. There have been exceptions, as of course there would be over the course

of thirty-two years: illness, travel, work, college. Dan understands. Dan comes, it's nice to be four instead of three, some balance restored, contra the God they don't believe in, the one who
killed her brother. This Sunday Dan's not there, he's at work;
there's always that, because work is respected in this house, particularly Dan's work.

"You saw that the Westons are putting their house on the market?" Lulu flits. She doesn't like to sit. She'll eat three bites, get up
and start cooking dessert. They never eat in the dining room, these
nights, just the family: That's for formal affairs, when there's a
caterer on hand. Sundays, they eat in the kitchen, talking while
Lulu stirs and chops and takes breaks to dash back to the table for
another bite or to get a sip of water. "There's bread, I bought it at
a stand in Union Square just for tonight, I almost forgot it." Lulu
gets up again to fetch the bread.

"Where are the Westons going?" The same roast potatoes, the
same crunch. It's comforting, as it's meant to be. Sarah sips her wine.

"The Westons are what we in the industry call 'cashing out.' "
This is a classic of Huck's: references to the "industry," no matter
what's being discussed. It's not funny, though Sarah accepts that
he means it as a joke.

"Empty nest!" Lulu deposits the bread on the table. Slick and
oily, a cross-hatching of rosemary on it. "The twins are out of college now, what do they need with that big old house, just the two
of them? This looks good, doesn't it?"

It does look good. Sarah tugs at the end of it, no need for the
knife—they're not formal. It's surprisingly gummy. "I'm out of
college, Mom. What do you need with this big old house?"

"Can't break bread when the bread won't break, Lulu." Huck tugs at the loaf.

"I'll get the knife." This, said as she's already across the room, doing just that. "Don't think we haven't had offers on this house, Sarah. But I'm sentimental."

"I would be lost if we sold this house. Lost!" Huck, mimicking horror. "You've lived your entire life here, you don't want to see it sold, do you?"

She wrests a piece of the loaf off before her mother is back, chews it thoughtfully. "I'm teasing, Papa. No. But the Westons. I mean, I get it. Hey, this bread is good, Mom."

Lulu beams as if she's made it herself. "I know, they had free samples, that's why I bought it. Free samples. I ate three!"

Sarah chews thoughtfully. She wishes, not for the first time, for Lulu's metabolism, but we don't get to choose what we inherit. She peels the skin off the chicken, which is unfortunate, because it's the best part.

"We need this house for our parties, of course," Lulu says. "And I love it here."

"Speaking of our parties, your mother's had a good idea. I don't know why we haven't had this idea yet, but leave it to Lulu."

"I wonder where they'll go, the Westons." Lulu slices into the bread. "Not Florida? People don't actually do that, do they?"

"They do, Mom. Maybe you and Papa should do that. Go somewhere warm."

"We'll buy in Cuba the second Castro dies. Any day now!" Huck raises his glass in salute.

"Ridiculous." Lulu reaches for the brussels sprouts.

"Okay, then, I'll bite." Sarah looks at her parents. They've always been this way. The Huck and Lulu show. "What's the big idea?"

"I should add it was cheap, this bread, seven dollars, imagine, you'd pay seven dollars just for the rosemary, to be honest." It's unclear to whom Lulu is speaking.

"Well, it was your mother's idea, but I'll do the talking. It's about your wedding, your nuptials, the ceremony; you should do it here, at home, don't you think? Why haven't we talked about this possibility yet?" Huck looks at her. He's in professorial mode. "I mean, not a church. There's the club, but you and Dan, you're not club people, are you? That's so old-fashioned."

"So society page," Lulu frowns. "The club. High WASP. Ridiculous."

"We are not club people." It wasn't just Chelsea Terrace. Sarah's been to see other venues—a woodsy old factory in Brooklyn, a tacky ballroom on the Upper West Side. Lack of space is the essential quality of life in the city. What space there is is expensive, and in high demand. None of those places is an option, not for next April, it seems. "At home?"

"You took your first steps in our bedroom," says Lulu. "You can walk down the aisle here, too, only fitting, don't we think? And save yourself the trouble of all this planning. It's too much."

The truth is it has occurred to Sarah, of course it has occurred to her, but she's hesitated. She wants this to be their day, hers and Dan's, not Lulu's.

"It's an idea, not a bad idea. I mean, venues are so expensive."

"Just think, in the backyard, how pretty, and we can fit lots of people."

"Two hundred, easily, definitely," says Huck. "I know we've had two hundred."

"I think we've had three hundred!" Lulu says.

"We are not having three hundred guests." Sarah frowns.

"An intimate gathering, then?" Huck drums his fingers on the dining table. "We'll have to really look at the list, make sure we don't forget anyone important. Weren't you going to get a planner or something? We need someone to oversee all this business."

"Not two hundred, not one hundred, more like seventy." Sarah's done the count a few times now. Seventy is on the low end, but still where she'd like to aim. "And I'm working on the planner. I'm supposed to talk to her soon. Willa. The one Ellen recommended."

Lulu purses her lips. She's filling the cobalt blue pitcher from the little spout by the sink that dispenses filtered water. "Seventy." She pauses. "Yes, Willa, she's the one. Ellen spoke so highly of her, and Rachel's wedding was so beautiful."

"A fine number, anyway," Huck interjects. Ever the diplomat. "A fine number."

"I told you we want to do something small." Sarah doesn't want to argue the point. And she doesn't want to bring up the obvious: that her parents are going to pay for this wedding, so they're within their rights to want to have it at their house.

"But seventy, that's minuscule. In my estimation. Much too small. I'm just saying." The pitcher comes down on the table with a thud. "Have it with the butter, it's the salty butter."

"It's fine, it's fine this way," Sarah says.

"You know, we still have half the bottle of that cabernet from the other night," Lulu says.

"That was a good one." Huck nods enthusiastically.

Lulu disappears up the stairs. Her father leans closer to Sarah. She sits at the head of the table, always has, since it was her high chair stationed there, decades ago. "Seventy people?"

"Maybe more. But small, Papa, intimate. It's embarrassing."

"What embarrassing? You're getting married. A community rite. That's what it is, you know. It's not for you. It's for—your people. Your mom and your papa."

"You eloped," she says. "You sidestepped this whole minefield."

He puts his hands up in surrender. "I'm only saying what your mother is too sad to say. She wishes her parents had been there, when we got married. She likes that whole business, the aisle, the flowers, the music."

Sarah nods. "Well, the flowers. The music. Everyone likes that stuff." She doesn't want to disappoint—she never has liked to disappoint.

———·———

Book club is every three weeks. A month was too long, by group consensus. You lost momentum. You didn't want to get together, or you didn't remember that you were supposed to or the nuances of the relationships in the group. Two weeks isn't long enough to read a book, or it can't be guaranteed. Three weeks is just about right. There's a page limit on the books they'll read. They're on Didion now. It's fine, but it's irritating, somehow. Part of Sarah suspects people only like to read Joan Didion because she's thin and glamorous, or was, anyway. The edition she's reading has a prominent photo of the author on the cover, looking chic.

Sarah's hosting tonight. It's good timing. The cleaning lady comes alternate Wednesdays, so it's only been a day, and the bathroom isn't covered in errant blond hairs, which proliferate, surprising even her, and the stove gleams. Even the inside of the refrigerator is orderly, clean, everything lined up in order of descending height. The cleaning lady has a touch of the obsessive-compulsive. Sarah leaves the house with a list: wine (there's always wine at book club), snacks savory and sweet (everyone will bring something, but her conscience won't allow her to be caught unawares should everyone forget their obligations), flowers (you can't have people into your house without buying flowers first, it's like putting on lipstick before a meeting).

She's read the Didion before: She went to college. Arrived there with dreams of reading books, smoking cigarettes, having sex, staying up into the night feverishly discussing something, anything, with someone, anyone. Lauren had gone into it with much the same expectation. They'd been on the same page about it. They'd chosen the college together.

High school was demanding, of course; they'd read *Pale Fire*, they knew about Marx, Ned Rorem, Watson and Crick, and the salon at 27 rue de Fleurus. Sarah didn't need to discover too much, didn't need scales to fall from her eyes, didn't need Judy Chicago or Cindy Sherman or Mary McCarthy (well, not her; they didn't read *her* at their college) or John Cage to give her a whole new way of thinking. She had that way of thinking. Mostly, Sarah looked forward to more of the same—lots of A's, the respectful pride of the professors—while she indulged herself in a little badness. A little exploration. A little shedding of inhibition. She could never get up to that, in high school. Her heart wasn't in it. But she would go to college, and no one would know what she was already like, no one but Lauren. So she'd cut her hair, maybe, or wear peasanty dresses, or learn to sing Joni Mitchell songs in a quavering, quiet soprano, or fuck a girl.

They knew so many girls like that. That's the thing about clichés. There's a reason they persist. So many girls—women, they were women, everyone said so, some of them even proclaimed themselves *womyn*—from so many schools like their own, from their city or other cities or other places, who arrived on a campus still drunk on summer, verdant and sunshiny. Thirty thousand dollars a head got you a lot in terms of landscaping: flowers everywhere, popping through fresh mulch. Huck, conservative hero, wasn't expecting much in the way of a welcome. He was used to visiting campuses and being met with creatively angry signs, or students disrupting his discourses to stand, turn their backs to him. They never discussed this, but he treated it, as he treated everything, with a mild bemusement, and preferred to spend his time with graduate students.

"You see, the drive is not so long," Lulu kept saying, then sighing because it was, actually, sort of long, the traffic of matriculating teenagers and their parents like the salmon congesting a stream. Her meaning was clear though: *You'll come home, often.* It was forbidden for freshmen to bring cars of their own, but the train was more than serviceable.

This parting was hard on Huck and Lulu. They were a small family, just the three of them, now, and of course, things had gone so horribly wrong with Christopher. Sarah was their second child and their second chance, the opportunity to redeem themselves, to do it right.

Her roommate was a delicate and angry girl named Ariel, who had grown up in Berkeley and was horrified when eventually she figured out who Sarah's father was. There was a damning assertion about Huck—an assertion, Sarah wasn't sure, she never investigated—in a documentary that was much talked about at the time, something about U.S. involvement in domestic politics in Latin American countries. Latin America was, for some reason, a pet cause of Ariel's—all of it, the whole continent. She read Marquez for pleasure and overly enunciated her Spanish words. After two months, Ariel requested to have her room reassigned. The authority overseeing this kind of thing was not pleased—the very idea of having a roommate, in college, was to further your experience of the world, to meet, and engage, and learn to live, in a very literal sense, with people different from you. Ariel was not buying this. Sarah wanted peace, prevailed on Lauren to swap, and for the next four years was wholly ignored by Ariel.

There's a great florist in the Sixties, so Sarah will end there, so the flowers don't get bruised and beaten on her other errands. Her to-do list isn't so long. Maybe she'll walk, she thinks. It'll be a nice alternative to going to the gym, which though she has time to do she doesn't have the will, just isn't in the mood. You go, you run, you sweat, you listen to music or watch the television, then you shower and it's hours later and you feel nothing in particular, or not different enough anyway, just a little smug, very hungry. Walking is good exercise.

She's always enjoyed this kind of time, the dead time in which her body is engaged in a pursuit for which her mind isn't required. Showering, walking somewhere, driving that familiar path from the garage to the house in Connecticut. In these moments, she makes her mental list, orders and reorders it. The list is, as ever, a hydra. For every matter that's settled—the house, of course it's the house—a new concern arises. She wants to tell Lauren about it, strategize on how to cram the cast of thousands her parents are evidently planning on inviting. Lauren knows the place, she'll have ideas. She should call her, adds that to her list. Not tonight: Tonight is book club. Lauren is not a book club friend; book club is something else: Meredith, who loves it—in fact, she organized it; Iris, a coworker of Meredith's; Valerie, an old friend of Iris's but also a friend of Meredith's; Simone, the wife of one of Dan's workers, who mentioned to Sarah once, at a party, that she wanted to join a book club. It's not Lauren's crowd. Not tomorrow: Sarah's supposed to go to Carol's for a working dinner, Chinese takeout and grants and details. Not Friday: work, then in the afternoon, a tasting at a caterer's; in the evening, dinner with Dan's coworker Steven and his wife, Amy. Not Saturday: Lulu's birthday is coming and she's going to get her a present—what she's yet to determine—and then meet Dan when he's off work—he always goes into the office Saturday afternoons, while she shops or reads or whatever. Not Sunday, sacrosanct, reserved for just the two of them, first at home, then dinner with her parents. But soon. And then she can tell Lauren about how they'll be having the wedding at the house, and how Lulu mentioned that maybe she'd like to sing a song at the reception, and how Lulu has started asking questions about what it's appropriate for the mother of the bride to wear. Basically everything that's happened around the wedding, Sarah's first thought has been to tell Lauren about it.

She's tired of this preoccupation with the circumstances of her own life. It seems petty, all this wedding talk. A night last week, dinner with Michael and Bethany, Dan's coworkers, and their spouses, Andrea and Elias. Lovely people, with the same palpable affection for Dan as everyone who knows him, and now, by some transitive principle, for Sarah, too, since they're getting married. A ring still means something. And that ring, what it symbolized, the conversation kept turning back to it—talk about work, then talk about the wedding, talk about real estate then reminiscences of their own weddings, then swapped details about honeymoons in Namibia, the necessity of providing guests some late-night snack (doughnuts, it happens; both couples had served doughnuts, this before they even knew one another), the perils of the registry and the importance of writing thank-you notes.

The wedding hasn't even happened yet and she's exhausted being the center of attention. Being a bride is apparently a solo effort. For example, she's not heard anyone ask Dan any specific questions about what he'll be wearing or what the guests will be eating. In a way, it's an improvement over the general tendency to only talk about what people do for a living—the first thing everyone asks someone they've just met, isn't it?

Her unsatisfactory answer to that query is that she's always thought of herself as a solver of problems. She just isn't clear on how to make this a career. Anyway, there never seems to be time to think about what she's going to do, because she's so busy doing it. Because there's no noun for what she's doing now, she tries to steer the conversation away from it. There's no noun, not really, for what Huck does, but he does so much. This is the family business, these things that Sarah does, the connecting of dots, the solving of problems, though she's aware that not everyone understands this, and she envies that friends like Fiona and Lauren can explain in one word what their business is.

At the moment her business is this wedding. Sarah doesn't mind it and doesn't expect Dan to be any more helpful than he is already: It's her responsibility, she gets that. It's not sexist, simply a measure of which of the two of them has the bandwidth to think about things like flowers and cake. It's not some kind of betrayal of a deeply held feminist conviction, that she has to now think about this shit—it's a reflection of the kind of relationship they have, the kind they want to have, one in which they take turns helping each other. She knows that if she complained, Dan would slip away on his lunch break to sample wedges of cake.

The truth is that she cares fuck all about cake. She'd have gone to the courthouse. But it's too late now. This is how they're getting married, and she's got to take it seriously, give the people what they expect, what they want: to put on a tie or a not-too-pretty dress, to eat lukewarm salmon, to tap a champagne flute with a dessert spoon, to take pictures, to dance, to say hello to the older relatives, to see friends from college and high school, to eat warm doughnuts from sticky boxes as the clock strikes midnight. She'll get through this, and make it perfect, too. She will not disappoint.

———·———

There's Halloween candy on display in the drugstore across the street from the office, the one that's more like a grocery store, or a boutique, that sells nail polish but also cantaloupe or a sweatshirt. It's a confusing but seemingly successful business model. Lauren had gone to get a yogurt, a midafternoon snack, that Greek yogurt with a little compartment of strawberry jam you can squeeze into the cup and mix up so it's like dessert. She's hungrier lately; the body responding to the calendar, presumably.

She's been looking forward to dinner, because of that hunger, if at the same time dreading it, because of Sarah. Not that she doesn't want to see her, not exactly. She's uncertain, actually, why she's reluctant.

Sarah's chosen a restaurant downtown, she always does, because, Lauren thinks, of a tirade she once went on, about how restaurants uptown are all terrible. Lauren stands by it, but at the time wasn't talking about Sarah at all, was relaying an anecdote about a party for one of her books, held in a too-bright spot in the West Seventies, where the air-conditioning was powerful and the food charmless. But she's fairly certain that Sarah made a note of it. She knows how her mind works.

Walking from the subway, Lauren is rather enjoying the chill, though she knows what will come next and thinks of warmer climes. One of the essential conditions of living in New York City is thinking wistfully about living in California. It's the opposite coast, therefore presumed to be the opposite in every other way. She's only been there twice, herself—that cookbook conference in San Francisco, where she went to some nice restaurants, drank a lot of thin, local wine, and spent a lot of time wishing she was outside. And Los Angeles once, years before that, a postcollege vacation with Sarah where they stayed with friends who shared an adorable little house. They couldn't get over the novelty of it: an actual house, all your own, a driveway, a table on the patch of concrete outside the kitchen door, bougainvillea shedding like mad. Greg, her college boyfriend—though it seems insane to use that word to describe their relationship, they were in college, they never went anywhere, just shuttled back and forth between his apartment off campus and her room on campus, fucking—had moved to Los Angeles after graduation to begin his career in the film business. He worked at a production company vaguely associated with a well-known director. He was mostly responsible for ordering lunch, unwrapping it, and placing it in the center of the table in various conference rooms. Greg was what that trip had been about. She couldn't afford it, but Sarah had urged it: a break from the rigors of their first jobs, a break from the shitty apartment they shared, plus a taste of an alternate life. Sarah had never wanted Lauren to break up with Greg, but what was the alternative: to have married him? He's married now, anyway. He's gained seventy pounds since college, not fat, but mass. He was so slender and hard, now he's positively burly, with a big jaw that he developed at some point in his midtwenties. He still works in film, as a line producer, though Lauren doesn't know what that means. His wife is a prop stylist, they live in Silver Lake, they have a daughter named Violet, whose existence he's lovingly documented online.

She couldn't have gone to California, those years ago, because she would have been going only for Greg, and that seemed idiotic, pathetic, would have been vastly overestimating what their relationship had been, never mind that he hadn't asked her to. College ended, their romance ended, and they'd both known that was coming. In fact, if they'd broken up, formally, a conversation, in bed one morning, she can't remember it. He was very sweet, and she had loved fucking him, but life had a lot more in store for her, in New York City, in publishing. Adventures. Now it's eight years later and far too late for her to move to California. And on the good days, she retains that sense that life holds something in store for her. On the bad days, she is not so sure. On the average day, the day like today, she can let her mind wander. But what would she do for a job? She can't style props, whatever that means. Still, on a chilly evening it's nice to think of bougainvillea.

Sarah is there before her, sitting, looking at her phone.

"Am I late?" Lauren doesn't want to start the evening off on the wrong foot.

Sarah shakes her head. "I'm early."

Lauren falls into the chair. If there's a ladylike way to sit down, she's not mastered it. "How are you?"

Sarah puts the phone into the bag on the banquette beside her. "I'm good! I'm actually superhungry."

"Me too. It's the fall. Hibernating season."

"God, this is the last thing I need, I'm supposed to put on a dress that you can be damn sure is going to be sleeveless. I can just see myself, arms wiggling in the breeze."

Lauren makes a sort of tsk sound in response, to register that she's heard and that she disapproves. "You look great," she says, but so close on the heels of what Sarah's said it doesn't sound sincere.

A pained smile. "How are you?" Sarah asks.

"I'm good, actually. Today was a good day." As Lauren says it, she marvels at it: She can't believe it's true.

Sarah looks surprised. "Do tell."

"You don't need to look so shocked," she says. "Am I such a downer? I have good days."

"I'm just happy for you," Sarah says. "Anything noteworthy or just generally a not bad day?"

That afternoon, the remnants of the expensive prechopped salad bar salad (spinach, chickpeas, broccoli, tuna, carrot, sunflower seeds, balsamic vinegar, $11.95) still on her desk, Mary-Beth had toddled over, which is how Lauren now thinks of her gait, and paused there behind her chair for a moment laden with meaning. "Lauren," she'd said.

This was not of itself worth note—she was her boss, of course they talked—but there was something in it, her pronunciation, some suggestion, some clue. "Do you have a second?"

This too: the implication that they needed to speak privately. Lauren had followed Mary-Beth to her office, worrying about the tuna salad on her breath like someone out of a commercial for gum, or an unimaginative television show. Mary-Beth even asked Lauren to close the door, or anyway, nodded toward it meaningfully.

The short of it: a promotion, and a significant one, the shedding of the epithet associate, a standing invitation to pitch projects, an expectation that there would be travel, and meals out, and even occasional reimbursements for such. The imprint is quite firmly in the black, it seems. Dallie will be leaving; the organization, lean though it is, will be reorganized; and Lauren will find herself, suddenly, quite near the top of the structure. And more— further changes coming, something unspoken but suggested, Miranda taking on a different role, one in the parent company, quite literally kicked upstairs, to the hushed, glass-walled thirty-sixth floor, where all the very most important meetings in the building take place. Mary-Beth had always liked Lauren, told her so, just like that, acknowledging that this change is big, unlikely, amorphous, a gift, a reward, for being good, for being liked. Mary-Beth even mentions the celebrity chef, the quarrelsome Cuban. They've been keeping tabs on Lauren, it seems.

Lauren shrugs. "A good day, is all. I don't know. There's this chance that I'm going to get some new responsibilities. Which I think is good. I mean, more work, but more interesting work."

"You mean they're finally realizing that you're incredibly overqualified for your job," Sarah says. "Thank fucking God. Congratulations. A raise?"

Once, years ago, when they were roommates in the city, unable to stop herself, Lauren had peered into one of the fat envelopes from Prudential that arrived for Sarah monthly. The sum—

the only sum she was able to divine, amid all those numbers and charts—was astonishing. "A raise," she says, but doesn't say what she wants to, which is that Sarah would consider the sum in question inconsequential. "A decent one." It's not much to speak of, really, but it's hers.

They order drinks: a martini, both of them; it seems retro, and celebratory, and somehow funny, and when they're delivered, precariously, the liquid spilling out over the lips of the unwieldy glasses, Sarah takes a sip, as if for strength, then raises the glass. "Huzzah," she says.

"Thanks," Lauren says. She sips her drink. "Editor. No associate."

"Not assistant?"

"Editor," she says.

"Fucking great," Sarah says. "I knew it." She pauses. "By the way, I just should say it, so whatever, but if you've been mad at me since the last time we hung out, I'm sorry."

Lauren has never known how to deal with a compliment and she's never known how to deal with an apology. It seems better, in both instances, to change the subject. "I'm not. No, I was just . . . You know."

"I didn't mean to keep talking about Gabe," Sarah says.

"I was in a bad mood," Lauren says. It's funny because now, hearing Sarah mention Gabe's name, she feels nothing, not even a glimmer of recognition. They could be discussing anything at all. Maybe she had been in a bad mood.

"It's a sensitive subject. I get it. You should have just told me to shut up, you idiot." And now: back to normal.

"Please, like anyone ever in your entire life has ever told you to shut up, and like you would." Lauren knows she loves this, the compliment disguised as an insult that Sarah is strong-willed, that Sarah will have her say. "How's Dan?" Lauren often forgets to ask about him. The giant ring, though, reminds her.

"He's good. He's the same. He's busy, he's working a lot lately, like more than usual, but it's good, like the good overworked, not the bad kind. How are your folks?"

"My folks? Um. They're fine. It was my mom's birthday two weeks ago. I got her a cookbook, one that we don't even publish, which is so lame but my father insisted it was what she wanted. I don't know if I believe him. Are you going on a honeymoon?"

"We talked about it. It's hard for Dan to get a lot of time off. But everyone is like, oh you have to go on a honeymoon and so on." She shrugs her shoulders.

"You're probably going to want like . . . a vacation from your parents, right?" Lauren knows the intricacies of that family's life well enough to be able to tease.

"Dan's got to go to L.A. at some point for work; I thought maybe I could tag along on that and we could schedule a real honeymoon later. Like Africa maybe? Africa. That's what everyone keeps telling me."

"L.A., God that is so weird, I was just thinking about when we went out there after school, do you remember that?"

"Do I remember that, of course I remember that, what am I, brain damaged? Holly and Christina and that tiny little house."

"You just wanted me to see Greg again, right? That was the ulterior motive."

"I don't know what you're talking about."

"Bullshit, you're the worst liar. Wait." Lauren has an epiphany, a small one, if there's a word for that. "This is just like that Gabe thing. From our last dinner."

"I don't know, I loved you guys together. And it's not like there was so much awesome stuff going on for us here at that point in our lives."

"The same stuff's still going on though," Lauren says, "all these years later."

"That's not true." Sarah looks wounded by this.

The waiter returns, they order more drinks. Sarah asks for a salad and some fish. Lauren asks for a salad and some ravioli.

Sarah clears her throat. "Okay, maybe that was my secret agenda."

"God, you are obsessed with me having a boyfriend."

"Gabe was great. That's all." The final word.

"But, like, Greg?" Lauren laughs. "I mean, what was I supposed to do—marry him? They even have the same name. Gabe, Greg. God, what's wrong with me?" Sarah has only ever had Dan. Maybe she fundamentally doesn't understand that it's possible to have a boyfriend you don't mean to marry, to fuck a guy and not have it mean forever.

"You could have married Greg." Sarah is drunk now, and her gestures have gotten bigger. She points accusingly, hilariously, at Lauren across the table.

"Please, the idea that I could have married the skinny guy from Art History is ridiculous. Even if that is, let's be honest, how most college romances turn into failed first marriages."

"You make it sound like it was so unserious," Sarah says. "He met your parents."

"Once, Miss Marple." How does Sarah remember these things? "We were kids!"

"People do that, you know, Lauren. People marry the people they met in college. It's not as ridiculous or out of the question as you'd like to pretend."

"You're my life partner," Lauren says. She reaches across the table and drapes an affectionate hand over Sarah's. She's tipsy, but it's not a lie. She cannot imagine sitting in this restaurant across from Gabe or Greg, not the way she can imagine sitting here now with Sarah, or a year from now, with Sarah, or ten years from now, with Sarah.

"People gave up lesbianism at graduation, however."

"Speaking of lesbians, I saw Jill. Shit, Jill what's her name? With the twin brother?" Now she's drunk, too.

"Jill Hansen? You saw Jill Hansen? And she's a lesbian?"

"No, just her haircut. But her brother is gay."

"Of course he's gay; remember junior year he gave that presentation on *Giovanni's Room?*"

"No, how do you remember this shit?"

"I take my vitamins. Where did you see Jill Hansen?"

"She's my neighbor. Married, moved here, I can't remember all the details. She asked about you. She gave me her number but I mean . . . am I supposed to call her? It seems very bizarre."

"Call her, she's nice." Sarah rolls her eyes.

"Two kids. What would we talk about?"

"Wait, Jill Hansen lives near you?"

"There goes the fucking neighborhood, right?"

"Seriously. I think she might actually be a billionaire. Listen. Before our food comes, there's something I need to tell you, or ask you."

"Okay."

"Don't be insulted, first of all. But you know, as maid of honor, you're supposed to be in charge of this whole bachelorette situation."

Lauren nods. "I was once at a store in the West Village that sold pasta shaped like little tiny dicks."

"I'm serious. Hear me out: I found this place. Tropical island. Nice hotel, actually nice, not tacky. All inclusive. The five of us can laze around, order room service, sit by the pool, get massages, the whole cheesy stupid thing."

Lauren considers this information. Pros: sun, a hotel bed, a massage, swimming. Cons: everything else. The groupthink that attends every gathering of more than two women that she's ever been a part of. She doesn't bring this up. Now is not the time. She smiles. "Five?" She pauses. "This sounds amazing, by the way."

"You think so?" Sarah looks relieved. "I was worried you were going to be, like, not into it or something." She pauses. "Yes, five. You, me, Meredith, Fiona, Amina."

"Cool," she says. She likes Fiona well enough, her smooth accent, her weird way of dressing. She thinks Meredith is quite silly, though, and Amina has always seemed to her like sort of a bitch. But they're Sarah's friends, and it's Sarah's thing, and actually, they're sort of her friends, too, by association, and she understands her responsibility at this particular moment. "The beach," she says, blankly, though she does love the beach.

"I was thinking, actually, Thanksgiving," Sarah says.

Thanksgiving. This is a stroke of genius. Lauren relaxes, immediately. This gives her the perfect excuse. "Thanksgiving. Yes. What a great idea. We'll go for Thanksgiving."

"Good, that's settled. Now, where is our food?"

———·———

At a certain point in her youth, back when it wasn't inconceivable as it now is that she'd be out late, Lauren had decided that if it was after 11:30 she would, by default, take a taxi. The subway was not safe at that hour, nor was it reliable. She couldn't afford a taxi, but neither could she afford to be raped or vomited on on the subway. So this was simply the rule. And she followed it faithfully, never even screwed the driver on his tip, even though she could have used those one-dollar bills probably just as much as he. Now her rule is 8:00 P.M. Any later, and no public transportation for her, certainly not all the way between Chelsea and her apartment. She can afford it. Not really, not in the big scheme of things, but she can, and she knows she'll be almost happy to hand over the twenty-four dollars at the end of this ride, to send it back out into the world. It will symbolize something, this transaction.

The taxi nudges into place among its compatriots and competitors on the bridge. The Manhattan is the uglier of the bridges, but it affords the superior view. She's drunk. She opens the window, gulps at the air. She's so thirsty.

The night is cool, but Lauren doesn't care. She's going to a tropical island soon, she thinks, but she doesn't even know which one, because Sarah didn't tell her. She's laughing at herself, laughing at the whole enterprise. Getting married is a silly business. It might be the catalyst or conclusion of all that Shakespeare, but it's still idiotic, in its way, or idiofying—it makes idiots of us all. She has the strangest desire for a cigarette, though she's not smoked in years. There's a shop on the corner, she'll stop and get a pack. She can smoke on the fire escape, that won't stink up the apartment. She can sit and smoke and think about nothing at all.

It's wet, anemic, and sort of pathetic, but it's snow. The view from the apartment is nothing special, normally: the void of the sky, there just beyond the staggered buildings, the blankness of the river, a suggestion of New Jersey. The snow, such as it is, gives Sarah something to look at, makes her grateful for the view. Anyway, staring out the window is preferable to reviewing résumés for Carol, who has requested Sarah's input. She's been moving the stack of papers around on the coffee table for an hour, not reading or understanding any of it. The day feels over, somehow. She picks up her telephone.

As a teen, getting a telephone installed in her bedroom was a hard-won privilege. They were probably the last generation of American girls to have to lobby their parents for that specific perk. Only two decades later, it seems as antiquated and impossible as traveling by blimp. But the negotiations: They had been brutal. Sarah had begged and promised, and the good behavior and good grades with which she bargained were finally accepted, this though she reliably delivered both without any added incentive.

In retrospect, it's less that her parents were duped than that they didn't actually care. The telephone line was installed. She was charged with monitoring her usage—the bills, in those smaller-than-standard-size envelopes, which she studied looking for what, exactly? They recorded every call she had placed, the eight cents that she would be required to pay for the time she called Hannah at her apartment and had had to leave a message with the grand-mother Cho. Sarah didn't have a checking account, of course, and her parents paid the bills, and never made any particular fuss about the number of minutes she spent on the telephone.

How did they find the time, she wonders? Two-hour phone calls with Lauren: When were they even apart for two hours, and what did they talk about? One of her stronger memories of child-hood: the hot plastic of the telephone receiver pressed up against her ear.

She's still a telephone person, though she can't now concen-trate on both a telephone call and some other task, as she had as a girl. She used to do her homework that way. The ubiquity of tele-phones hasn't done anything to change the fundamental intimacy of a telephone call. A little miracle, is what it is. She pushes the résumés away, calls Lauren.

"Hi." Lauren, familiar.

Another lost aspect of the old telephone culture: never know-ing who was calling. "Hi." Sarah's surprised Lauren picked up. She's usually harder to get.

"I was just thinking about you. That's so weird. But so perfect."

"Good things, I hope."

"The greatest, actually. Do you remember our Goth phase? Please tell me you remember our Goth phase."

"That hardly qualifies as a phase," Sarah says. "We bought some Urban Decay and went to a Nick Cave show."

"We were so dark and mysterious." Lauren laughs.

Sarah shrugs, forgetting Lauren can't see it. "Adolescence is a dark time. We were experimenting."

"It's funny to think about. It was unlike us. It was unlike you. You were . . ." Lauren trails off.

"I was . . . ?" Sarah asks.

"You were, you know, you were the alpha. The leader. The role model, the head of the class, the girl most likely."

"Bullshit." Sarah's laughing. "I was not. I was just some girl. Just a teenage girl trying things on, like you were."

"So what's up?"

"Nothing up." Sarah stands. Pacing has supplanted homework as what she does when she's on the telephone. "I felt like calling. Do you remember how much we talked on the telephone when we were kids?"

"My parents hated that."

"I remember you insisting that they get call waiting."

"They refused. Eight dollars a month! An outrage."

"But what did we talk about, Lauren? What was it that we had to say to each other, so urgently?" Sarah stares out at the snowy night. Snow makes you feel more cozy, always, and she doesn't even care about having to go out into the stuff tomorrow. The tickets are bought, the rooms reserved: four nights, a pool, a hot tub, a spa, room service, a bar, golf, if for some reason she decides to take up golf. Having this to look forward to makes everything else seem possible.

Lauren sighs, or exhales, it's not clear, the weight of her breath surprisingly loud. "I'm glad we don't know. I'm sure it was idiotic. Did you ever read anything you wrote in a journal as a kid? It's all garbage. Thank God I never had the discipline to write in my journal more than three times a year."

Sarah was the same way. A journal as a birthday gift, two or three dutiful entries, then the book sat fallow in an old shoebox in her closet where she kept secret possessions: notes from friends, old boarding passes, playbills, useless foreign currency. That box must still be there in the house on East Thirty-Sixth Street. "I don't know," she says. "Whatever we were worried about then, it's probably so sweet and unimportant."

"It probably didn't seem that way at the time, though," Lauren says. "We wore black nail polish. We had real problems. The problems we have now pale in comparison."

"You have problems?"

"I have no problems. How about you?"

"Wedding planning problems. Boring problems."

"What's the latest? Lulu been practicing her repertoire for you? She should do something with a mariachi band. Mariachi bands are so festive."

"That's cute, actually. No, the music is up to her. I just need to show up and get dressed. That's the problem. The dress."

"The dress, yeah. Have you been trying stuff on?"

"It's all terrible, Lolo. Giant and puffy or like . . . slutty. I had no idea slutty was such a big thing in wedding dresses."

"I think you should go slutty. I think it would be a real departure for you."

"This is just one of those things. You can't go in alone. I think I know what I want then I step inside and I turn into a babbling idiot and start trying on the most ridiculous things and I look at the salesgirl and she's like 'You look great!' and I think maybe I do look great and should just give her four thousand dollars so I can be done with this torture."

"The problem is you're going in alone. Why don't you take me? I'm rational."

"Why don't I take you?"

"I am the matron of honor," Lauren says proudly.

"Maid."

"Oh, didn't I tell you? I got married. Sorry! I should have mentioned it. I just really wanted that *matron*."

"If you want to come, please come, that would be so great. I could use the help," she says.

"Why don't you just ask? Yes, I will come. Duh. Don't be a moron."

"Talk to me about something besides this wedding." Sarah's eye falls on the stack of bridal magazines on the coffee table, several pages dog-eared for reasons she can't recall. It just felt like what she should be doing—folding down pages and mentally filing away: mason jars for cocktails, Polaroid cameras left with the centerpieces, a basket of flip-flops by the dance floor. "What happened with temp?"

"Temp is fine. Temp is the same. Temp and I are working together on something, actually."

"Just be careful," Sarah says. "Your promotion probably means you're his boss. A sexy complication." Sarah's teasing contains her own happiness: five years Lauren's worked there, making cookbooks; it's about time this happened for her.

"I just think he's cute is all," Lauren says. "He wears shoes. I've barely actually spoken to him."

"Shoes are good."

"No, I mean, like, shoes. Man shoes. Driving shoes. Moccasins? Drivers? What are they called, the ones that have the little buckle over the top? He might be the first man I've ever been interested in whose dressiest shoes aren't Chucks."

"Oh yeah. Drivers? Wait, are those loafers? Dan has a pair of those. Horsebit. It's called a horsebit."

"Of course Dan has a pair of those. He probably wore those in the second grade."

"Shut up." Sarah laughs. "Maybe. But yes. Man shoes, for a grown man. So the temp is a grown man, only without a grown man's job."

"Hey, it's competitive out there, cut him some slack."

"So you're working on something. Mixing business with pleasure yet?"

"Nothing like that, Sarah. I'm trying to figure it out. I think maybe it's not a good idea. I wouldn't want my bosses to know that I was fucking some guy in the office, you know?"

She's impressed. Lolo, her Lauren, making the responsible decision about a guy. "Maybe you're right, maybe an office romance isn't a good idea. Besides, guys, whatever, but this job thing, I mean, it's about time this happened, really. You should enjoy it."

Lauren is quiet. "It's not that long coming. I mean, don't make me sound like some kind of loser."

"No, come on, all I meant was that it makes sense, I think, for you to be thinking about how this would look to your bosses. Versus your own wanting to date a guy who wears real shoes."

"Okay." Lauren is not convinced. Lauren sounds wounded. This is her way of punishing: monosyllables.

"I didn't mean anything." Sarah is quiet. "I shouldn't have said it like that. If it's real shoes you like in a man, we can find you real shoes. Let's start looking. You'll need a date for the wedding!" This last—a way to change the subject, to make herself the butt of the joke, to make herself seem the pathetic one.

"Yeah. Fine. So, okay, wedding dress. Let's make a plan."

They make a plan—next Wednesday, at Bergdorf's—then they talk, more, almost an hour longer, and later, falling asleep, Sarah realizes she has no idea what it is the two of them talked about for so long.

The water looks the way Lauren expects it to: unreal. Seen from above, unfolding all around them, the color of toothpaste. There's an impossibility to it, but also that disappointment she's thought, until this point, specific to the experience of encountering a famous, much-reproduced work of art in its original form. Come face-to-face with the *Pietà* and feel nothing profound. Gaze upon those Bacon triptychs and feel no more disturbed than any other day. So now, leaning forward in her seat to peer out of the window that is, for some reason, set a couple of inches in front of the seat rather than comfortably abutting it, she takes in the expanse of the sea and thinks the things you're supposed to think (like jewels, like silk, so blue, etc.) but feels unmoved nonetheless. Not that she isn't looking forward to getting into that water. She's not insane.

It's the day before Thanksgiving, and the airport is crowded, but so, too, more surprisingly, is the plane. She did not know about this, before; that a significant subset of our fellow Americans say fuck all to grace and grub with their racist great-uncles, get onto planes, and fly off to resorts where the only concession to the holiday is a turkey and cranberry sandwich on the lunch menu. Lauren's parents were unthrilled when she bailed on what's one of the family's last remaining rites.

"Oh, a bachelorette trip, that's nice," her mother said, meaning the same thing every mother says when she uses the word *nice*.

It's the latest way she's found to disappoint her mother: denying her the pleasure Lauren knows she derives from seeing all three of her children, arrayed around the table, just like old times. Lauren feels sorry for her mother, a terrible truth. She'd gone to college, married a sweetheart, and taken a job at the doctor's office thinking of a future of three or four children, vaccinated and checked up, *gratis*, by the Doctors Khan. That had all come to pass. Why the pity, then, if everything had gone swimmingly? Because it wasn't enough. Even with the scholarship, there was scrimping related to Lauren's schooling. Her parents consider Macy's a splurge.

They had singled her out for this not because she was smart, though she was not dumb, but because she was theirs, and therefore special. Plus her mother had in her, deep somewhere, a feminist feeling about the thing. Lauren suspected that her mother harbored fantasies of being a doctor herself, and that filing insurance claims for the Doctors Khan was the closest she had come to it. Bella wanted more for Lauren. She still did, needled her about things like a title change, and flextime, and business cards, things she must have studied up on, having no personal experience with them. At least, then, there was some concession, some good news.

"The good news I won't be able to tell you in person is that I'm getting promoted," Lauren had told her mother.

A squeal, a sigh, and so many questions: more money, more responsibility, a new title, a new role, her own office, new business cards?

She's happy she's got this to give back to her mother. She's made it! Or she's making it. It was worth it! Or at least it seems more so now. Lauren's always been held to a standard different from the ones against which her brothers are measured. Theirs is more forgiving, and against theirs, well, they're both sort of succeeding. Ben believes in real estate. Alexis helps him with staging: fluffing pillows and putting a frozen apple pie in the oven to evince a sense of hominess. Just picturing them in their hatchback, the magnetized door sign advertising Ben's credentials and telephone number, is depressing, though in truth they probably make more money than Lauren does. It's true that Adam had broken their dad's heart by foundering in community college, then giving it up to work at a nursery and landscaping business that belonged to the father of a high school friend. He lives at home, but this seems, in some odd way, to please them.

Lauren tries to imagine what the Brooks family's attempt at togetherness in her absence will look like, but can't dwell on it because it makes her feel too guilty. She's a terrible daughter.

———·———

The resort has sent two black SUVs. The drivers (one smiling, one stoic) load their bags, and they pile in: Lauren, Sarah, and Amina in one, Meredith and Fiona in the other. Amina has endless arms and legs, thin, brown, bangled. Her jewelry clangs and clatters as she moves. Amina's specific combination of grace and ungainliness makes Lauren think of a giraffe. She's known Amina since high school, not particularly well, but in that school, in that circle, even simple acquaintance came with a certain intimacy, one that could last for years. It wouldn't have been perceived as a breach had Lauren called Amina, after years of their not having spoken, to ask a favor.

"It's beautiful, my God," Amina is saying, peering out of the tinted windows. She speaks with the oddest of accents, Amina does, a cocktail: her father's Etonian English mellowed by her mother's distinguished Dhundari, to say nothing of the parade of schoolteachers who conducted her education in American schools the world over—first Istanbul, later Berne, then Addis Ababa, finally New York. She came to the States at ten; indeed, it was from Amina that Lauren assumed the role of "new girl" in sixth grade. As Amina shades her eyes to get a better look, her bangles clatter against the glass. The effect is ladylike.

Sarah's cheeks are flushed, and her hair wavy, though the air isn't all that humid. Eighty-eight, the average high in late November—Lauren looked it up. Forty degrees warmer than back home at midday, where the office is empty anyway and no one cares that she's on a tropical vacation instead of eating that thing called stuffing that comes from a box that's secretly Lauren's favorite part of the meal, precisely as it was designed to be by the chemists who came up with it. Thanksgiving is perhaps unique in being the holiday where people defend the specific eccentricities and nuances of their family's way of doing things and spend years reifying them, re-creating them with their subsequent replacement families. Lauren has sentimental feelings for certain things, of course (cinnamon toast, an indulgence permitted when she was home sick; the smell of chlorine and the memory of visits to the indoor pool, a winter ritual), but Thanksgiving isn't one of those things.

The resort looks like a gigantic house, which is precisely what it once was. A *plantation,* they say the word proudly, it's not as shameful here as it is back home. The thing is perfect, naturally. The palm trees have been planted to achieve symmetry. The sea is an even more preposterous color, seen up close. The woman behind the desk greets them with convincing sincerity.

They have only just arrived, of course, but it seems almost like the others have been there for a few days, or been here before. They seem relaxed, they seem unfazed, even as they coo over the resort, check their phones, Fiona actually gripping Lauren's arm and squeezing it with an enthusiasm that seems feigned, and anyway, odd, because they don't know each other that well either, she and Fiona. She was the girl in college (there's one in every college) who was almost suspiciously well dressed. She transferred away to Parsons after two years, but she and Sarah have remained close—her presence here surely means they're closer than Lauren realized. Lauren admires Fiona's fashionable eccentricity. She's wearing a hat.

Everyone seems at home, or more at home than Lauren is. She always feels a bit odd in hotels. It's true she hadn't wanted to come, is deeply skeptical of spending days on end with a gaggle of girls. Over that arc of time, conversation becomes consensus, and groups turn into something else, gangs, almost. Still, as wedding rites go she has to suppose this is better than a night out in one of those neon underlit limousines, drinking champagne, singing karaoke. Now that they're here, Lauren is excited to go to her room, to shower the plane off her body, to put on a bathing suit, to sit by the pool with a book. She's brought two, even though she suspects that everyone else will expect there to be a lot of group conversation. She doesn't particularly have anything to say.

Even after the grandeur of the lobby, the room is a surprise. The floor tile is cheap, the wall color offensive, but the bed sprawling, and the bedroom spills out onto an indoor-outdoor room and from there, just the outdoors: green grass, a winding path, and that sea; it's still there, it wasn't a dream. The air-conditioning is on with conviction. The porter deposits Lauren's bags and she realizes she doesn't have any currency, whatever it is they use in this country. She gives him a five-dollar bill, hopes that's enough, or not too much to be an insult. Anyway, he doesn't say anything. The bathroom is strangely old-fashioned, but the water in the shower is wonderfully hot. Her skin feels oily and her hair smells like fast food. She uses the shampoo provided for her convenience, not caring what effect it might have on her hair. She can't afford this, none of this. It's a little faded, the luxury, but it's luxury all the same. Sarah is paying for the hotel, for all five rooms. She insisted and in the end no one fought her on this. It's not as though she doesn't have the money.

Lauren rubs sunscreen over her body. You have to work at sunscreen or it just sits there on you. There was mutual consent that they'd meet at the bar, where the woman at the front desk told them they could order snacks or sandwiches until the restaurant opens for dinner. She is hungry, actually, almost starving. She puts her bathing suit on, then a dress over that. She wants to eat, quickly, a shrimp cocktail—which sounds suitably tropical and ridiculous, the sort of thing you'd only order if you found yourself in a hotel—then she wants to lie on a chaise by the swimming pool, fall into the cold water, wrap herself in a big and ridiculously fluffy towel. She wants to read and then fall asleep and then wake up and continue reading, but in the end she leaves her book in the room and finds the bar.

Fiona is already there. She's involved with a cocktail, taking pictures of the view with her phone. She's wearing the same hat, an exclamation mark to underscore her height.

"Amazing, right?" This by way of hello.

Lauren sits at the table Fiona has commandeered. The bar is empty, only the bartender behind the bar. A beautiful smile there, too. Maybe it's because they're black that their smiles seem so bright. Maybe this is a racist thing for her to think.

"To be sure," she says. Which is, she realizes as she says it, an insane thing to say, some accidental attempt at Englishness. She gets that way with accents sometimes.

Fiona doesn't seem troubled by this. She's wearing dark glasses. Her hair looks reddish in this light. She's pretty, Fiona. "I'm having a mai tai," she says, the tone confessional.

Lauren laughs, because she thinks she's supposed to. "That sounds good."

"It's good, my friend, highly recommended."

So Lauren signals the bartender and orders one, as well as some french fries, called chips here, a colonial holdover.

"You're in food, yeah?"

"Cookbooks."

"I'm a terrible cook," Fiona says. "I'm English."

Lauren laughs again. "I don't actually cook, either," she says. "Not much. The cookbooks we publish, they're by celebrities. Easy recipes. Chocolate cakes with mayonnaise in them, tacos made out of store-bought rotisserie chicken."

"My husband does the cooking." Fiona sips her drink. She's graceful. "He's always trying to do these ambitious things from magazines. Recipes that begin with things like 'Dig a hole in the backyard.' He makes a terrible mess. Dirtying every bowl in the house, that kind of thing. You're married?"

"No." The bartender brings her drink. Lauren shakes her head for emphasis. "Not spoken for!"

"Last woman standing." Fiona sips her drink.

"Something like that."

"But you have a serious boyfriend, right? I remember Sarah saying something about that."

"Had. We're not together anymore."

"Sorry."

"It's okay," she says. The chips have arrived. "Anyway, been a couple of years."

Fiona nods. Her eyes have wandered out to the view.

The weird thing about travel: You go, and then you're there. You've been looking forward to it, or dreading it, or thinking about it, whatever, and then all of a sudden there you are. It's been a month since Sarah told Lauren about this trip. Four weeks of worrying about the expense (and there was that: bathing suit, sunscreen, taxi to the airport; her paychecks have yet to reflect her new salary, and anyway, the change won't be that dramatic), yearning for the sun, bristling at the thought of an expanse of quality time with these four girls, but delirious with the thought of free-dom from routine. She hasn't left New York in three years. Those three years ago, she went with Gabe to Denver for the wedding of an old friend of his. That was the last time. She needs a change.

She met Gabe through Sarah, though Sarah did not know him, not exactly. Huck had been one of the featured speakers in a series of lectures at the Museum of the City of New York, where Gabe worked as a curator. He and Sarah had happened to meet at a reception after one of the talks, and she'd just asked him—it's always easier to ask for a friend—if he was "seeing anyone," that genteel parlance, and hearing that he was not, insisted she set him up with Lauren. Gabe assented, because that was the sort of guy he is. Easygoing, easily led. Lauren didn't have high hopes for it, figuring first that Sarah didn't exactly know her type and, second, that anyone willing to go out for a drink with a stranger's best friend, sight unseen (though later she learned Sarah had shown him a picture of her, on her phone), would be mentally or in some other capacity deficient. But Gabe was not. He was nice. He'd gone out with her, he explained to her, much later, simply because he'd been asked to, and this was easy to reconcile with the Gabe she came to know, the sort of guy who did what people asked of him. He was unerringly obedient.

Lauren jokes, sometimes, that the relationship lasted four years because that was how long college had lasted, and high school before it. Four years and her mind is set, like a cake after forty-five minutes. Four years and the thing, no matter what that thing is, has run its course. It's true what she says to Fiona—there's no hatred, no spite, no revision. Hadn't they fucked on the floor of her living room, Gabe kissing every bit of her, her neck, her armpits, which she particularly liked? Hadn't they had brunch with her friends and his? Hadn't they paid those desultory visits to her parents and brothers in New Jersey?

Gabe is big, broad, the body of an athlete despite his near complete devotion to bookishness. Gabe, his glasses always slipping down the bridge of his nose, his distracted air, his terrible seasonal allergies. Gabe, with his big hands, and a penis that curved charmingly to the right, angled so it struck something in her just so. They haven't spoken but a couple of times in the two years since they broke up, broke up because he wanted her to marry him and she didn't, though she's not told anyone, especially not Sarah, especially not her mother, who loved Gabe, thought him just the kind of man she'd imagined her only daughter settling down with. Gabe had wanted for them to marry. She had not. That's all.

"I think I see Amina," says Fiona. She fiddles with her watch.

They reconvene at the table. Showered, changed, ready for leisure. It seemed so late in the day when they arrived. Now it seems early, because there's nowhere to go, nothing to do. Mutual agreement that they won't bother leaving the grounds of the place tonight—maybe not all weekend! ventures Meredith. She and Fiona reorder drinks while everyone else is on their first. The french fries do not last long.

Within the hour, on the beach: this despite the fact that the sun is setting. Lauren thinks of her book, the way a criminal must his gun: Using it could change everything. It's not all that warm, but they've come all this way to dig pedicured toes into white sand, and so they all are.

Later, she is tired from this residual sun, from the travel, from the dinner, which was fish, but unexpectedly buttery. It makes her stomach ache, slightly, either it's that or the daring mix of cocktails and wine she's spent the day consuming. At least they are all tired, so there's no peer pressure when she begs off after dinner.

"I'm exhausted, you guys," she tells them, and there are sympathetic nods.

Meredith actually yawns.

"Let's make a plan for the morning!" Amina likes a plan. She's already booked manicures for all of them.

"Let's relax," Sarah suggests. It's her party so this suggestion carries a lot of weight.

"Agreed," Fiona says. "Whoever gets up first, grab a good spot on the beach. Then let's all meet up there."

"We can have lunch on the beach," Meredith says, in awe. There's a ten-dollar surcharge per head for this particular extravagance, but who cares. "Doesn't that sound amazing?"

To Lauren, this simply sounds sandy.

"That does sound amazing," Sarah says. It's settled.

There's more chatter and kisses before Lauren folds up the big cloth napkin, deposits it on the table, and says her final good night. She jabs the plastic key card into the slot above the doorknob. The light flickers red. She tries again, and then again. Finally, it turns green. She's inside. The door falls heavily behind her. The room is quiet. She opens the door to the terrace. The muted sound of the sea. It's almost hard to believe it's out there. This is what people talk about when they talk about a tropical paradise. She slips out of her shoes. The hotel staff has been in for the turndown service. Turndown service has never made much sense to her. The housekeepers have been in to make the room look like no one's ever been there, then they return and leave all this evidence that someone's been there: a bucket of ice and a sweating plastic bottle of very cold water, a little square of chocolate Lauren unwraps immediately; she cannot not eat chocolate, even though this particular specimen is subpar. She lies on the bed, fully dressed, something she'd never do at home: Fully dressed you're covered with the filth of the city, and her bed, her real bed, is a space she considers almost sacred. This is a stranger's bed. It's belonged to a thousand people before her. In a few hours, someone will come in and fix the sheets, so it doesn't seem to matter if she gets sand on them.

———·———

A long time ago, about a year into their relationship, Gabe had taken Lauren to a hotel. There was no particular special occasion to mark; any occasion becomes special when a romance is that new. They were past the point of brushing their teeth before kissing in the morning but had not reached the point where they'd leave the door open while urinating. The hotel was nice, though the room was surprisingly small.

"Oh," Gabe said, tossing the overnight bag onto the bed. They'd packed an overnight bag, even. "This is nice." The *oh* implied that he had expected otherwise.

The bathroom was very near the bed. There was no good place to put their bag. But there was a minibar, eleven-dollar doll-size bottles of vodka kept just a hair below room temperature, because those minibar refrigerators are never all that cold. There was a tray with chocolate bars riddled with almonds, a paper cylinder full of mini chocolate chip cookies, two bags of fancy potato chips with retro-looking logos. Later, after some particularly athletic fucking, even for them, even for that stage in their relationship—it must have been the hotel, its powerful suggestion of sex—they'd eaten it all: stale chocolate bars, salty chips. They didn't have ice, so mixed the vodkas with a sparkling water. The room was small, but the view was impressive. Lauren had never understood real estate listings that trumpeted their views before that night. The city lights, then the darkness of the park; the choreography of the traffic lights and the pedestrian crosswalk signals. At that height though—not a sound. There was a helicopter in the distance, and even that, its insistent thrum, could not penetrate the room, which felt hot and smelled of their sex, a little animal, borderline un-pleasant, or so it would have seemed to someone who just came in. They spilled the crumbs of aged-cheddar-cheese-flavored po-tato chips across the soft white sheets, and she swept them away with her hand. She lay on her stomach, and his mouth was on her ear, her neck, her spine, her waist, her ass, her thighs, the backs of her knees, the bottoms of her feet. They fucked again. There was a television in the bathroom. She turned it on, a sitcom she hadn't seen in years: four old women sharing a house in Florida. She watched it through the wet glass of the shower door, stayed under the cascade of water for eleven minutes, twelve minutes, maybe fifteen. Gabe had ordered room service while she was in there, and he was in the shower himself when the dinner arrived, the rolling table guided by a smiling, heavyset woman with curly hair. One Caesar salad, a little parcel of bread, two cheeseburgers, a pile of onion rings, a bottle of cabernet. He left his wet towel in a puddle on the carpet, climbed onto the bed naked and started eating the salad with his fingers. They watched a terrible movie, finished their dinner, ordered ice cream sundaes, and fell asleep at eleven, the room's curtains wide open, so the room filled with sunlight in the early morning, but they were so hungover they slept in, paid the extra money for a late checkout. He fucked her again, in the shower, then they dressed and slipped out into the city, where it was another normal Sunday afternoon.

That first year, they held hands on the sidewalk. Gabe's fellowship ended. He became Doctor Lawrence. He gained twenty pounds. He ran the half marathon. He flirted with vegetarianism. He took a job at the Cooper Hewitt. He decided to give up his apartment, because the commute sucked. He asked her if they could get a place together. She suggested he move in with her. He did. He studied the cookbooks she brought home, learned to make scrambled eggs, very slowly, over a very low flame. He never did start leaving the door open while he peed. She did, sometimes.

He wanted to get married. He wanted to marry her. Lauren listened for it, the voice that would tell her what she was supposed to do, but she never heard anything. That's what you were supposed to do, with big life choices: Listen to your instinct, listen to your inner voice. Hers had gone silent, or she didn't have one after all. Lauren imagined that everyone but her had them, voices, cartoon guardians perched on their shoulders, saying *yes,* or *no,* or *try this,* or *run.* She tried creative visualization, which was something like prayer: a new last name, a child, a station wagon, a move to Riverdale. She wasn't opposed to any of this, strictly speaking, nor, though, was she tempted by it.

She didn't know what to do, but in the end, not knowing what to do is a way of doing something, too. Gabe lost patience. Finally, two years ago, he moved out. His brother helped him carry his things down the two flights of stairs. He called, from time to time, that first couple of months after. They met once, for a drink, at an unremarkable and dark bar on the Upper East Side, something near the museum, and convenient for him, since he'd moved to Queens. It should have been comfortable, but was not. It was as though they were strangers, or cousins, or their parents had been good friends and they'd been raised together with the assumption that the friendship would continue through the generations. It seemed impossible she'd ever known him, in a way. It seemed impossible that he'd lived in her apartment, that he'd shaken hands with her father, that his tongue had been inside her ass. They had two drinks, and then he stood to leave. He hugged her tightly, and there were tears in the corners of his eyes, and then, horribly, they were spilling onto his cheeks, which were bare. He'd recently shaved that beard. "I don't know why this is happening," he said, and then "Good-bye," and then he was gone, so abruptly he forgot to pay the bill or offer to split it. She paid it and left.

———————

There's a knock on the door. Lauren's eyes were closed, but if she'd fallen asleep, she feels very awake now, almost like it's morning, though it's only been moments. She stands. There's sand on the tile floor. She must have tracked that in this evening. She puts her hand to her hair, touches it, primping by force of habit, trying to look glamorous for the maid, the waiter, come to tell her she's left her phone at the table.

"Hey." It's Sarah. Cheeks a little red, a dead giveaway that she's been drinking. If her parents had been the type to care about that sort of thing, her adolescence would have been much more difficult.

"Hi." She pulls the door open wider, and Sarah steps inside. Lauren sits back down on the bed and looks at her. "What's up?"

"Ugh." Sarah slips out of her shoes and falls onto the bed next to her. "Ugh."

"Too much to drink?"

"I need some water."

She reaches over her friend's body to the bedside table, blessing the faceless women responsible for the turndown service.

Sarah drinks. "Fucking Christ. Why did I do this?"

"Drink too much? It's fun." Lauren shrugs. "You're celebrating."

"It's day one and I'm exhausted already."

"You just need to sleep it off." Lauren pats Sarah's knee.

"I can't drink like I used to." Sarah squirms around on the bed. Their heads are almost touching. "I'm old."

"You need to pace yourself, is all," Lauren says. "We're not old but we're not seventeen. God, how many times have we ended up like this? Drinking bottled water, trying to fix what couldn't be fixed?"

Lauren remembers: Hannah Cho's apartment, on Park, in the Nineties, just below where the train escapes from underground, a big bed in an unused bedroom, she and Sarah curled up just like this, after drinking a bottle of the Chos' red wine out of little porcelain teacups from the china cabinet in the dining room. Hannah was in her bedroom with Tyler Oakes, the rest of the party had drifted away hours before, and Sarah and Lauren were drunk enough that standing was risking vomiting.

Then, freshman year of college, a house party so crowded they spent the night on the porch, drinking the beers they'd brought themselves to avoid having to stand in line, show stamped hands to one of the guys who lived in the house. They left the party after two beers each, drank their thirds on the walk home, their breath misting in the October air, sat on Lauren's bed in the outside room of their shared double, windows opened wide, blowing cigarette smoke into the darkness.

In London, that liberating season in another country, another city, another life, a preview of adulthood, sipping whiskey on ice as a gentleman at a pub—a gentleman, he seemed impossibly old at the time but was probably in his forties—had shown them. He was taken with the two young American girls, had treated them to the good stuff. Falling into bed, laughing hysterically at something, at nothing, at being alive, at drinking like a grown-up, at being wanted by a grown-up, the way that man, that night, had commanded the publican, the way he produced the beautifully colored pound note from his fat wallet, then went home to jerk off to the memory of the two of them, picturing four breasts, two mouths, one tongue timidly meeting an unfamiliar clitoris. Lauren thinks of that guy, sometimes, when she orders a whiskey in a bar.

"I feel a little better, actually." Sarah sits up. She yawns. "Are you glad we're here?"

"I'm glad," Lauren says. She is.

"I knew it." Sarah, triumphant. "You had your doubts. You were reluctant. But you came, and I was right, and it's amazing."

"I never said I didn't want to come," Lauren says. "But yes, it's amazing here."

"I can see what's on your face, you don't have to say it." Sarah laughs.

"It's just that." Lauren sits up now, too. "I was just worried about money. And work. And stuff. I don't know. I'm not a bachelorette party kind of girl. But it's not about me. You're getting married. This is your party!"

"It wouldn't have been a party without you here, so I'm glad you came."

Lauren's quiet. She never knows what to say when people say nice things to her. There's never any response that seems to make sense. "So. Meredith."

"I know." Sarah shakes her head. "She doesn't mean to be like that, she just . . . is."

Meredith had steered the conversation, at the beach, and then over dinner, back to the long, complex saga of her breakup with her boyfriend, Ilan. Her face had grown dark but also more animated, as she gestured wildly with her hands, the pitch of her voice rising as she detailed some slight, the fervor of her words betraying that her feelings for him linger.

"They broke up, like, a year ago, am I right? I mean, she was explaining something, I was barely listening, and then it was, like—wait, we're talking about ancient history."

"I know." Sarah shakes her head sadly, then bursts out laughing. "It's ridiculous, I'm sorry, oh God, I'm a terrible person."

"I mean. Months." Lauren is laughing now, too. "And she's still, like—talking about the intricacies of some e-mail he sent her in response to some e-mail she sent him in response to, oh my God, I was, like, please shut up."

Sarah shushes her, starts laughing more loudly, almost choking.

"The whole time she's talking about this, and just going over and over every detail, and I said, and I know I'm such an asshole,

I said, 'Gosh, Meredith, it's hard to believe he could do this to you,' and she says 'I know!' She's so deep in herself she can't even detect sarcasm."

"That's nothing." Sarah composes herself, suddenly serious. "You know, I wouldn't even know Dan if not for Meredith. Remember, her brother, blah blah blah."

"Right." Lauren nods.

"So, like two months ago, we're talking, about the wedding, about me and Dan and how she and her brother are the ones who introduced us in the first place, and she goes off on this tangent about how her brother loves Dan so much and how he'd always kind of wanted her and Dan to end up together."

"No."

"It gets better! And how like, in an alternate universe, it should have been her and Dan who ended up together, like even that night, the night we first met, how he was so nice and she felt such an instant connection to him but then of course I did, too, and she saw that and didn't want to interfere."

"Please tell me you're making this up. How can you be friends with this person?" Lauren is aghast.

Sarah shakes her head. "She means well. I know, it's ridiculous, but she's just like—she's obsessed with being single. It's her thing right now."

"No man in his right mind would be able to go on a date with her. Maybe we should chip in and get her a hooker while we're down here. I hear that's a thing."

"God, we'd be doing her a favor."

"Fuck, that is such an insane thing to say. And she's your friend. Your good friend." Why were they so mean to their friends?

"I know." Sarah nods.

"And it's like—obviously, Dan and you belong together. You're crazy about each other. I mean, I can't see Dan dealing with her, not even in her bizarre alternate reality."

"You think so? You know that." She pauses. "Yeah. He's good, Dan."

"I know that," Lauren says simply.

"Sometimes I'm not sure." Sarah pauses. "I mean, I know you're not crazy about Dan."

"When did I ever say that?" Lauren takes the bottle of water from Sarah.

"Come on, Lauren."

"What come on?"

"I'm not stupid. It's okay."

Lauren doesn't say anything.

"I'm just excited that it's finally happening, we're getting married, and my friends are going to be there, even if they're secretly wishing they were the ones in the ridiculous white dress with everyone looking at them."

"Do you want me to be in charge of Meredith? I'll get her trashed, make sure she doesn't say a word to you the whole night."

"She's harmless," Sarah says. "She's so deep in the pit of her own despair she has no idea what else is going on."

"You won't know what's going on either. Isn't that what people are always saying? Like their wedding is just a blur of kissing relatives and posing for pictures and eating terrible cake? That's what I always hear it'll feel like."

"Posing for pictures." Sarah's face darkens. "We need a photographer. I need to add that to the list."

"Forget about the list for a minute." Lauren knows all about Sarah and her lists. "They call them mandingoes. A mandingo?"

"Who does what?" Sarah is confused.

"Guys from the islands who fuck old white ladies? Get their groove back."

"Christ, is that a thing? That's terrible. And that word sounds suspiciously racist to me. I wouldn't mention that in mixed company."

"Mixed company is genders, not races," Lauren says. "Like if we were talking about asshole waxing or something, that's a non-mixed-company conversation. As in, you can only talk about that with ladies. Boys can't handle waxed assholes."

Sarah doubles over with laughter, or would if she were standing. She bends her body, almost fetal. Her laugh is loud; it's always loud but louder, significantly, when she's been drinking. "Fuck," she says. Catching her breath. "Let's have another drink."

Lauren opens the minibar, weighs the options. "Brown or clear?"

"Brown, I think? Nightcap. Is there ice?"

"There is ice." Lauren fills two of the glasses, which are fitted with little paper sleeves so you know no one's sipped from them. She drops the emptied miniature bottles onto the table, their tiny metal caps into the trash can, where they land with a ping.

"Thanks." Sarah sits up and accepts the tumbler, a half inch of amber inside. "After-party."

They clink their glasses together. Lauren gestures over her shoulder at the terrace. "Should we go outside or something? I mean, since we're in a tropical paradise, et cetera?"

"Fuck the tropics," Sarah says. "I'm so comfortable."

Lauren shrugs, steps up onto the bed, and sits, legs crossed, in what was once called Indian style but she knows, because of a friend who teaches middle school, is now referred to as crisscross applesauce. Settling down, this feels familiar, that stab of déjà vu. It's elusive, it slips away. Something then, about this: a room this temperature, a bed once freshly made, a glass of something to drink, even the suggestion of the ocean just beyond because when you are near the ocean it's always present.

"Are you tired?" Sarah asks.

"No." Lauren shakes her head. "Actually, I feel weirdly, bizarrely awake."

"So do I." Sarah stares up at her. "This feels familiar. I remember this, somehow, the two of us, doing nothing, just sitting somewhere in the middle of the night and the night didn't seem to matter and we were just wide awake. Do you know what I mean?"

"Sleep is wasted on the young." It's uncanny how this happens, sometimes: how Sarah can seem to see what Lauren is thinking, then give voice to it, then look to Lauren to hear her confirm it, to acknowledge that she's—what, read her mind? Impossible, but it seems to happen. Lauren resists admitting that they are thinking the same thing. She prefers to think of them as wholly separate people.

"We were never tired," Sarah says. A trace of awe.

"You make it sound like we're in our fifties," Lauren says, chiding.

"Tell me you don't feel a little bit old these days. Just a little bit. Ever so slightly." Sarah's tone is confessional.

"Maybe." Lauren considers this for a moment. "Like, if you're thirty-two and you haven't yet bought a sofa, a real sofa, there's something vaguely sad about you."

"You've bought a sofa," Sarah says.

"I don't feel vaguely sad," Lauren says.

"Good." Sarah pauses. "You probably think this whole thing is stupid."

"What whole thing?"

"This." Sarah gestures at the room around them. There's a skill-less painting on the wall to the left of the bed: a sailboat. "Tropical weekend getaway with the girls. Hen party, that's what they call it in England. Hen party. Hen pecked. There's something sexist there, isn't there, women as fowl?"

"I thought maybe there was some implied double entendre there," Lauren says. "The opposite of cock, you know. But I don't hate this. The tropics! What is there to hate? I'll take this over Thanksgiving. Why did I never consider this before, actually? Destination Thanksgiving. It's sort of genius."

"But I bet your family misses you."

"Maybe." Lauren doesn't like to discuss her family with Sarah. Lauren knows and understands the nuances of the Thomas familial life. She knows the private language they speak at home. Sarah does not know the Brooks family way of life—even Lauren feels she no longer knows the Brooks family way of life. She prefers it this way.

Sarah is staring at the ceiling. In profile, Lauren can see a trace of Lulu in her. Something about the way she holds her head, like she's posing for a photograph, but it comes to her naturally.

At her chin, though, she turns back into her father, masculine, decisive, no longer Lulu, without whatever you call that quality that isn't quite beauty but is something approaching it.

"My mom wanted to come this weekend," Sarah says.

"No." Lauren shakes her head.

"She did."

Lauren laughs. "Of course she did."

"A girls' weekend, she just kept saying that, over and over again, finally I was like—Mom, you're not one of the girls," says Sarah. "I felt bad, but can you imagine if she'd tagged along?"

Lauren can, actually.

"Well, I'm glad you're not hating this. I'm half hating it," says Sarah. "But this is fun, just lying here like this, away from Meredith's travails."

"Maybe we just need to sleep? Like even though we're not tired. Tomorrow is another day and all that jazz? We'll get pedicures and order shrimp cocktail and eat lunch on the beach and do whatever."

"Read a book? That's what I feel like doing, reading a book. I feel like reading a book and thinking about nothing."

"Or talking about nothing." Lauren drains her glass. "That's what you want. To sit with our feet buried in the sand because it's cool and the sun is hot, and you want to talk but not about anything. About the weather. About what there is to talk about. About things you saw on the street. About whatever you heard on NPR."

"That is what I want." Sarah nods. "How did you know?"

"That's what everyone wants," Lauren says.

Knowing it all is a condition of being twelve. So it was something (strange, noteworthy, unfamiliar, odd) that at twelve, Lauren realized that she didn't actually know Sarah, didn't understand her. She had thought otherwise for some time; they'd been acquainted for a whole year, after all, a long damn stretch no matter how old you are. Sarah was not quite pretty but was quite popular, by whatever alchemy determined popularity. At twelve, popularity is as powerful a force as you can imagine, and it conferred on Sarah something like authority, the province of grown-ups. Sarah spoke; people listened.

Lauren had nothing, at twelve. Her chest as flat as those of the boys who made a big show of stripping out of their shirts during their basketball games—what, it was hot! Her hair, unremarkable; makeup, forbidden—hell, pierced ears were forbidden. Plus she didn't know any of these kids, didn't understand the things they talked about: the Hamptons, their big sisters' drug dealers, their mothers' plastic surgery, their fathers' indictment or promotion or book deal. One of her classmates came to school daily with a bodyguard; this was never remarked upon, which drove her insane. Who were these people?

Sarah was an ambassador from this strange world. Lauren could not understand Jonah, the boy whose father was running for mayor, or Kathe, the girl whose stepfather had three Oscars on his mantelpiece, or Bee, the girl whose portrait appeared in *W*, but she thought she could understand Sarah. Little kids arrive in this country speaking only Vietnamese and after two weeks of *Sesame Street* they're telling their parents how to pay the gas bill. You can learn, and Lauren tried to, studying Sarah, listening to her, mistaking the chemistry between them for comprehension.

By seventh grade, they had worked up to regular Friday nights together; eventually, they convinced Lauren's parents to let her take the train home alone, rather than having her mother trek into the city to fetch her, which often entailed a quiet cup of tea in the kitchen, Bella Brooks's fingers tightening around Lulu's white porcelain cups, garishly painted with birds. Lauren listened intently and began to understand: that Barneys was better than Bloomingdale's; that East Hampton was better than Water Mill; that Daniel was the nice one, William the mean one, with respect to the Jones twins; that the cool cigarette to smoke was a Camel Light, if you were a girl, and a Marlboro Red, if you were a boy, and American Spirit, if you were a hippie.

One night at Sarah's, after enough of the same had happened that Lauren could think of them as just another fact of her existence, a new development: Sarah, armed with Lulu's credit card, took them out to dinner. A few caveats pertained—the restaurant had to be nearby, on a preapproved list, so there was the Indian on the corner or the Bangladeshi opposite, the sole difference between the two the presence of meat on the menu of the latter. There was the Chinese place, which had been called Jade Garden, then closed and reopened unchanged save the name, Forbidden City, which they found hilarious for a reason she can't remember now.

At twelve, Lauren got comfortable. She understood how to get by in conversations, she knew that there were boys who thought she was pretty, and that was one of the more important things. Then one night, around Thanksgiving, that's why she's remembering it now, something about this time of year, even here, in the tropics, she found the photograph of Christopher, tucked away, largely forgotten in one of Lulu's many photo collages, this by the guest bedroom, then occupied by William Li, the Chinese graduate student who had come to stay for three months.

"Who's that?" Lauren's curiosity. He was cute, whoever he was.

"Oh." Sarah matter-of-factly sipping a soda through a straw. "That's my brother, Christopher."

Never, in the year plus, a mention of this brother. Lauren wasn't even sure how to ask the question.

"He's dead," Sarah said, still dispassionate.

The story took a long time to learn. Lauren knew by that point that you don't ask questions, you don't demand details, you don't ask for clarification: You dance around, you act, you feign understanding. This tactic worked at school and it worked, over time, with Sarah, and Lauren got to some understanding about Christopher, ghost brother, eleven years Sarah's senior, dead when she was only seven, and in the second grade.

Lauren played coy and eventually Sarah showed her other pictures beyond that one—Christopher, polo shirt, gap in his teeth; later, safety pin through his septum, unwashed hair. Christopher was, she learned, political, only his way of doing things involved throwing vials of pig's blood at the feet of the closeted mayor. He was young, but he was a savant. The apple fell near that tree, but on the far side of it. Ironic.

Lauren understood, later, that Lulu was a young mother, and she inferred that Huck was probably an absentee father; surely this explained something. Christopher had existed, there were photographs, but he was out of focus, he was off the page, he was ahead of his time, out of time as well. AIDS, which they blamed on drug addiction, but Lauren had studied those photographs, and divined in those eyes some sparkle, in that body, some softness. She had her doubts.

Sarah had been sent off to a psychiatrist that year, smart enough to understand that what was ostensibly a playdate was in fact an evaluation. She passed with flying colors, as was her wont. If they were stung, Huck and Lulu, by the fact that their friend in the Oval Office couldn't do anything to spare their son, by the fact that the newspapers carried no mention of his brief tenure on earth, by the fact of a funeral for a child, of all the unthinkable things, they were at least saved by Sarah.

Two-thirds of their lives they've known each other, and Sarah's told her so little of that brother. If Lauren complains about her brothers, Sarah reacts like Lauren is relaying something alien, something wholly unique. She had only been seven. Lauren remembers nothing of being seven: the sticky green vinyl of the bus seats on the backs of her knees, the fleshy gap in her teeth, the powdery smell of her second-grade teacher. Sarah's recollections, if she has them, must be as vague, as fleeting, as sensory. They've never discussed it but Sarah works, now, for AIDS patients. It's deliberate, but quiet, as she is. As a girl, Lauren almost begrudged Sarah her dead brother; hard to admit, as she was thirteen and old enough to know better. Like a cashmere scarf, a Tiffany key ring, a dead sibling was but another thing Sarah possessed that she did not.

———— · ————

Lauren sits up in the chair. Outdoor chaises aren't actually all that comfortable, or she's never sat in one that is, anyway. In the end, what you want is a bed. She's got a funny knot in her lower back, testament to the fact that she's just drifted away into sleep, this despite the chatter Fiona and Amina keep up. They're each flipping through a magazine, stopping every so often to jab at the thin, glossy pages with an accusing, greasy finger. Their talk is of the clothes, their cut, their color, their appropriateness for the occasion being pictured, the connotations and associations of the celebrity caught sporting said clothes by some intrepid shutterbug with a telephoto lens. Lauren's not opposed to such discussions; she knows quite well the pleasure of sitting, feet immersed in a hot, whirling bath while a penitent Korean woman trims her cuticles, and thinking about whether a certain personage has attained sufficient fame to wear a specific garment, or whether that garment's appearance on the frame of a reality star hasn't forever, in her estimation anyway, cheapened their good, Italian name. It's just she wants to sleep is all. She wants to let her mind drift up into the sky like a kite, bob and dip on the eddying air, go where it will.

Maybe she's being unfairly uncharitable toward Amina and Fiona. It's easy to be that. Fiona, in her unexpectedly straightforward bathing suit, reclines like Delacroix's odalisque on the fringed pink towel, a souvenir from a trip to Kenya. Amina, all those luxurious curves, that expanse of beautiful skin. Their every movement looks choreographed, something Lauren never knows how to do. She's sure everyone can see it, the strain on her face as she walks through a room, that awareness of being watched. Other people have it so easy.

At least Meredith has a headache. She threw up after breakfast, then disappeared into the confines of the former plantation in search of central air. Meredith can't hold her liquor, which is a problem as these celebratory rites naturally involve a fair amount of it, on top of which the poor dear is drinking to forget, though in her drunkenness she keeps bringing the conversation back to remembering. It's Sunday, a day that feels like departure, but they're not leaving until tomorrow afternoon, which gives the day a still more decadent feeling, if it's possible, after the lobster at breakfast, to amp up the decadence. The Sun King himself would probably have taken it easy on the champagne. But never mind: Someone else is paying, and they're all celebrating. That's the thing with the way we celebrate in this culture, Lauren's realized this weekend: Even if you don't believe it, at first, and don't mean it, eventually you get so drunk you feel celebratory. Then maudlin, but that can come later. They've agreed to take Sunday night off from one another, room service and pay-per-view, though she can imagine that Fiona and Amina might hit the town for dinner together. They seem to have much left to say to each other. A chat about their favorite mascara.

They are at the pool, where the breeze is less intense, because of the thoughtfully placed fence. Lauren stands, yawns, and slips into the water, which can be done in an instant, it's that warm. She does it with the same thought she puts into everything: reaching for grace, or to be like Esther Williams—is that her name?—and not a portly sea lion easing its way into the surf. Her bathing suit seems wanting, somehow, though the shade, something like pink grapefruit, had seemed appealing in the pages of the catalog. She slips under the water, eyes closed, and feels her hair drift behind her like an idea, like a trail of perfume. She stands. The tile underfoot is reassuring. The water comes to just below her breasts, which if not quite as shapely as Fiona's have always stood her in good stead. Gabe had liked them, anyway. They've been with her through a lot, these breasts. She'd wanted them, so badly, and then they came on, pretty quickly. She remembers standing before the mirror, shirtless, in profile, studying how they sprouted from her body, and they had, too, sprouted. No wonder we use fruit metaphors, Lauren thought; breasts nurture, yes, but they ripen on our bodies, too.

She blinks. The level of chlorine in the water has been perfectly calibrated. Her eyes feel fine. In a few weeks, the local newscasters will be delirious with joy as they estimate increasingly more dire snowfalls. The store on the corner will fill with people who never keep food in their apartments, desperate to buy milk. It's always milk. It's hard to fathom: In forty-eight hours, less than, she'll be borne back home; she didn't want to come here in the first place and now she wants never to leave. She'll move to the island, open a cooking school, lead chartered tours, run a bed-and-breakfast, plan destination weddings for a living. Every vacation comes to this point, doesn't it: visions of an alternate reality. Sell the house, quit your job. Tomorrow morning, the moment will have passed, and she'll be tired of drinking subpar coffee out of cups so small that the stuff loses its essential heat too quickly. Tomorrow morning, she'll miss the amiable chatter of the WNYC crew. Tomorrow morning, she'll be tired of the relentless fluffiness of the towels here, the weird softness of the water in the shower, the sweetness of the food.

There are eyes on her, and she catches them. The waiter, the same one who's been serving the guests by the pool all afternoon, the same waiter who brought them drinks—strictly nonalcoholic, they're all in the mood for Cokes—an hour ago. He's handsome, of course, hotels like this don't employ the ugly; he looks almost carved, though is that racist, only something she thinks because of the incredible blackness of his skin? She doesn't think so, or doesn't mean it that way, though of course, racists never mean their racist ideas in a racist way. Anyway, it's well intentioned: He's gorgeous, actually. He's a bit younger than they are, she guesses twenty-five. There's something about the ease with which he talks to them. They could be his big sister's friends. They're visitors from a world not his own, not New York, but their thirties.

He had arched one eyebrow, one only, as he handed her a glass of Coke. The wedge of lemon embraced the lip of the glass in a way that was sort of beautiful. Normally, the lemon is a bit of art direction Lauren can do without. Today, she squeezed it into the thing, and damned if it wasn't more delicious. In the alternate reality she's in now, she drinks soda with a citrus twist at eleven thirty in the morning.

"Thank you," she had said, because you say thank you, and you make eye contact when you do. A lesson learned over the course of many Friday nights at restaurants with Lulu.

That eyebrow, moving like it was independent of his face. What muscle did he manipulate to achieve this effect? It was a little flippant, not the deferential "You're welcome" offered to the rest of the girls with their Cokes—Diet for Sarah and Fiona. There were nuts, too, a sterling dish in the shape of a seashell, a bed of peanuts and cashews, a lone, gigantic Brazil nut. She took it.

He's got another tray, for an older couple, the only honeymooners at the resort, or so she assumes. She imagines theirs a second marriage, maybe a third. They're old enough that there could be older children, college aged. The man is a little dumpy and pale but with very happy eyes, the woman is redheaded and strangely vibrant, probably a yoga teacher, or an amateur ceramicist. The waiter places their tray on the table with a flourish, but is the flourish meant for her? His shirt, incredibly white for someone who works with food, his smile still easy, still convincing. Maybe he's stoned? Lauren sees his smile falter, waver for a second into something else, and she bends her knees, drops back under the surface of the water.

An hour later, she is the first to make her excuses. The empty glasses and bowls and remnants of the chicken Caesar salad that Sarah and Amina picked at together have been cleared. The umbrella is still useful, because the sun is so powerful, but Lauren wants a break and pretends that will be a nap. There are kisses, something she has given in to. Women like these kiss good-bye, it's one of those when-in-Rome situations. She knots the towel around her body, a stab at modesty. Here, they can lie basically naked, but a hundred yards from here, the hallway seems to demand more decorum.

She shoves her sunglasses up onto her head, one hand keeping the towel in place, the other gripping the flimsy cotton bag, the promising weight of the not-much-read paperback inside. Up

over the path, flip-flops in her bag, the grass underfoot. It's a wonderful feeling. Inside, the hallway is air-conditioned, if not as arc-
tic as she knows the room will be. Her flesh prickles. Her nipples
tense. She should drop the flip-flops to the floor, step into them.
She doesn't, though, hurries past the equine paintings toward her
room. And there is the waiter. He's bearing a tray, gives a nod
with that smile, a nod back, tipping his chin up high, holding his
face up for her to study. A nod not of deference, of servility; a
nod of hello, the nod of the man on the street. She knows this nod.
Then he's past her, rapping firmly on a door down the hall and
announcing himself in a cheerful voice. No accent to speak of.

She fumbles into her room, tosses the bag onto the bed, so
lush that the impact makes no sound. She drops the towel to the
ground, kicks it out of the way. Absurdly she wants a hot shower.
The mind-boggling waste of a hot shower on a hot day. She's
thirsty, too, ready for another eight-dollar bottle of water. A little
shiver from the cold, or the heat, or the shock of the one after the
other when, just as firmly as on the door down the hall, a knock.
Actually, three. No explanation offered.

She doesn't bother trying to hide behind the towel, actually
kicks it out of the way so she can open the door.

"Miss," he says. His voice a little softer. "Did you need something?"

His dick fits into her mouth much as she had hoped it might.
Something familiar in the arc of it, and he's so excited he pushes
perhaps a hair too far—which tells her that he is young, after
all—into her throat, into that spot where the pleasure turns into
discomfort, but a discomfort she finds strangely comforting. She's
thirsty but her mouth finds the saliva.

His shirt still so white, and still all buttoned up. He picks her up off the floor, sets her down on top of the bed. They are quiet, they are focused, then, fourteen minutes later, they are finished. He pulls his clothes back on—his boxer briefs, what is it with men this age and boxer briefs?—grinning all the while. She doesn't try to cover herself, moves about the room naked, halfheartedly righting the pillows, taking a bottle of water from the minibar, and accepting from him the condom—pathetic, spent, sticky—he's peeled off his body. She wraps the thing in a fistful of toilet paper, but it still makes an unpleasant sound as it lands in the bathroom trash can. The immodesty, her nakedness, feels good. He says something, something unimportant, uninteresting, irrelevant.

She takes the damp towel from the floor, wraps it around herself just as he opens the door to leave. Every action has an equal and opposite reaction: The door across the hall opens at that moment, Meredith, still a bit green, catching Lauren's eye. She seems on the verge of saying something, Meredith, as the waiter ducks out with a final nod. Lauren lets the door close, then stands for a moment, considering the back of the door, the helpful diagram showing the path to the nearest exit, in case of emergency. This is an emergency, of a sort. She lets the towel slip down once more, uses one corner to dab at the inside of her thigh. She goes into the bathroom. At least Meredith will have something new to talk about.

———·———

The French toast tastes different. Not as good. Even the little slice of papaya is less appetizing, seems to be grinning at her, menacingly. Lauren pushes the plate away after a couple of bites, where only yesterday she devoured the whole thing, and even briefly considered ordering something else, a side of potatoes, fried to crispness, a plate of bacon, pink and slimy.

There are hours until they leave, and she's already packed, leaving aside the clothes she plans to wear on the plane, after one final shower, because suddenly the sand, omnipresent as sand tends to be, is starting to drive her mad. Her hair, which gets luxuriously wavy and full from the salt water, suddenly feels dirty, oily, a hindrance. She'll miss this, she is sure, a few weeks from now, or even upon arrival: waiting in that taxi line at JFK, her breath visible in the evening chill. She'll miss this when the sky grows dark at an hour when Britons could conceivably be taking tea.

Meredith settles in across from her. She's dressed for the beach: a too-big white T-shirt she's knotted at her midriff, a skirt fashioned from a long scarf. Her hair is pulled up into a high, girl-ish ponytail. She yawns, then smiles. It is early. "Good morning!"

Lauren's never been good at remembering to say good morning. It seems like something people should just assume. She sips her coffee. It's not as strong as she wants it to be. "Morning."

"It's thirty-six degrees in New York right now. Thirty-six!" Meredith looks at her joyously.

"Yeah." There is no other obvious answer.

"I tell you what, I could stay here for another week, two, three, whatever." Meredith unfolds the menu, which is comically over-sized, though much of it is just white space. She must have it mem-orized at this point, they've had breakfast here every morning. "What about you, Lauren?"

"It'll be hard to go back to reality," Lauren says, though she doesn't mean it and misses her reality, her mornings alone: opening her eyes seconds before the alarm clock rings, dressing while watching the newscaster on the local channel who does that segment where he highlights interesting stories in the day's local newspapers.

"We have been spoiled," Meredith says. "All these amenities." She pauses. "Sometimes I think I should run away, you know? Start over. Like seriously."

"Everyone thinks that sometimes. Or all the time. I don't know." Lauren studies the dining room even though she knows he's not working.

Meredith waves over the waitress, asks for a cappuccino and a mixed-berry muffin. "I just don't even know what I have to go back to, to be honest," Meredith says. An audible sigh.

Meredith is so deeply within her own agony she doesn't even have it in her to properly tease/needle/blackmail Lauren about what she's witnessed.

Lauren pokes at the flesh of the papaya with her fork and feels ill. "It's that time of year," she says gamely.

Meredith looks puzzled. "What time of year?"

"Oh, the holidays, you know." Lauren gestures helplessly. "That time of year. The bad time of year. Family. Office parties, presents, money, Christmas music, tourists, love and joy, all that shit."

"Oh, you mean it's hard to be alone this time of year." Meredith nods. "Yeah, I guess that's true."

In fact, that's not what she meant. What she meant is what she said, general as it was. The warm air outside means she feels disconnected from the time of year, but the awareness lingers: It is that time of canned love and joy and peace and it's irritating. Even as a girl, well, not a girl, but a sullen preteen maybe, she disliked Christmas. The sight of mangled wrapping paper across plush carpeting makes her heart sink. All the meaningless giving, all the mindless getting, all the nothing. Her mother, as mothers do, loves Christmas. Lauren doesn't want to think about it at the moment.

Meredith has more to say. Lauren can see it, in the tense hunch of her shoulders, the expectant gleam in her eye, which is trying to fix on Lauren, hold her, as a magnet might. Meredith is lonely. Lauren has been lonely, of course, everyone has been lonely. But she's not sure she's been lonely in the way that Meredith is lonely, in this public, ravenous way. Her loneliness is like a smell, it's there, you're aware of it. Lauren is relieved by her own imperviousness to this kind of loneliness. It afflicts so many women it seems like it's the normal way to be.

Sarah and Fiona come into the restaurant, join them at the table, beckon for the waitress, exchange their good mornings. They, too, are dressed for the beach—they're enjoying every last minute of this.

"I've forgotten about every part of my real life," Fiona says, dreamily. "I guess that means this has been a very successful vacation."

"Yeah." Sarah studies Lauren's face, then turns over her shoulder to consider the sea. "It's nice to leave reality behind. Get away, drink. Misbehave." She pauses, looks back at Lauren. "Don't you think?"

So Meredith has told her. This is not surprising. Meredith doesn't seem like the secret-keeping sort. "I guess so," Lauren says. "No hangover, at least." She taps her temple. "I hydrated."

"You're so smart, Lauren. I'm in awe." Sarah smiles, not a real smile. It's not a rebuke. It's something else. Discomfort, embarrassment.

Lauren knows how Sarah feels about sex. Her embarrassment, that hint of awe, they don't mask a curiosity—they are symptoms of a disinterest. Lauren knows, she's fairly certain, every guy Sarah's ever fucked: Alex Heard and Dan Burton, yes, as well as the two in between them. Only those four, fewer than a handful. Lauren's not being teased, she's being scolded. Sarah's so reluctant to talk about sex that this is how it will come out: oblique conversational jabs that would sound odd to Meredith and Fiona were either of them listening.

"You know what?" Lauren slides away from the table. "I think I'm going to head to my room and pack up before the beach. So I don't have to later. I'll meet you out there?"

She's wrong: Sarah is capable of more than veiled verbal sparring. She knocks on her door only ten minutes later. Lauren knows it's her before even opening it.

"What's up?" Lauren's already packed, so she's just been lying on the bed, half reading an issue of *The New Yorker* from several months ago. She's very far behind in her reading.

"Hi. Can I sit?"

"Sit. Obviously." Lauren doesn't sit. She stands by the door, looking down at Sarah. "You ready to go home?"

"Look, I—" Sarah stops. "Meredith told me what she saw, and I am just. A little surprised, or something. I don't know."

"Well, I don't know what Meredith saw, but . . ." Lauren barely has it in her to protest.

"Meredith saw enough. She's annoying but she's not stupid. You fucked the waiter, Lauren? Seriously?"

"It's a vacation." She is surprised they're discussing it at all, but not surprised by the tone in Sarah's voice: disgust. She's barely trying to conceal it. "It's not a big deal."

"Embarrassing, though, right?"

"Embarrassing for whom, Sarah? Am I embarrassed that Meredith, who is your friend, not mine, saw something, and gossiped to you about it like a prude? I don't know. It's her choice. But you know. It happens. I fucked a guy. If this were Afghanistan, you could stone me."

"It's just embarrassing. It's just . . ." Sarah pauses, looks around the room as if willing the right word to appear. "It's tacky. What about that temp? I thought you were interested in him."

Lauren laughs. "The temp?" She can only barely conjure his face. "What does he have to do with anything?"

"You liked his shoes," Sarah says, ridiculously.

"What can I say? I'm tacky. I'm so sorry. I'm so sorry that this private thing that has nothing to do with you, and certainly nothing to do with Meredith, is so tacky. You know. I'm sorry that it makes you feel so embarrassed."

"God, that is not an apology." Sarah stands up. Her anger is unusual. She's whispering, but it's a loud whisper. "I am so sick of apologies that are like . . . *I'm sorry that made you feel this way.* That is not how you apologize. You're not supposed to be sorry for having made me feel a certain way. You're supposed to be sorry for doing the fucking stupid thing you did in the first place. So don't try that, okay? You are better than that."

"I see. I'm better than a bad apology but not so good, because, I'm still a tacky slut who . . . fucks the help. Is that accurate?"

"You know what? You can play it that way. That's totally fine. It's obviously not about the help, and you know it. It's obviously not about being a slut, and you know it."

"It's about what, then? It's about me being me, and not being you. This is what it's about, Sarah. I am me, and you are you, and there was no difference there for, I don't know, a decade? But now there is. And you get mad at me, for being me. And I get mad at you, for being you. Except you never actually get mad, you just get, morally superior. And smug. And I don't know what else. And I get mad. And then we don't talk and it's a whole fucking thing."

"What are you even talking about now?" Sarah is pacing the small area of the bedroom.

"I don't know." She doesn't. But she does. Lauren means what she's said and can't totally believe that she's said it. Sarah seems, on some level, to disapprove of almost everything she does. She's still bringing up Gabe's name, years after the fact. "Is this friendship or is this force of habit?"

"I don't know what that means." Sarah is still whispering.

Lauren looks at her. She's more tired than angry.

Sarah shakes her head. "I don't know what you're saying."

Lauren sighs. "I shouldn't have . . ." She doesn't know how to finish the sentence. She's not sure what she's apologizing for.

"I'm going to the beach," Sarah says. "I'll see you there." She leaves via the room's private terrace. Lauren lies on the bed for twenty minutes, staring at the ceiling, before joining the rest of the party in the cabana they've reserved until noon. The car will take them to the airport at one thirty.

She will shower, one final, hot shower in this glorious bathroom, though her hair will still feel salty, her feet still sandy. She will put on the jeans and the shirt and the cardigan, though it's too hot for a cardigan, because it will be cold on the plane, she knows. She will leave behind the three issues of *The New Yorker* that she'd brought with her, having read them entirely, except for one article about baseball. She will leave behind twenty dollars on the nightstand, for the housekeeper. She will scurry through the lobby and into the car quickly, but she won't see the waiter, so it's fine. She won't watch while Sarah signs the bill, which she's already told them all repeatedly she's going to do and therefore none of them will put up any kind of fuss about it. She will be quiet on the car ride to the airport, they will all be quiet on the car ride to the airport, studying their phones, already thinking about work, and boyfriends and husbands or lack of boyfriends and husbands, about winter coats and the way the city smells when it's cold outside. The sky will grow dark as the plane continues north, and the city will come into focus as light, a glorious array of lights, as the plane dips below the clouds and the pilot gives his well-rehearsed speech about not moving about the cabin and so on. And she will know that when the pilot says the words *Flight attendants, prepare for arrival,* that will mean arrival is truly imminent, because the approach to the city is a long one, the lights misleading; you will think you're there but you're still a ways off, and then there it is, nearer, nearer, so near it seems you'll plunge into the sea, it seems the plane's wheels will skim the roofs of the cars on the highways, but none of that will happen, all will be well.

The people on the street—the disappointed-looking business-man with snow on the cuffs of his pants, the Chinese grandmother moving very slowly, umbrella doing little to protect her, the post-man in his cloudy blue fatigues—seem defeated. A sadness more persistent than the snow seems to settle on the city. We think of January as winter's heart, but in truth, it's only its beginning. There is much yet to get through.

Sarah doesn't succumb to this sadness. She feels liberated. Christmas had been so much distraction. One of Huck's timeworn jokes: Their religion is gift giving. For Christmas, you didn't ask for humble, stupid things, common, cheap things, because those you'd get anyway: stockings stuffed full of card games and candies, tiny, plastic things meant for Barbie; later, earrings and bracelets and rolled-up pairs of tights; later still, gift cards and jewelry with a more adult seriousness, no charms in the shapes of cats. At ten: a horse, a beautiful young thing, called Bellatrix. She boarded in the Bronx, and Sarah's mother drove her up twice a week to ride. That had been her year of the horse. Her clothes were equestrian, the books she read heroic narratives about girls riding through danger or somehow, with the intercession of their fearless steeds, saving the family farm. Her allowance was saved for a dreamt-of new saddle, so expensive that it would have taken her literal years to accrue enough, but somehow that never occurred to her, as a child.

She lost interest, of course. Kids lose interest, and Bellatrix was sold three years later. Later, at fifteen, she'd realize how weirdly sexual it is, this thing with girls and horses, and she'd feel strange. That year: Cartier watch. Again, much desired; she wears it even now. She had wept viciously the day she'd misplaced it in the locker room before swim class, but one of the custodians had seen it on the bench, taken it to the main office for safekeeping, and her anguish had lasted only an hour or so. Then at seventeen: the car, the compact BMW she'd wanted, but in blue, which Huck had deemed more sensible than red, and not a convertible, because Lulu was convinced that in an accident you'd be decapitated.

This year, Sarah had prevailed on Fiona to accompany her to Barneys, and they came up with an asymmetrical necklace, something between a collar and a bird's nest, set with gems in an array of pastel shades. Lulu loved it. Huck was harder, but also somehow easier: A book would suffice, the rarer and odder the better, but this year, she'd wanted something to communicate her as-yet-unspoken thanks for shouldering the expense of the wedding and the attendant hassle as well. She'd been mindful of this for months and had poked around online to see what was at auction, had almost splurged on some first editions (Updike, signed; Shaw, pristine) but had then done one better by purchasing, from a small auction house based in Dallas, a handwritten letter from Winston Churchill to his brother.

For Ruth, Dan's mother, retired after years in private practice as a psychiatrist, from her and Dan together, a set of illustrated volumes surveying the work of John Singer Sargent. Ruth was going to devote her retirement to painting. She did watercolors and was very good. She had the sort of precise eye and steady hand required by the medium. For Andrew, Dan's father, a pair of leather gloves: truly beautiful, horribly expensive. This came after much discussion with Dan, who seemed as puzzled by his father as she was. Fathers are a mystery. Anyway, it gets cold in Michigan.

They spent the day at Huck and Lulu's, the whole new family together. Lulu did the cooking, feeling too guilty to employ temporary help. She spent hours on hallacas, wrapped lovingly in banana leaves. They sat in the dining room, set with the best china, and Huck told stories while Ruth, conscientious Emily's List donor, gritted her teeth. Sarah hadn't bothered to implore Huck to keep it nonpartisan; it was worse if you admonished him like that. Ruth took two very healthy whiskies after dinner and hurried out, after dessert, claiming a nascent headache. It had been, overall, a success.

——— · ———

Willa's office is in a strange corner of the city with no particular character: a small hotel, a kitchen supply showroom open to the trade only, a shuttered Turkish restaurant, heavy maroon curtains still draped across its doors. The office is on the second floor, with big windows looking out over the quiet street and lots of potted orchids that are miraculously thriving despite the dry winter air.

"How are you holding up?" Willa has a bemused, I-told-you-so demeanor. Wedding planning is her calling; her business depends on making it seem an impossibility.

Sarah sees Willa not as a mechanic or plumber, an expert called in to address something she couldn't possibly do herself, but rather as one of the caterers Lulu trusts: someone to do a job she's capable of but can't spare time for. "I'm holding up," she tells her. It's not a lie. She feels fine.

"Things are going wonderfully on this end," Willa says. They're at a small, round table, set with a teapot and little cups, like girls playing at tea party. The place is full of this kind of frippery: slipper chairs, coffee-table books, doilies under the orchids' terra-cotta pots, stuff chosen to appeal to the average bride, the Willa bride.

"That's great," says Sarah. There's a pad of paper and a cup of sharpened pencils on the table, in case she needs to take notes. She doesn't feel any particular need to take notes.

"Why don't I get the cakes and we'll get started then?"

"That's great," Sarah says again. She was expecting the table would be laid already. She's impatient. She doesn't enjoy being around Willa: She thinks her forceful empathy conceals something—condescension, bitterness, it's not clear what. But she is efficient. She disappears into the backroom to retrieve the samples of cake.

There's vanilla, with a thin band of raspberry between its layers; there's chocolate, with a coating of crushed, salty nuts; there's coconut, with a suggestion of banana, somehow; there's another chocolate with mint that tastes like a Girl Scout cookie. They're all good. Sarah likes dessert but getting through Christmas while being mindful of her regimen, her plan—*diet* is such a disgusting word—was so hard. It seems crazy to be sitting in this strange room on Twenty-Fifth Street eating seven pieces of cake in the middle of the afternoon, but you make concessions. She ate the papaya dulce that Lulu made for Christmas dinner, even though it wasn't all that good, and she had one accidentally fattening meal with Lauren, their own holiday celebration.

It's a ritual with precedent: just the two of them, the chance to swap gifts and get drunk and talk shit before disappearing into family and obligation. She texted Lauren a couple of weeks after coming back from the island, banter, though Sarah was still— *mad* wasn't the word, but there was a word for the feeling, somewhere. Still, tradition is tradition. Lauren must have felt the same way, because a plan was made, and kept, a bar in Tribeca: subway tile, mustachioed bartenders, one-dollar oyster specials.

"I'm not sure I understand the appeal of oysters." Lauren fiddled on her stool, the puffy coat hanging on its back taking up too much space.

"They're erotic, right?" Sarah made a face. "I think people just pretend to like them because it seems sophisticated."

"How's the wedding coming along?"

Sarah shrugged. "It's coming."

"I had the best idea. I'm actually so excited to tell you. I wanted to tell you face-to-face. Are you ready?"

Sarah nodded.

"Here it is: rehearsal dinner. I was thinking we should do something totally different, basically the opposite of the wedding. Like you don't want a fancy meal, you don't want place cards and tablecloths and all that, you want fun, light, festive, delicious. You want Mexican!" She paused, triumphant.

"I already called Ventaja," Lauren went on. "They've got a private room, holds up to forty very comfortably, and we've already done a menu. Tacos, guacamole, that sort of thing. And I was thinking, because we don't want to go too crazy the night before, we could do churros for dessert. Anyway." She reached into the pocket of the coat perched behind her and handed Sarah a piece of paper. "Here's the menu we did. You can nix anything you don't like obviously. Or the whole idea. I don't know. I put down a deposit, but it's refundable. So be honest, like, if you hate the idea."

Sarah was surprised. She took the piece of paper, didn't read it. She looked up at Lauren. She still had a trace of the tan she'd replenished on their trip. "You know, technically, the rehearsal dinner is the groom's family's deal. Ruth had some idea, I can't remember the details. But obviously your plan is going to be a million times cooler than whatever she's cooking up."

"Who cares about technicalities?" Lauren shrugged. "Don't worry about your mother-in-law. I'll talk to Dan. I'll take care of everything. If. I mean, if you're into it."

Sarah had been so mad. It didn't disappear, but it no longer seemed fair to be mad at her, or as mad. "Thank you." She meant it. "Thank you."

This is Lauren's way: disappointing, and then far exceeding, expectations. Even now, Sarah still doesn't get it—why she'd fuck someone, not just someone, a stranger (and, as she'd admit only to herself, as she'd never say out loud: a waiter, it's worse that he's a waiter), and turn what was supposed to be a trip about the five of them, together, having stupid, harmless fun, into something about herself.

"Any favorites?" Willa looks down at her, expectantly.

Sarah can't remember how any of them tasted, particularly. She chooses the vanilla. She likes that pretty little slash of red in it.

———

She's taken on more shifts at the store, lately. One of the long-time employees has left and they've frozen hiring. Sarah doesn't mind, in fact enjoys having more demands on her time, since she's shifted so many of the responsibilities—finding the tent, ordering the cake, checking the response cards against the invitation list, figuring out the outdoor lighting scheme—to Willa.

It's a dead time for retail, but a boom time for their store: People deaccession once-prized possessions to make room for their holiday loot. Paper bags full of books in particular, but also: vases, unwanted pillows, lamps, picture frames, the occasional painting or sculptural oddity. The pink sale was her brainchild, and it's proven a success in the two years past: The store transformed into a sea of pinks and reds, a nod to Valentine's Day. She poured pink foil-wrapped chocolate kisses into a Blenko bowl ($400) and stationed it by the cash register. The first day of the sale, an interior designer came in and swooped up two thousand dollars' worth of stuff, destined, she told Sarah, for the bedroom of a teenage girl whose parents are renovating their five-bedroom in the Apthorp.

Sarah still needs to find a tuxedo for Dan. She needs to coordinate with her future mother-in-law the details for the postwedding brunch on Sunday afternoon, which she'd like to have in this bistro on Park Avenue South that has a lovely, sky-lit garden room. She's bought a small weight, ten pounds, and curls it up toward her head, sixty times on each side in the mornings, before her shower, hoping to tame the subtle wiggle of her upper arms. And there's honeymoon research: She's trying to figure out the best time of year to go to Botswana. She's reading Norman Rush in preparation.

Understaffed as they are, she knows they need her, but today something more important has come up. She telephones the store, tells Jacob that she won't be in that afternoon. Jacob is flustered but she is impatient and thinks, for the first time ever, *Oh for Christ's sake, it's only a shop*. She's so overwhelmed, she doesn't pause for more than a second to feel satisfied by the fact that they do need her there, after all.

Then she calls Dan, pacing nervously on a stretch of Thirty-Ninth Street, making a circuit from the free newspaper kiosk to the fire hydrant. A Sikh shopkeeper studies her suspiciously, and she stares him down icily. Dan is in the middle of prepping the big presentation, which is due to go off to The Hague next week. Their conversations when he is at work are never that fulfilling— monosyllables, nodding—so when she hangs up, she calls Lauren.

Years, what, more than a decade ago, a long-ago January night, drunken, because what else was there to do in the dead of the upstate winter, after some party in some person's house, she and Lauren had been making their way across that well-lit campus, the reassuring blue glow of those security telephones, the pools of light meant to discourage attackers. They walked with too much confidence: The snow had melted, the water had frozen, and ice was everywhere, and they were too drunk to care. It was Lauren who fell, all of a sudden, that's how these things happen, about to step and then prone, not hurt, because it was the heel of the foot behind her that had foundered, so she landed with a graceless thud on her ass.

"Ouch," she said, first, then started to laugh, tears mixing in, not from pain, or shame, but from the cold, the preposterousness of the situation.

"Promise me," Lauren had said later, "if you are my friend, if we are friends, let's make a deal. From now on, when one of us slips and falls on the ice, the other one will, too."

"Why?" Sarah had asked.

"We're in this together" was Lauren's answer, and it somehow made sense.

"Lolo," Sarah says, when Lauren picks up, efficiently, after one brief ring, answering with her name—"Lauren Brooks"—so terse, so professional. "Lolo, I fell on the ice."

———·———

The first place Sarah could think of is this strange hotel near Bryant Park. It's in Midtown, and it seems furtive, the place you'd go for an extramarital martini. She's forgotten that the old hotel has undergone a modern renovation. It's a ghost of its former self, a suggestion of columns and grandeur, the patina of slick woods and velvet. It's a pastiche. It's ugly, but classy. It's not yet quitting time and well past lunchtime; the place is deserted. The host has olive skin and beautiful features. His hair has a subtle wave to it, and some kind of product to hold that wave in place. She's seized by a desire to touch it. He shows her to a booth, delivers a glass of ice water, which she drains, and a menu.

Lauren arrives after only a few minutes; true to her word, she must have left as soon as she received the call. She is there, as Sarah has asked her to be.

"Hey!" A jocular tone, concealing an edge of worry. Confusion.

"Hey yourself," Sarah says.

Lauren slides into the banquette opposite, pushing off her coat and scarf and bag in one graceless motion, shoving the bulk onto the bench beside her. "What's going on?" She pauses. "You fell on the ice."

"Our distress call." Sarah nods at the menu. "Drink?"

"Drink, why not." Lauren smiles. "It took me a second there, the ice thing. But I remembered."

"Of course you remembered, Lolo."

"So you want to tell me what's going on? Why we're drinking?"

"You're drinking." Sarah hesitates. She's grateful. "I'm pregnant."

"Oh. Oh!" Lauren stares at her. "Congratulations?" She looks down at the closed menu on the table in front of her. "Jesus. Who's the father?"

"You know, I tried to guess what joke you were going to make." Sarah smiles, crazily. She feels like laughing. "I had *Who's the father?* on my list. I also had *Again?*"

"That's pretty good, actually." Lauren laughs. "So I guess wearing white is out?"

"That was on my list, too."

They order drinks.

"I'll take two sips," Sarah explains, defensively, as the waiter disappears in search of their drinks.

Lauren holds her hands up in protest. "I didn't say anything."

"I'm fucking pregnant." She stares at Lauren. She wants something from this exchange but has no idea what. She's looking to Lauren to tell her how to react.

"That's amazing." This time, no joking. Lauren smiles.

"The miracle of life." Sarah frowns. "I don't even know what to say."

"I take it this is a surprise?"

She's only been off the pill a few months, the doctor's advice. If they were going to start trying, the doctor suggested, it was time. They'd been sure it would take a while. "This is a surprise," Sarah says. "I mean, it's good, generally speaking, though the timing is a little . . ."

"Did you know?" Lauren sits up, leans forward a little. "Wait, *do* you know?"

"Went to the doctor. The usual visit, but like—I've been tired. I thought it was just the wedding stuff." She shrugs.

"Shit." Lauren is still smiling. This is the right response, Sarah knows: shock, but also joy. "How far along are you?"

"I'm four weeks, she thinks, maybe six. Can't confirm as yet."

"Which means that two months from now, you'll be three or possibly four months pregnant."

"I'll be fucking showing." Sarah feels her shoulders seize up. Her biceps are sore, as they have been for weeks. All those dutiful curls.

"You won't be." Lauren takes her hand. "Three months, you'll be fine."

"I've been fucking starving myself for months, doing those fucking arm exercises." Sarah can feel she's about to cry: that terrible heat on her face, that damp in her eyes.

"You've been doing arm exercises?" Lauren's tone is mocking.

"Hired a goddamn trainer. Jake. He's expensive." Sarah starts laughing.

The waiter brings their drinks. She picks three ice cubes from her water, drops them into the wineglass, cooling it but also diluting it. She tastes it, and it is wonderful. The very taste of relief. "I was working really hard at this. It's stupid. I am excited about being a mother. For Christ's sake, I realize that's more important than being skinny at my wedding. But I just wanted to be skinny at my wedding. To drink champagne, and do tequila shots with the caterers when everyone had gone home."

"Tequila shots?" Lauren sips her gin. "Isn't that kind of racist?"

"I'm sorry I took you away from work." She's not crying. She's not laughing. She just is.

"Please. Work is stupid. This is much more exciting."

They are quiet for a moment.

"Are you going to find out the sex?" Lauren asks.

"I don't know." She hasn't considered this: it being not an it, but being a he or a she. "I guess I should talk to Dan."

"Wait, what did Dan say? Is he excited?"

Work Dan isn't the greatest at having conversations but he knows Sarah well enough to interpret that there was something behind the terseness of her "Hello." Dan had excused himself from the office, she could hear him, stepped out into the hallway then, finding people there as well, gone into the stairwell, his voice echoing in the emptiness. *You're sure?*, Dan had wanted to know. *I love you. This is wonderful. I'm so happy. I hope you are, too. This is the greatest.* All the right things to say, but Sarah had wanted more, which is why she'd called Lauren. "Well, he's thrilled of course. I mean, he sees how this isn't the best timing, but yes, he's excited."

"It's great news, Sarah. It's magic." Lauren dips a finger in the trail of condensation her drink has left on the table. "You're in shock. You'll feel totally different in about one day."

"I'm not mad about the wedding, it's just . . . Why do anything if you're not going to do it the right way? I was trying to do it the right way."

"You always do."

"I'm supposed to be jumping for joy at this news, but it's supposed to be separate news. My two milestones are blurring into one." Another sip of the wine. That's three. She wants a fourth, but not brain damage. She pushes the glass toward Lauren. "Drink this please, so I don't."

"Glad to oblige. I'm double fisting it. Because this is cause for celebration. Fuck the wedding. You'll look beautiful. Who cares?"

"I'll look beautiful." Sarah pauses. She is not the kind of person who likes to spend a lot of time talking about what she looks like. It's like Meredith, talking about being single. It's a bore.

"I'm going to be Auntie Lauren," Lauren says, then, "You're not telling Huck and Lulu."

"I am not telling Huck and Lulu. This is going to be complicated, though. I'll need to keep this under wraps for . . . ten weeks? It's going to be like a British sex farce. Mistaken identities, going in and out of doors."

"Just say you're tired from wedding stuff. You're golden."

"Huck's already bought a case of wine he wants at the rehearsal dinner. At your rehearsal dinner. He says the rehearsal dinner is always more fun than the wedding. It's the A-list. The out-oftowners and the friends you actually like. There's less dress code and more drinking and better speeches."

"That's why your amazing matron of honor is in charge of it. Because he's right, it's going to be more fun than the wedding. And if Huck wants a case of wine at this thing, he better call me and we can get that sorted out."

"Maid of honor, you idiot. But if I don't drink the special wine it's going to be . . . suspicious."

"Oh, come on." Lauren sips Sarah's wine, then goes back to her gin. "We used to be very accomplished liars. You're forgetting."

"We did lie." Sarah remembers: missed curfews, forged excuse notes, twenty-dollar bills from Lulu's purse.

"All little girls lie, it's what little girls do. So lie. Do teenage Sarah proud. Besides, if Huck loves this wine that much, he'll be trashed. People never notice if other people are drinking, unless they're alcoholics, and if there are any alcoholics watching you, they're going to think you're an alcoholic, not knocked up."

"I find this weirdly reassuring."

"As you're meant to. A few months from now this will all be a distant memory, and you'll have a baby and you'll be a mom and holy shit, I need this second drink all of a sudden." Lauren pauses, then, almost accusingly, "Wait, what about names?"

There's a short list. Sarah's had it for some time. "I wasn't exactly all excited to have this big wedding. I only recently started to come around and sort of . . . enjoy the thought of it. Thinking about how all these people I like are going to get together one day in April and be in the same place and eat this good food. It sounded nice. Now I feel like an asshole for not feeling excited about the baby and saying fuck all to the wedding, and I mean, sure, fuck all to the wedding and yay babies, but how did this happen?"

Lauren is quiet. "Well, when a sperm meets an egg."

"I mean, we're old, Lauren. We're old now. This is it. Life is happening to us. I called Jill, you know? After you told me you ran into her?"

"You did?"

"I did. I'm not even sure why, I was curious or something. And she was like—the baby this, the baby that, and she said, the thing about having a baby is you're never alone again, ever, in any meaningful way, ever for the rest of your life."

"She can't say that. Her kids are babies. They'll turn out to be teenagers like us and we had nothing to do with our mothers for a while there. I still have nothing to do with my mother, really."

Sarah shudders. "Envisioning the baby inside me as us as teenagers is not exactly reassuring. All I mean is, suddenly it's happening to us. Life is happening to us."

"Life is always happening to us." Lauren finishes her cocktail, pushes the glass of wine back across the table. "Have another sip, he won't grow a third leg or anything."

She takes a small sip. "Okay, now seriously, take this away. Do you want to get dinner?"

"It's five o'clock."

"Early bird special?"

"Yeah, let's get dinner." Lauren signals for the waiter. "I'll get this. Celebratory drink on your big day."

"Do you really think life is always happening to us?"

"I do," Lauren says.

Lately she feels so stupid. It's the pregnancy, Sarah tells herself, then remembers she's pregnant, and gets angry. For days, she vacillates between those two states: idiocy and rage. Joy—about the pregnancy, the wedding—it's out there somewhere, she tells herself.

At the moment, nothing holds her interest. The fat paperback she's been picking at is lying splayed open on the coffee table. It's good, but the television seems more appealing at the moment. *Jeopardy!* is on, and she's playing along, talking out loud, unembarrassed. Dan doesn't care. He sits at the little desk by the window, tapping away, oblivious.

"Who is Vanessa Bell? What is Eminent Victorians?" Dan chimes in with the answer that eludes her: the Abyssinian hoax.

She's not prone to exaggeration so Sarah wouldn't say she's exhausted, but she's tired. She's not used to working so many hours in the store: labor that involves much standing, much cheerful chatter. She's good at *Jeopardy!*, but she's not smart. They're two different things. Younger, she'd have called herself smart, because she was raised to believe she was. She was raised to believe she was perfect. The shock of college wasn't the usual—discovering radical politics, lesbianism, Kathy Acker. It was discovering her mediocrity. She'd always been adept, before, at seeming smart: asking the right questions, asking questions at all, maintaining an air of propriety, of friendliness, of openness. The ingredients, she thought, of intelligence. Teachers loved her, and so did the students. She was active, which she took for a type of intelligence. Her college professors, though, were not swayed by this activity, this performance of intelligence. They had no context for knowing her. She was one of a few hundred.

As a girl, she'd been loved, indulged, and aware enough to understand that this meant she was, in a word, spoiled. She took pains to remember that. It was unbecoming, she learned quickly, to whine, to brag, to push. The thing to do was wield her power subtly. Never a tantrum, whether over a doll or, later, a saddle, later still a CD changer for the car, a credit card, tickets to Florida, because she understood that these would come, by virtue of the fact that she wanted them to. So, too, at school, deemed academically one of the best in the country—the country, understand— she'd managed A's almost across the board simply by expecting them for herself. And if, on occasion, she forgot to read the book, she would expect, and receive, a reprieve.

The October of her freshman year of college, Doctor Diana Baker had startled her, during office hours, by saying a firm *no* to Sarah, supplicant, come to inquire about an extension on a paper. She had her argument ready, should it come up—something to do with Huck, but not a name-drop.

"We're all adults here. You don't want to or can't get to the work, that's your concern. I'm not in the business of keeping tabs on my students."

Sarah must have sputtered or begun to speak, apologetic, embarrassed, her cheeks growing hot.

Then this. "I can't help you. No one can, no one but you. Thanks for dropping by."

The good game show has ended and is followed, as it always is, by the stupid one, which she loves anyway. It's got a comforting cadence to it, spin the wheel, mention a letter, take a stab, win some prizes. The winning contestant today, the one who's advanced to the final round, is a portly guy in a purple button-down shirt with a raspy voice who can barely contain his excitement. The camera pans to the crowd as he introduces the two people in the audience rooting for him. His friends, a woman with very alert eyes, wearing a dress more suited to a cocktail party than being in a studio audience, and another friend, goateed, gray haired, heavyset, probably a coworker. Poor thing, to have no spouse, no family there to cheer him on in his moment in the spotlight. The clue, the answer, is a phrase: *Better to have loved and lost than never to have loved at all.* He gets it right, wins forty thousand dollars. Good for him, she thinks.

Sarah had always confused a proximity to excellence for excellence. She had confused the expectation that she'd be exceptional with the reality that she was not exceptional. She got the paper in on time, after all, got a C, finished the class without ever speaking to Doctor Diana Baker again. This wasn't a turning point, the kick in the pants Doctor Baker might have thought she was giving; Sarah looked deep down into herself and saw there was nothing else there. She did fine in college, got the degree, naturally, on time. She met Dan, which affirmed that her suspicion that she was not, herself, smart, was well founded. Dan was smart. Maybe it was enough that she was nearby. That was how she'd felt about Lauren, first meeting her; she was so pretty, maybe it was enough to be within that. That had never faded, that love of Lauren's prettiness, the love of sitting firmly within the confines of its spotlight, its halo, its shadow. Now, she's blaming the stupidity—and let's be honest, it's more absentmindedness—on the pregnancy. She'll need an extension on everything. She'll get it done in eight months. It'll be fine.

This resignation manifests itself as a sigh, one louder than she'd intended, but isn't that always how they come out?

"What is it?" Dan turns his gaze from the computer to her, even though he's fully capable of maintaining a split focus, indeed seems to focus better when he's doing two things at once. Some of their best conversations have taken place while he's driving, or typing, or cooking.

"I forgot to do something," she says.

"Wedding thing or life thing?"

"Work thing," she says. "I need to e-mail Carol about this grant, and the fall, and I don't feel prepared to answer any questions."

"Because you can't, because you feel like it's dishonest to discuss this with her without disclosing that you're pregnant," Dan says.

"Bingo." She impatiently picks up a fat bridal magazine, which has slipped from its perch atop a pile of four others on the shelf under the coffee table. "This place is a mess."

"We should get Aga in," Dan says. "A deep clean."

"She was here a week ago," she says.

"Maybe she should come weekly instead of bi-," Dan says.

"That seems excessive. How much mess could we make in a week?"

"This much," Dan says, gesturing around the apartment. "Aga is happy for the work, I think. I mean, we pay her well, we treat her nicely, I hope. I would like to think we're model employers. Besides, if she comes weekly, the house won't be as dirty each time she comes, so her job will actually get easier, even as she makes more money."

"Fine, we'll have her come weekly, then." Sarah is displeased by the fact that he's solved this problem so quickly.

"You don't need to be angry. You have better things to be doing with your time, I think. Your work. The wedding. The pregnancy. I have less time to spare, to clean, with my work, and honestly, when I'm home like this, I would rather hang out with you than clean the bathroom. It's not an ethical dilemma. It's not even a financial imposition."

"Fine, I don't know why we're talking about it." She shrugs.

"We're talking about it because when you, or anyone for that matter, says 'fine' they usually mean something else entirely, and we're talking about it because you were just complaining that the apartment is messy and I was trying to offer a solution."

"Okay." She's angry now for no particular reason. She counts to three, as she was advised to by her mother, once, and it works: The anger dissolves like a tablet in water. She sighs again, and it's noisy again.

"You're stressed." Dan gets up from the desk, settles onto the sofa beside her.

"I am that," she says. She looks around the room. The jade plant needs watering.

"What's on the list?"

"There's nothing on the list," she says, though this isn't the truth. She needs to remind her mother that their cleaning lady will have to come the day before the wedding, and she'll have to bring a whole team with her. They'll need someone to help with shifting around some of the furniture. These are things she can't ask Dan to do, it doesn't make sense for him to do them. They're not impositions on her, even, just facts.

"Maybe you should take a day off," he says. "See a movie, go shopping, walk in the park, it's nice enough out. Go to the museum. Hell, go to the theater, isn't that one of the reasons people are always giving for living in New York, the proximity to the theater? We never go to the theater."

She laughs. "I don't need to go to the theater, I'm not eighty years old."

"David, at work? He told me we have to be sure to go to the movies and out to dinner whenever we feel like it, until the baby comes. That after, those things, those small things, those last-minute let's-go-out-for-Indian-food whims, become impossible."

"I'll feel fine when this wedding is done with, I think. Coordinating, it's fine, it's what I do."

"Yes, it is. You're very good at it. You're very good with a task."

"But a meaningful task," she says. "Not the task of throwing a party, with my mother and father, to celebrate our love."

He laughs. "We should have eloped. To Paris. Or Vegas, do people still do that?"

"It'll be fine," she says. She gathers the pile of bridal magazines, walks to the kitchen, and dumps them into the can under the sink where they keep the recycling, where they land with a satisfying thud. She won't be needing those anymore.

"Let's go out." Dan stands.

"What out? We were going to order Thai and watch that show."

"Screw that show," he says. "Screw this presentation, screw the world. Let's put on our coats and go somewhere. Let's get a cab. We'll go to the Odeon."

"Are you serious?"

"Dead," he says. He's already stuffing his feet into his boots. "I'll even look the other way if you want to take a sip of my martini."

"Yeah," she says. He's right. She'd been looking forward to Thai and TV, but now that's not what she wants at all. She wants to be out of this apartment, in the cold wintry night. She wants someone to bring her food, then take away the dirty plates. She wants to look around a crowded restaurant and try to imagine the lives of all the people around her. She wants to sit in a taxi, next to Dan, next to the man she loves, and remember that she loves him, and marvel at that, and think about the fact that they've made a human being, and that is a miracle. She doesn't care about her wobbly biceps, she doesn't care about what she's wearing, she doesn't care about the fact that they might run into someone they know; she only washes her hands at the kitchen sink, then wraps herself in her coat, and they go. She doesn't even bother looking in the mirror by the door.

She's relieved to get to February. January is cheap gym memberships and best intentions. It's atonement. For Lauren, a product of the American educational system, the year begins in September. The Jews had this one right, she remembers her dad saying, which sounds vaguely anti-Semitic in the retelling and so she never retells it. She can't muster any of this self-improving spirit, because it's the same instinct as its ostensible inverse, the greed and gluttony of the holidays. Some of the girls in the office brandish their juice fast bottles, numbered, multicolored, as proudly as if they were designer bags. The fridge in the kitchen is full of them, and when she's getting milk for a cup of tea one particularly overcast Thursday, she briefly thinks about taking out one of the bottles, pouring its contents down the drain, just to see what happens.

Lauren doesn't love the winter, but accepts that it exists, which makes surviving it much simpler. She's trying to find something beautiful in the purple of the sky, in the way the city's ambient lights swell up in the late afternoon. It's terrible outside, yes, but weather like this, light like this, makes inside seem so much lovelier. Though the workday ends at six, six thirty sometimes, she's there later tonight: problems with a gluten-free cookbook. She's the last one there, but that's okay. It's her responsibility. Things have changed: Miranda's corner office is mostly empty, as she's decamped for the executive floor. There is slack, and Lauren is tasked with picking it up. This feels good, and associating good feelings with work feels new, almost shocking. It's near eight, and the exhausted-looking cleaning lady shuffles in, emptying the garbage cans and whispering into her cell phone. The bulk of the overhead lights click off, and the office looks so different. In the bathroom, spotless now that the lady has done her thing, Lauren brushes her teeth, tidies herself, and finds a strange satisfaction in knowing she'll be back in so few hours.

She's meeting Rob, at a place in the West Village, his choice; she's never good at picking restaurants. They all seem the same: a cheeseburger for eleven dollars or a cheeseburger for twenty-one dollars. Rob's not in the office anymore. The journeyman's life. He's copyediting a special issue of one of the remaining city magazines, a guide to the boroughs' best doctors. It's a paycheck, though he's optimistic about a prospect at a more literary newspaper, where he'd get to edit a sportswriter he particularly loves. He enjoys reading *The New Yorker*'s articles about baseball.

It had started after Thanksgiving, after that tropical hiatus, after the bad blood, after the waiter, whom she's mostly forgotten. Rob had stopped by her desk in the morning, flimsy cup from the office kitchen in his hand.

"Hey, Lauren," he said. "Just wanted to touch base on that thing we were working on. It's all set. I sent you everything. I wrapped it up yesterday."

"Oh, you did?" She spun around in her chair to look up at him. Then, correcting herself: "Hi."

"I did. I noticed you weren't in. But it was kind of a slow day for me so I just finished it up."

"Cool. Thanks for doing that." She was practicing sounding like a manager: supportive, grateful, acknowledging.

"Long weekend?"

"Long weekend," she said.

"Looks like you got some sun," he nodded at her forearm. "Jealous."

"Oh, yeah. I was away this year. My friend is getting married, my best friend. Turks and Caicos."

"Nice. Destination wedding."

"No, this was just the, you know, the bachelorette weekend or something? I don't know what you call it. Just girls."

"Girls' weekend." He nodded approvingly. "Sounds fun."

"Well, it wasn't exactly a girls' weekend. I mean, it was but. We didn't see the Chippendales or anything like that."

Rob cocked an eyebrow, which had the effect of making him seem like he was grinning, though his face was serious. "Your loss, I'd say."

"It's just that I'm not exactly a girls' weekend kind of person, is all."

"What kind of person is that?"

"Never mind." She shook her head. She was blabbering. The truth was: She'd imagined this. Just this, a casual conversation, Rob in his cute shoes, smiling and flirting, that crackle of energy, that sense of possibility. She'd felt it, even then, on the plane, the idea that she was going home, yes, but also going home to him.

Rob. Rob Byrne. She knew his last name, and that knowledge felt like a certain kind of progress. Things happen in her mind, and then they come true; it's discomfiting.

He chuckled. "It's cool. I think it sounds fun. More fun than Thanksgiving in Maryland with my mother and my sister."

"Oh, I don't know. Thanksgiving isn't so bad, right? At least you don't have to buy anyone a present." Then, that last bit: She was flirting.

"My sister is doing this gluten-free thing, it's a real drag."

"That's a coincidence," she said. "I'm waiting on a gluten-free manuscript to come in. I'll have to get you a copy. It's going to be one of our big fall releases."

"I'm sure by the fall she'll have moved onto a new obsession, but that's so nice of you." He paused. "What is gluten exactly?"

She shook her head. "One of the wonders of the world, actually. Anyway, thanks for taking care of that. I'll let you know if I need extra hands on anything else, if that's okay?"

"It's what I'm here for," he said. "Hey, let's have lunch today?"

They had lunch. Lauren was going to ask Karen to join them, which would have made it feel slightly less unprofessional, but she was out with the flu, so it was just the two of them, at the diner across the street, the one so authentically New York that tourists rarely ventured into it, the one not long for the world, the one that would someday soon be transformed into a drugstore, or a quiet, efficient lobby holding blinking, beautiful automated teller machines and nothing more.

Rob had landed the temporary gig because his old boss was friends with Kristen, recommended him as a capable set of hands to help out in her absence; he wasn't an aimless, career temp, but being adrift is a condition of being a certain kind of bookish dude in the contemporary economy. He had moved to New York to do his MFA at Columbia, finished that with minimal debt, worked at a magazine aimed at the collectors of yachts and race cars, left that to work at a literary imprint of one of the big publishers, lost that job in a round of belt tightening, and gone to work as a research assistant to an academic writing a popular biography of a pioneering art dealer, but that book's research was finished and now here he was, on the assembly line at their office. As this story came spilling out of him, she saw more clearly what this thing was. It was as she had imagined. We only tell these stories about ourselves to those to whom we need to give some context, some understanding. These are details we offer to those we feel might find something meaningful in them. He wanted to be known by her, to be understood by her, and to kiss her, to sleep with her, to—whatever the verb is. He wanted her, and she had known he would. She is good at that, at being wanted.

That Friday, he'd asked her for a drink, and a drink meant something different than lunch during the workday. They left the office together, went to a bar in a Midtown hotel, where she ordered a Manhattan and held the glass as seductively as she knew how. He kissed her when they were leaving, stepped toward her as they waited for a taxi on the curb, pressed into her, held her by the chin and brought his face to hers, and their mouths met, and his tongue grazed hers, and then he took her by the hand, held the taxi door open for her like a gentleman, and saw her again Monday morning at the office, where they pretended that nothing was amiss. They maintained this game, and only Karen knew otherwise, because Lauren had confessed to her one day over lunch at the very same diner.

"I knew it." Karen took a pink envelope of artificial sweetener out of the little ceramic dish and threw it at her accusingly. "You tramp."

"Shut up." Lauren grinned. It was part of the game: She wanted to be teased.

He had stopped working with them at the end of December, and so they'd abandoned the complex dance of pretending not to know each other as well as they did. One Saturday before Christmas, he'd come home with her, to order Chinese and watch a movie, but as soon as they entered the house, they'd fallen onto her bed as if it were a familiar place for them both. She wanted this out of the way before dinner; sex is never any good when you're full of food. She took a shower after, came into the living room to find Rob opening the door to receive a plastic bag containing a paper bag full of oily Chinese from the middle-aged man who did the delivery for Hunan Delight. They sat on the floor, not watching the movie, talking about the quality of the dumplings. When the greasy plastic containers had had their lids snapped back on and were stowed in the fridge, Rob left; having sex was one thing, but it was still too soon for him to sleep in her bed.

He has slept there, twice now, the first time another Friday night, just after starting his new gig, and his cool shoulder in her back that Saturday morning wasn't as strange as she thought it would be. They'd dressed that morning and gone to the indoor flea market, where they ate fresh doughnuts and looked at people buying garbage. They'd walked around in the unseasonably mild chill, had lunch at a terrible Frenchy place on Atlantic Avenue, and ended up back at her place, Rob still in the clothes he'd worn to the office the day before. He mentioned this, then stripped out of his clothes and fucked her on the floor of the living room. They showered together, she cooked a frozen pizza, and they sat in their underwear and ate it, then he left the next morning, kissing at the front door. Now, seeing Rob waiting, hands in his pockets, in the front of the restaurant, which is dark, and very warm, feels familiar. A scene she's lived before, the scene of meeting him in a place they've never been together before, but recognizing him, the slope of his shoulders, the long arms, the beginnings of a bald spot, the easy grin. Rob always looks satisfied.

"How was work?" Rob had joked to the hostess—*Give us the best seat in the house*—and it had worked. A back booth, out of the way, giving them a command over the whole room, candlelit, hushed despite the crowd, some trick of the acoustics.

"Gluten free," Lauren says. The waitress brings them cocktails, and they knock their glasses together before they take a first sip, and Lauren can't tell if the gesture is ironic or not. "You?"

His face brightens even further. He loves his job. "Great. We got the green light on that profile. So that's exciting. And spring training starts soon. I think that'll be good."

"Awesome," she says, and that, too, sits awkwardly, somewhere between irony and sincerity. She is excited for him; his excitement is infectious. She wants good things for him, and that seems surprising. It must mean she likes him more than she was aware of liking him, to this point. She is not one of those women who frets about what it all means, who is always checking the present against some grand game plan. She thinks of poor Meredith, her ravenous desire to use those nouns: boyfriend, fiancé, husband. Meredith would love Rob, who is handsome, but accessibly so: not beautiful. Beautiful men are horrible. Much better, a man who looks like a man, a man who is generically handsome, well proportioned, unfeminine, a man with faults, though it's early enough that Lauren's not privy to Rob's faults, not yet. She's never heard him burp.

"It is, right? What are you going to order?"

They have settled into a pattern of consulting each other before ordering in restaurants, exercising the right to reach across the table to the other's plate. She opts for fish; he asks for lamb, even though they both agree it sounds cruel, and that there ought to be some euphemism for lamb, something nonpartisan, like veal, or something misleading, like sweetbreads.

They order a warm dessert—apples and caramel in a salty pastry, topped with saltier ice cream, this vogue for salty desserts is a winning one—and she pays the bill. This is something they're still feeling through, this question of paying, but it's idiotic to expect him to pay simply because he has a penis. She has the better job, after all. She puts down her corporate card—she's allowed, it's research, they're scoping out the hotshot Korean chef who runs this place—and he says nothing, then thanks her when she's signed the bill. It all feels like something they've done a million times before, but in the best possible way.

They walk to the subway, not holding hands but not far apart on the sidewalk, their shoulders brushing occasionally, and when they stop at the corner newsstand so he can buy a copy of a literary journal he likes, he asks if there's anything she wants, and he buys her a copy of *Elle* and carries them both like a high school sweetheart in the 1950s, clutched to his chest. As they walk down the steps into the station, he offers her his hand—there's ice, hidden beneath the puddles. She takes it. They push through the turnstiles and sit on the bench, knees pushed together, despite the intercession of the little wooden partition meant to offer commuters a modicum of personal space. The train arrives, and she finds a seat and he stands above her, both hands on the overhead bar. She holds the magazines on her lap, looks up at him. His face looks different from below. She likes this view of him, from below, his body near enough that she can pick up his scent—deodorant, faded by the day, chewing gum, something vaguely like pine, which might be his shampoo. There, on the bench, his dick so near her face, his dick that feels like it's hers now, her special province, her territory. Tonight, she will sit like this, below him, and kiss his balls, and breathe in his smell deeply, and tomorrow morning they will kiss good-bye at the door and she'll do the laundry and go grocery shopping. She's out of yogurt, she noticed that morning.

———— · ————

A thing like Valentine's Day can poison a fledgling relationship. In truth, forgotten tulips can undo even a marriage. Women are weird about these things. So, too, are men, though. Rob brings a box of chocolates, heart shaped, the next time he comes, but it's meant to be a joke, and Lauren gets it. They eat them all, though they're not very good.

Even if she's not using any nouns with respect to Rob—and she's not, or hasn't, she's been careful—he is going to be her date to Sarah's wedding, which implies a certain seriousness, at least to Sarah. That afternoon, after Sarah had announced her pregnancy, they'd left the hotel in Midtown and just walked, past Mr. Morgan's library, past the Empire State Building, through that weird intersection near the Toy Center, through a Union Square filled with slush instead of skateboarders. They'd kept walking, past the smoking undergrads at the New School and the smoking undergrads at NYU, past counterfeit handbag sellers and praying Muslim cabdrivers. They turned toward the bridge, slipped down streets lined with seafood markets and fruit vendors and the odd, colonizing art gallery. There was an organic restaurant Sarah had read about somewhere.

"You haven't sent your response card in," Sarah said.

"I haven't decided if I'm coming."

"I'm serious, you're going to fall afoul of Willa, which I would not recommend." Sarah smiled. "I assume you're bringing the temp?"

"We can call him Rob now," Lauren said. Sarah's invitation had arrived: thick stock, postage in a denomination she'd never before encountered, flawless calligraphy on the envelope, and on the card itself, the vague promise of herself, Lauren Brooks "and Guest."

"I'll need a bit more information. Like his surname. You know Lulu needs to know everyone's last name."

Lauren did know this. Lulu has a thing about knowing a person's first and last name, some weird colonial tic, a strain of old-world formality. "Well, it's Rob Byrne."

"I'm glad you're bringing him," Sarah said.

"Well, I'm sure he's glad to be going." This was a lie. She wasn't sure how he felt about it at all. Their relationship wasn't old enough to handle Valentine's Day; a best friend's wedding—it was asking more than she'd like to. She was doing it for Sarah. She knew Sarah would be happier to have a relative stranger in attendance at the wedding, because she wanted Lauren to have a date. This was like the rehearsal dinner party: a gift.

"Lolo?" Sarah looked at her, pantomimed rubbing a hand over an extended belly. "I'm pregnant."

"I remember," Lauren said. They laughed.

There is what you think, and there is what you say. Of course, Lauren's heart is warmed by the idea of mother and father and baby, that unbridled joy, those sweet infant smells, the softness of new skin, and those pliable, plastic faces. Perpetuating the species is all important. But she cannot brook the smugness of a certain class of parent, the mother in yoga gear pushing the Brobdingnagian stroller, vaguely Scandinavian and overly efficient, the mommy sighing and eyeing passersby, her face now a beatific smile, now a suspicious glower. Lauren's neighborhood is lousy with such women, and it's not always women, indeed it can be worse when it's men, men eager for you to notice that strapping baby Hazel to their chest makes them different from, and better than, other men. Having a baby, she often wants to tell these parents, is no cause for sanctimony. Doing what the body is designed to do; teenagers the world over do it. Girls can bake up babies in rapid succession; boys can get boners moments after ejaculating.

Lauren isn't certain Sarah will end up one of these smug sorts, but she does know that she'll be the friend Sarah calls when she's got to report a transgression by one of her other mommy friends' horrid children. And she will have mommy friends: Fiona will one day pop out a Quentin, Amina will birth a Nikhil, and the babies will enjoy a friendship based only on the fact of parentage; no more random, in the end, than a life-long relationship based on having once sat next to someone at the school orientation when you were eleven years old. An undercurrent of hostility, the inevitability of competition when Max crawls/takes solid foods/develops teeth/speaks clearly/poops on the potty/rides a scooter/learns Mandarin/loses his virginity/gets into Yale sooner or more easily than his pal Theo. Lauren knows what women are like. She is one. Sarah will get through it though. That much she knows. She always wanted to be like Sarah, when she was younger—to be loud, and listened to, and smart, and comfortable dealing with adults, and able to solve problems on her feet. She never knew Sarah to get into trouble, not once, not ever.

"You are that," Lauren had said.

"Hey, we should get together, don't you think? The four of us? He's going to be at my wedding, it would be nice if I got to know him and his dapper shoes before that, no?"

Lauren had been expecting this. Sarah loves a double date. She and Gabe, Sarah and Dan: seeing whatever nonsense was at the Guggenheim followed by pasta someplace uptown, three hours of Matthew Barney at the Film Forum, then drinks and shared confusion at a bar in Soho. Not bad times, even though she never looked forward to them. Sarah was Lauren's, not something she wanted to share with Gabe and Dan. They made it into something else entirely.

"We just got through Valentine's Day, man," Lauren said. "I'm taking him to a wedding. Let's not tempt the gods, okay?"

Sarah shrugged. "A night out with friends, it's not exactly meeting the parents, Lauren."

"Baby steps, Sarah. They're not all Dan. Some guys, they get spooked."

"Men." Sarah rolled her eyes. "God. What if it's a boy?"

They both laughed.

———·———

Lauren likes clothes, but Lauren hates shopping. Why does it make you so tired? The small talk with salespeople, the visual stimulus, the chemical, perfumed smell of department stores or the bouquet of the boutique: flickering fig candles and the proprietress's takeout, somewhere backstage. There's never anywhere to sit, unless you're trying on shoes. It's a bore.

Of course, she'd swallowed this, fought it, not mentioned it, and gone with Sarah to that appointment at Bergdorf's. Then another, for good measure, at a smaller salon downtown, then a second appointment at Bergdorf's. She's due to go back with her again, for the second fitting. Sarah's had to confess the pregnancy to the seamstress. The seamstress has seen it all. It comes with the territory. The dress is the right one, though: long but not trailing (what was the sense in that?), sexy but not whorish, modest but not dowdy, modern but not boxy, romantic but not ridiculous. Standing on that little velveteen-covered cube, spinning around, the three-way mirror reflecting her a thousand times over, Sarah looks like a bride, Sarah looks as she should, Sarah looks pretty.

Today: more shopping, and on this, the first sunny day in March, that first day you sense that spring isn't a delusion but an eventuality. They should be strolling down the West Side on that path overlooking the river, the one that leads to her favorite underattended movie theater in Manhattan. They should buy the paper and then only read the Week in Review and the magazine. They should stop at a diner and order french fries for no reason. That's the point Lauren and Rob have reached in the relationship; they are not at the clothes-shopping point in the relationship, but here they are.

Rob says he could use a suit. He's only got one, and it's harder to button the jacket than it should be. She worries that he's going to think of her, annoyed, when he's reckoning with this thousand dollars on his Citibank card. This is about Sarah's wedding, naturally.

"I like this one?" He sounds unconvinced. The salesman has pinned the pants' unfinished hem up under itself on his left leg, so they can see how it'll look. The suit is black, and it looks the same as every other suit he's tried. They're all the same, suits; isn't that the point?

"It's great," she says. "It's the shirt and tie that will make it, I think."

"And the shoes," Rob adds. The salesman at the previous store had said this, noting, disapprovingly, Rob's mottled winter boots.

Later, at his place, the suit paid for and sent away in the stern, capable hands of the Russian woman who will finish the pants and bring the cuffs up at the wrists, Lauren takes off her shoes, curls into a comfortable spot on his bed, watching as he moves around the room, disposing of his new purchases. He moves without a hint of consciousness, with something like grace, a quality you rarely observe in a man. But then this is his room, his home. It's like watching a chef in his kitchen, an artist in his studio, watching Rob tear little plastic tags off the shirt and ties (he bought three, he said he needed them anyway), slip collar stays out of their tiny pockets.

She's seen worse boy apartments than Rob's. It's true that the sofa is actually a futon, but it's not too horribly ugly, and the futon has been pressed into service as a sofa because Rob has a real bed, or, actually, a queen-size mattress, on top of a box spring, sitting on the floor. The bedroom is too small, he tells her, to get a bed in there. She thinks the mattress on the floor gives the apartment a bohemian vibe. Rob's tidy and has been thoughtful about certain things, like stashing the plastic-wrapped quartet of toilet paper rolls inside a closet rather than leaving the whole thing sitting out on the floor of the bathroom. She'd once known a guy—twice fucked a guy—named Jesse whose bathroom floor had been sodden and sticky with what she could only assume was urine, flicked off his and his roommate's dicks and left to molder on the linoleum. There's a fuzz of dust under the bookcase, but the books are tidy and organized. Rob's apartment has gestures that imply the homey: a vintage poster for a Smiths record, framed, on the living room wall, a striped throw pillow on the futon, a reasonably sized television. There are no video games, she noted the first time she went to his home. A lot of men she has known still play video games.

"You're okay with this, right? The suit, the shoes, fuck, you didn't have to buy the shoes."

"I'm okay with it, Lauren. Stop asking."

"It's just a lot of money." It's a considerable sum, but she's long been in the habit of spending impulsively. Now, those impulses are a little easier to justify. The raise wasn't much, not when you stretch it out over twenty-six paychecks, but it is something, and Mary-Beth has said something about a bonus. Lauren's trying to look at it from his perspective, though.

Now he's just tidying up. He shakes a crumpled sweater out, lays it on the bed, folds it. "It's fine. It's a work thing. Dress for the job you want, and so on." Rob grins, more to himself than her. "Besides, I want to look awesome at this wedding."

"Well, it's a pretty nice suit," she says.

"Wait until you see my dancing."

"That bad?"

"A fancy suit will only partially make up for it," he says.

She shrugs. "I just don't want you to, I don't know, feel obligated. You can wear whatever."

"That is total bullshit, but okay. Seriously, don't worry about it. My sister will get married eventually. I'll have to go to funerals. A man can use a black suit."

"Future funerals, do tell me more." She picks up one of the tags he's snipped from one of the shirts, a heavy rectangle of cardboard, and throws it at him. "Maybe I can recommend a good psychiatrist?"

"God, you're so pretty, you know that?" He drops the sweater on top of the dresser. "You are so pretty."

Junior year, coming out of a classroom, maybe European history, but her memory can only manage the general feelings, the atmosphere, she heard a snatch of conversation, not directed at her but not necessarily meant to be kept from her. Patrick Adler, finishing something he was saying to someone, some guy named Shane or Shawn. Speaking of her, and Sarah, she knew that, though she can't remember the context that made it clear that it was them he meant: something to do with a party, a concert, a plan for a coming weekend. "You take rich, I'll take pretty." She's always remembered that. She's always known which she was. She's never been quite sure which of them came out better, in the end.

"Thanks," she says. What can she say?

"You don't have to thank me. You are." He hurls himself onto the bed, leaps onto it, like a boy into a pile of leaves. The mattress quakes under the force of him.

She thinks he is going to kiss her, thinks he is going to fuck her, thinks she should suck his dick, do something, he deserves something, he's spent more than a thousand dollars on something he thinks is going to please her, and done it with a smile on his face. But he doesn't. He reaches up for her, pulls her down toward him until she's lying on the bed next to him, the two of them staring up at the ceiling, where a little patch of late winter sunshine still lingers. The apartment is quiet. It smells of him—detergent, maleness, something hard to place. He doesn't say anything, and neither does she, and after a few minutes she realizes he's fallen asleep, abruptly. She lies like that, next to him, for what seems a long time, not wanting to wake him.

They lie there, his snore soft, like a baby's, then she sleeps, then wakes, notices he's not there. He's in the kitchen, because they've made a plan. He's promised her a meal, promised to use one of her books, by a celebrity Italian chef, small as a bird, whose signature touch is putting lemon zest into everything.

"Veal," he says, triumphantly. He sweeps an arm over the counter, proudly, as she comes in from the bedroom. He's bought the good stuff, wrapped in white paper and tied with twine, from the old-school butcher. Those used to be everywhere in this neighborhood—as well as plumbers, coffee roasters, funeral directors. You still see statuary (the somber virgin, the lamb of God) in front of the homes of the more devout, though most of the old Italians have moved off to Long Island, sold their brownstones to enthusiastic millionaires of no particular faith. One of the churches has been turned into condos.

"How cruel," she says. She yawns and crawls onto one of the kitchen stools.

"Cruelly delicious," he says, flicking through the twine with the end of his sharpest knife and unrolling the paper, like a child at Christmas.

The kitchen counter divides the kitchen from the living room, nominally; in truth, the kitchen is a wall of the living room. Rob likes to cook or is learning that he likes to cook, anyway. The cookbook is splayed open on the cheap stone countertop. An NPR quiz show is playing softly in the background. He probably didn't want to wake her. He rents this apartment. It's nice enough.

"I have a secret," she says.

"Do tell." He's not wearing an apron, but there is a striped dish towel draped jauntily over his shoulder.

"Maybe you should sit down," she says. "Sarah is pregnant."

"Sarah, friend Sarah, the Sarah who's getting married? Premarital sex?"

"I was shocked, too," she says.

"Congratulations to Sarah, friend Sarah whom I have never met but whose wedding I will dance at. We should have a toast. Pour some wine, would you?" He gestures at her with his meat-contaminated hands.

She pours the wine, which has been breathing, though she can't see how that would make any difference in the thing. The wineglasses are very tall. She clinks her glass against his, which is still sitting on the counter. "To Sarah and baby," she says.

"Seriously, though, is this a surprise? It must be a surprise."

"It's a surprise," she says. "Which is unlike her. She's usually got everything under control. I guess she thought she had this under control, too, but you know, sperm, they're dogged little suckers."

"There but for the grace of God," he says. He washes his hands, sips the wine. "Is she excited?"

"I think so," she says. "It's the way it was meant to be. Just early. I told her not to sweat it. I don't think anyone will know it to look at her. She's got a body for childbearing. She can disguise it."

"A body for childbearing," he says. "Ouch." He sips the wine. "Cheers."

"Well, I'm just saying."

"I've never even met her," he says. "Am I going to meet her before this big fancy wedding?"

"Probably," she says, though she has no real idea.

"Sarah with the important father, whose parties are attended by members of the Supreme Court, that's all I know about her."

She shrugs. "I've known her for a million years," she says. "She's my best friend."

"So you don't want her to meet me," he says. "What am I, your sexual plaything?"

"And personal chef, don't forget personal chef."

"Seriously, though, we should all get together, do something, don't you think? I think. Invite them over. I'll cook." He looks at her.

She tries, fails to imagine Sarah and Dan here, in this kitchen. There are four wooden folding chairs pulled up to a shabby table Rob also uses as a desk. A jar that once held organic strained tomatoes has been repurposed as a vase. The flowers are a nice touch though. "Dan," she says.

"The fiancé?"

"He's unbearable," she says. "I don't know. Maybe we can all get a drink or something."

"He's unbearable, but your best friend is marrying him," he says. He's slicing mushrooms, pushes his slipping glasses back up his face with his shoulder.

"He's not so bad, I guess. He's not my favorite person in the universe, but they're very well suited to each other. It makes, like, one hundred percent sense that they're getting married."

"Because he's a loser?"

"He's not a loser." She pauses. "I don't know."

"You described him to me, like two weeks ago, and I quote, as a 'loser.' "

"I didn't realize you were taking notes. He's fine. He's just such a . . . I don't know what the word would be. A nerd?" She knows that's not right.

"I'm a nerd."

"You like baseball," Lauren says. "Dan likes medical ethics."

"I like medical ethics."

"You do not."

"I could." Rob reaches into the fridge, removes the butter.

"You couldn't, trust me, it's horribly boring." The wine is good.

"Can I just ask though, seriously, it's not me, right? You're not ashamed of slumming it with the lowly editor type? Fucking the temp."

"You're not even a temp, anymore," she says.

"I'm asking a serious question here, Lauren."

"Don't be insane," she says. "I'm not hiding you from them. I'm protecting you from them."

"Well, you can see how a guy might get the wrong idea," he says. "It's not like I'm saying take me home to meet the folks."

"The folks," she says. "Let's talk about something else, okay?"

"Are you sure Sarah is your best friend? You never sound all that psyched about her."

"I don't? Yes, I'm sure. Obviously. Look, we've known each other for years, and maybe we're a little different now, as grown-ups, but there's a long history there. We go way back, as they say."

"You seem a little on edge, though, when you talk about her. You know what I mean?" He's dicing garlic.

She isn't sure what to say. She's annoyed. She's known Rob four months, she's known Sarah twenty-one years.

"I'm just saying, sometimes it doesn't sound like you're best friends. You seem a little . . . annoyed by her," Rob says.

"Everyone's friends annoy them sooner or later, right?" She drinks. "She's my best friend. I can't explain it."

"I didn't mean to make you mad," he says. "I thought we were just talking."

"We are just talking." She's being short with him but she can't stop herself. "I'm sorry. I don't know. It's—" She doesn't know how to complete the thought. It's complicated. It's her way. It's private. All of those things, though this last is too mean—she doesn't think Rob should be allowed to talk to her about Sarah. Four months, fine, but they don't know each other. She can't be known in so short a time.

"Hey." He puts the tongs down on the counter and looks at her seriously. "You there? I'm sorry if I said the wrong thing. I'm just curious about Sarah. I'd like to meet her. She's a big part of your life. It seems right that I would know her."

She looks down into her glass. He is right. "You're right. Never mind. Let's focus on the task at hand. Can I help?"

"I don't know, Lauren. I run a pretty serious kitchen."

She climbs off the stool and goes to stand beside him in the kitchen. Things are very organized in there: cutting board, bowls, the pepper mill. She's seized with a powerful urge: to take him by the hands and pull his arms around her, to feel the weight and warmth of his body behind her, to feel him, there, a real human being, hers, to just stand there for a moment, quietly. She doesn't do this, though she doesn't know why. She reaches up—he's taller than she is—and grabs the towel from his shoulder. She tosses it over her own with a flourish, like Isadora Duncan with her fatal scarf.

"Let me show you how it's done," she says.

―――・――

The morning is cool. Sarah is in the library, waiting for it to be eleven past the hour, when the local channel recaps the forecast, but also hiding from Willa. It doesn't work.

Willa sweeps in with purpose, takes Sarah by the hand. "Don't worry, darling, it's going to clear." Willa shakes her cell phone in the air triumphantly. "I've got an app. Hour by hour. It's saying noon. So don't you worry."

Sarah isn't worried, in fact; it's April, what did they think? She no longer cares about whether the weather will hold, but Willa seems almost to want her to be unhappy. If Sarah is petulant, that will give Willa something to do; if Sarah is grumpy, that will reinforce Willa's value. Sarah doesn't want it to rain, obviously, but she wants Willa to somehow be proven wrong. After tomorrow, she'll never have to see her again. She turns the television off before the weather report even comes on and goes upstairs to wait.

Willa has been calling the bedroom "the bridal suite" and "the staging area" alternately: the former possessed of too much grandeur, the latter too silly. Neither can elevate what is, after all,

Sarah's childhood bedroom. In this room, what can she be but a girl again—all that childish ephemera: years' worth of yearbooks, framed certificates for this or that accomplishment; a Lladro figure of a horse; a sterling, hollow pig, filled with Kennedy half-dollars. Behind the door of the walk-in closet—the only space where Sarah was allowed to exercise her decorative instincts, her adolescent psyche made visible. There, glamour shots of horses torn from the pages of magazines gave way to a parade of soft, shirtless lads, interchangeable really, the stars of screens large and small, Jonathans and Tylers and Aarons and Eriks, who were then ripped down, supplanted by postcards of paintings, stolen from the gift shop at the Met, an Avedon portrait of Allen Ginsberg ripped from the pages of Huck's *New Yorker,* though she never managed *Howl,* a photograph of Sylvia Plath she found God knows where. Even here, this assemblage wasn't necessarily the real Sarah. There was an artifice to it, she was aware even as she had assiduously set about Scotch taping.

Danielle, the hairstylist, is waiting for her, sipping a gigantic paper cup of coffee, as is Lauren, sitting on the edge of one bed and reading an old *Vanity Fair.* Danielle arrived half an hour ago, rolling a suitcase, black, efficient, the sort a flight attendant uses, in her wake. But now she's unpacked, the tools of her trade arrayed neatly on the bureau, atop clean, white towels that she must have brought with her.

Danielle came recommended by Willa. Sarah had only glanced at her portfolio, a panoply of dewy brides with stunning updos and tousled manes, but upon meeting her, Sarah knew she was the one: It's hard not to be impressed with a woman like Danielle, a hairstylist who wears her own hair shorn to the scalp, something black women are uniquely capable of pulling off. Danielle wears a black tank top and black jeans, and Sarah considers, resentfully, her well-formed biceps. After all these weeks of dutifully lifting and dropping those stupid pink barbells, she doesn't have much to show for it. Danielle had listened carefully at their meeting and seemed to agree that what Sarah envisioned—hair back, not up— was the right thing to want. Danielle had taken Sarah's face in her hands, studied the shape of her head, and the whole thing was so intimate, so loving, her warm, strong touch. Danielle was the kind of woman you'd let do anything to you.

"You look lovely this morning," Danielle says. "How are you feeling? Nervous?"

"A little," Sarah says. Why lie? She can admit to Danielle what she won't admit to Willa.

"First things first," Danielle says. "Have you eaten?"

Sarah shakes her head. She hadn't even tried. Not morning sickness, thankfully, just a disinterest in her usual bowl of yogurt and cereal.

Danielle frowns. "This is your job," she says, accusingly, to Lauren.

"She doesn't want to eat," Lauren says. "I tried!"

"You didn't tell her she has to?" Danielle shakes her head. "You have to."

"Maybe I should eat." Sarah's still not hungry, but if Danielle says she must, then she must.

"You should. A boiled egg, something with some protein, and some fruit, just because." Danielle sips her coffee.

"So should I . . ." Lauren trails off. "Should I, like, go down-stairs and boil an egg?"

"You should," Danielle says. "That would be the right thing to do."

Lauren puts the magazine aside and stands. "Okay. One boiled egg, coming up."

"Make it two," Danielle says. "One isn't enough. And find some fruit."

Sarah finds it reassuring that even Lauren is cowed by Danielle. Lauren stands, sort of shrugs, leaves the room. Danielle's tone isn't unkind, but she's clearly someone to whom other people listen.

"I'm all set up," Danielle says. "You're going to sit here. The light is good right here." Danielle has pulled one of the little benches from the end of the bed to a spot in the sunlight, by the window.

"Sounds good," Sarah says. "Are you ready for me now?"

"No, no," Danielle says. "Once you've eaten, we'll start."

Sarah wonders what Dan is doing, if he's taken a shower yet. The guests are due to arrive at four. The ceremony itself is supposed to take place half an hour after that. It's early, but she knows how quickly these hours will fall away. Time being relative, of course, and speedy on a day such as today. Dan will send some last work e-mails, take a shower, dress, take a taxi to the hotel to meet his parents, fetch them, take another taxi downtown to her parents' place, come inside, chitchat, fuss over the arrangements, retie his tie, and then guests will start trickling in. What seem like hours will turn out to be minutes. She's excited to see him all dressed up. She likes the way Dan looks in a suit.

Last night was fun. More fun than she'd anticipated, and genuinely celebratory, which had been her biggest concern. She'd worried that everyone would gather in a room and it would feel like an office birthday: sheet cake in a conference room. But it was the kind of night people remember, will be the thing they remember when they think of her and Dan. *Remember the night before your wedding, we went to that taco place downtown? That was so great!*

Sarah didn't eat much, something every wedding magazine told her would happen. She nibbled on a piece of corn, sodden with cold cheese, but did her duty—to circulate, to hug and kiss the guests who had made the trip in from out of town, her mother's cousin in from Miami, her father's sister's widower and her cousin in from Los Angeles and New Haven. Willa kept bringing Sarah plates of food, but she mostly ignored them.

Sarah had been dreading the toasts, but in the end, they were sort of charming, even heartwarming, and she'd endured them with as much grace as she could muster. She felt like the actresses at the Academy Awards must: It's hard to manage poise when you're so conscious of wanting to seem poised. But there were moments the smile, practiced, conscious, slipped into real happiness. She can't remember much of what was actually said, now, but never mind. Everyone had a great time, which is what matters.

The party was a gift, her gift from Lolo, the best gift, better than the handblown footed glasses, the Conran plates, the Porthault napkins that the people she knows less well than Lauren will give them. Better because she could never have come up with it on her own. Who would have thought of tacos? They didn't talk much—Huck or Lulu pushing and pulling her into obligatory hellos and kisses and catch-up conversations. She caught sight of Lauren, in red, across the room, nodding at something that Lulu was telling her, then later, when Huck had the floor, expounding upon his theory of love, a speech that was moving, that was persuasive, because that's what he does for a living. Sarah watched Lauren, who was listening, reach out and put her hand in the crook of one of Rob's arms, which were crossed against his chest. Leaving, Lauren had leaned in close and whispered into her ear, twice (it was noisy): "That was so fun."

"Thanks to you," Sarah had said. It wasn't clear if Lauren heard.

Lauren smiled. Next to Rob she looked tinier. Her breath was citrusy, from the wedge of lime the waiters had forced on the participating guests of one round of celebratory shots. Her eyes were the way they got when she'd been drinking, bright, a little wild, wider than normal. "See you in the morning," Lauren said, leaning in for an actual hug then, surreptitiously, gently, placing her hand against Sarah's stomach.

Sarah doesn't especially want a boiled egg. "Danielle, would you like to know a secret?"

"Hit me," she says. The tone of a woman used to being confided in. People love to confide to their hairdressers.

"I'm pregnant." Sarah pauses. It feels less odd to say it aloud now. It's a secret but it's still the truth. "You can't say anything in front of my mother, though, promise me on a million Bibles."

Danielle clasps her hands together. "You're pregnant! Congratulations. You are so lucky. Pregnant women have the most beautiful hair. Your hair will never be better. It's something hormonal."

She's read the exact opposite but doesn't disagree, only nods, smiling. "I planned it this way so my hair would look amazing."

"It's good news, though," Danielle says. "A big year for you. Married, baby. It's wonderful. And you must be early, you're not showing at all. So your secret is safe, I think."

"I'm not far along, no. This wasn't exactly the plan, knocked up on the wedding day, if you want to know." Sarah laughs. "I think I'm just getting in under the wire. I feel like tomorrow I'm going to wake up five hundred pounds heavier. I think she's waiting, trying to be polite. She doesn't want to ruin my big day."

"A girl?" Danielle turns her back, fusses with the accoutrements on the table, but catches Sarah's eye in the mirror.

"A hunch."

"Does your fiancé know?"

"He knows. Just me, him, Lauren, and you. Top secret, swear to me."

"Sworn," Danielle says, in a tone that makes clear that she's to be trusted.

That's not quite true, though: The doctor knows, the seamstress from Bergdorf Goodman knows, and she knows that Lauren must have told Rob. It's clear they've reached the secret-sharing stage in the relationship. She doesn't mind.

She'd finally laid eyes on Rob a few weeks before. "You should meet Rob," Lauren had said, calling from the office one afternoon, using that hushed and inexpressive tone she used when she telephoned from the office. "He's coming to your wedding, after all."

This was something Sarah had been waiting for, had asked for, but something she'd not wanted to insist upon. She was thrilled. The four of them met for a drink on a Thursday evening after work, a restaurant in the West Village, equally inconvenient for all of them, but a place that Dan's fond of. She wasn't sure what she expected from Rob—had to see him to realize that she'd suspected there'd be something distasteful about him, some reason Lauren had kept him hidden away. But there was nothing.

He's handsome, Rob, tall, with tousled hair and those smart eyeglasses that everyone wears nowadays. His eyes crinkle shut when he laughs, his voice has a bit of a creak, an almost adolescent squeak, and he makes no attempt to disguise the extent to which he's smitten with Lauren, always touching her, casually stroking her thigh, resting an arm on the back of the banquette and with his right hand teasing a bit of her hair. His manners are old-fashioned, the work of a vigilant mother: He'd stood to greet Sarah, stood again when Dan, late at work, finally arrived, a firm handshake and lots of eye contact. He'd kept signaling the waitress whenever their glasses were near empty, insisted on ordering appetizers even though they'd all said more than once that they were just going for drinks. Sarah, unable to drink, of course, had happily eaten everything that came to the table, and Rob had ordered more. When it was over, he paid the check, flatly refusing to discuss the matter. He didn't have a tattoo on his neck, wasn't dressed like a hobo, wasn't preoccupied with some delusion like being in a band.

Nor was he just normal; he was interesting. Their conversation was about books, about the media, about his job, about baseball, but he'd had several questions for Dan about medical ethics, and his inquiries were informed, his interest genuine. Rob might be better than Gabe, and she loved Gabe, remembers fondly what Lauren was like when Gabe was in her life. Sarah saw a suggestion of that, with Rob, noted the way Lauren leaned into him, their bodies occupied with each other even as their minds were not.

Lauren speaks more loudly with Rob around, or did that night, anyway, and a smile seemed to play across her lips when her face was at rest, when the rest of them were talking and she was silent. Rob is good, Rob is great, and more important than that, the Lauren that is beside Rob is good, is great, is happy. That's the Lauren she loves the best.

——— · ———

Lauren's read somewhere that the proper way to boil an egg is to put it in the cold water, bring the pot to boil, then cover it, removing it from the heat and letting it sit for ten minutes. So this is the method she follows. She must have dropped one of the eggs in too forcefully, though; a small fissure opens in the shell, and the albumen ribbons out, swirls and bobs on the surface of the agitated water. When she lifts it out of the pot after the allotted ten minutes, she runs it under cold water until she can bear handling it. The white has cooked into a little mass of lumps, like a flower, or a tumor.

She's not hungry herself, and in fact, dealing with the egg makes her less hungry. It's sort of disgusting. She tosses the brown shell into the garbage disposal, even though Lulu composts. There are bananas in an enamel bowl on the windowsill, and she takes two of those. She makes toast, too, because it seems like the thing to do, moving slowly, because she is tired.

She slept heavily, drunkenly, but also with satisfaction: The party was perfect. The private room was comfortable, the staff attentive. There were big stone bowls of guacamole and mountains of chips, warm from having just been fried. There were juices in glass pitchers you could have taken for alcoholic, though they weren't; she had insisted on those at the last minute, remembering that Sarah wouldn't be able to drink the special wine Huck was having sent over. There was corn slathered in mayonnaise and cheese and there were tacos, four kinds—fish, pork crispy and not, and chicken, all in floppy little tortillas stuffed with cilantro and radishes. The platters just kept emerging, take as many as you like, then there were toasts with both champagne and tequila, then churros, sugary and thick. Dan's dad spoke, Huck spoke, Meredith's brother Ben spoke, and it had occurred to Lauren, and then panicked her—as Sarah's oldest friend, as her maid of honor, was she supposed to give a speech? She'd asked Sarah this, the night they were out, the night Sarah discovered she was pregnant.

"God no," Sarah had said. "God no."

So, no speech. She thought maybe Meredith would be unable to resist clanking fork against flute (Meredith was the kind of girl who always had to drink champagne; it's curious how we consider it so ladylike to drink something that makes you burp) and tell some long-winded, discomfiting tale about how she and Dan were the ones meant to end up together. But no: She seemed occupied. Her date that night, and for the wedding, too, Jamie, a coworker of Dan's, arranged by Sarah out of some sense of obligation that only Sarah seemed to live with, held her attention nicely. Lauren got a good look at Jamie. He had a very young face, was clearly younger than they were, but a bald spot he had tried to atone for by wearing the rest of his hair longish. The desired effect had not been achieved, but Meredith seemed happy.

It had been fun. Lauren had suspected it might not be, and she had been wrong. Leaving, she'd taken Sarah by both hands, hugged her, told her just that.

"I was wrong," she'd said. "It was fun."

And Sarah had understood. Rob had fun, too, much more fun than Lauren, mostly because he'd spent much of the night getting hammered with Dan's lesbian sister. Lauren has no idea what they might have talked about—Rob was barely coherent on the cab ride back to her place, and this morning, when she left, garment bag slung over a shoulder, tote bag with (she hopes) everything she'll need, Rob was still asleep, snoring loudly, which didn't bother her, because she was awake. Nor was she bothered by the proprietary way he commanded the bed, the long, white bulk of him at an angle, taking up as much space as one person possibly could, the rise of his ass, whiter still than the rest of him, the sight of her pillow, the one she slept on, tucked between his hairy legs, his clothes abandoned on the floor the moment they stepped into the apartment, his funny blue-and-red underwear atop the pile. If he's awake now, he's probably thrown up. She's glad she missed that. She puts the eggs and toast onto a plate, one of the lime-green ceramic plates, from the shelf by the door. She'll take the food upstairs, maybe duck out for a coffee run. There's still plenty of time.

Lauren climbs the steps, balancing the plate carefully. There's a general air of hubbub in the house. On the stairs, she passes the cleaning lady and her minions—giving the powder room the once-over, aligning picture frames, straightening the rugs, which were beaten and then vacuumed only hours before. On the landing, where the staircase makes its turn, a place that's no particular place, Lulu has set a rattan plant stand, topped with two battered coffee-table volumes (Berthe Morisot, Kenneth Noland), on top of those, a clay bowl, bought in India, within that, a beaded necklace, from Haiti, the beads made of old paper, wound around itself in a complicated process by the women at a crafts cooperative supported by a nonprofit she and Huck have long given money to. In this tiny space, so much life, and that doesn't include the pictures on the wall, of Sarah, mostly, though you'll spot Huck arm in arm with Reagan, and a picture of Lulu with Mimi Fariña and Bob Dylan. The disordered detritus of their very well ordered lives. As a girl, Lauren found all this stuff enchanting; part of her still does. Her parents had stuff, but not nearly so much, not nearly so interesting: a couple of brass elephants you might be able to persuade someone were souvenirs from India but which were almost certainly found at T.J. Maxx, stacks of thick military thrillers, piled here and there throughout the house, family photographs, those awkward tableaux—fresh haircuts and best sweaters, the photo studio's logo embossed tastefully in one corner.

She wonders if it were her wedding, at her mother's house, would her mother have paid for a cleaning lady—visions of sensible Bella Brooks, running the rented shampooer over the mauve nap of the living room, warning them all to stay out of there until it dried. It feels cruel to think of this now. Were Bella a different sort of person, she might have forged a friendship with Lulu (as Amina's mother had, years ago, an early playdate). She might have been invited herself, today, though who knows what she would have worn, who knows what she would have made of the wedding registry.

Lauren suddenly feels ill. She's noticed this more lately: the delayed onset hangover. Her stomach tightens, churns: Why Mexican? What had she been thinking? She nudges the door all the way open with her shoulder, goes back into the room, sets the plate on the desk, which had been meant as a place where Sarah could do her homework, though it was almost never used as such.

"Who's hungry?"

"Ugh," Sarah says.

"You're welcome," she says.

"Trust me, eat," Danielle says. "You will be glad you did."

Sarah picks up the egg and takes a tentative bite. Lauren sits back down on the bed. Still not hungry, she does, though, have a very specific craving and is glad she's come prepared. She picks her tote bag up from its slump on the floor. "I bought these. Don't shame me." She reaches in the bag, produces a pack of cigarettes.

"Camels," Sarah says.

"Ultra Lights," Lauren says. "They're practically healthy. A drag won't kill you."

Danielle laughs. "I'm looking the other way, okay?"

"Finish your breakfast," Lauren says. "We'll sneak away for ten minutes and then you can brush your teeth and Danielle can work her magic."

At some point when they were in the tenth grade, Lulu had become concerned with property values. Huck was on the short list to lead the minority party's government in exile, a foundation situated in a handsome Washington, D.C., town house. Lulu made lists: National Cathedral School versus Madeira, where she discovered Brooke Astor herself had been a student, Bethesda versus Georgetown, selling the house versus renting the house. The agent had been dismayed to see that the occupants hadn't fully taken advantage of one of the house's frontiers: the roof. Lulu was sensible about these things, and the roof deck was built, completed not long after Huck had withdrawn his name from contention for the directorship of the foundation. Anyway, President Gore never came to pass, so it would have been an unexciting time to be at that foundation. In politics, in Huck's politics, it's better to be an enemy than a friend. They forgot all about the roof deck.

At least, Huck and Lulu did. By tenth grade, new privileges had accrued: Huck and Lulu decamping to Connecticut Friday morning, allowing Sarah to join them by train, Saturday morning, or skip the thing altogether. Lauren remembers Lulu, looking askance even behind her dark glasses, once, poolside at the Connecticut house, where the distinguished guest couldn't take his eyes off the dollops of Lauren's breasts, new enough then that she marveled at it; her nipples grew firmer just from the good professor's gaze landing on them. The country was for relaxation, and it had to have been more relaxing without Sarah and Lauren in tow.

Lauren hasn't been up to the roof deck in years. The last time: another party, a celebration of their graduation from college, or Sarah's graduation, anyway. Lauren had come by, a formality. At that point, their relationship had entered some never discussed cooling-off period. Anyway, they were going to be roommates in the city; they were going to live together, which changed altogether Lauren's relationship to the house on East Thirty-Sixth Street. Beautiful as it was, much as she loved it, that house was about Sunday dinners and little kid sleepovers and that first time sucking Ryan Harmon's dick in the upstairs bathroom while Sarah and Amy and Tyler and Jake and Sasha and Rachel sat one floor above, under the Manhattan sky, smoking Camels and dropping the butts into empty Rolling Rock bottles where they died with a quick little hiss. That was childhood, and it was over.

"I haven't been up here in ages." Lauren surveys the view, the only thing you can do from that vantage. In the context of the city, of course, the house does not seem that high, but there, on the roof, you feel like a giant, a minor god. "It's so nice today."

Sarah sighs, relieved. "Cross your fingers. I should have waited until May."

Lauren nods at Sarah's midriff. "You dodged a bullet there," she says.

There are four wooden chairs gathered around a round table, and they sit.

"I feel like we're at a spa or something." Lauren digs into her bag, removes the package of cigarettes and a small blue plastic lighter. "You know? All this primping, us in our gym clothes or something."

"I thought you quit," Sarah says.

Lauren lights a cigarette, exhales. "I'm not really smoking," she says.

"Optical illusion."

"I just thought, you know, for old time's sake." Lauren shrugs.

"We got our emphysema started right here on this rooftop," Sarah says.

"Shit beer, cigarettes, Friday nights," Lauren says.

"Ryan," says Sarah. "Ryan something."

"Tim Alhadef," says Lauren. A beautiful half-Arab, half-Swedish guy on the soccer team with whom Sarah had been obsessed for a full year. He had curly hair and thick eyebrows and wore shorts even when it was cold outside.

"Tim Alhadef," says Sarah, wistful. "God, he was fucking gorgeous."

"Those legs," Lauren says.

"Give me some of that," says Sarah.

Lauren hands her the lit cigarette. "Whatever happened between the two of you anyway?" She knows there was something—a kiss, more than, a makeout in a corner while the rest of them were drinking and talking, but she can't recall the specifics, and anyway, Sarah was always coy about that kind of thing. She could talk about sex in the theoretical, but not as it related back to her.

"Fuck," Sarah says, exhaling the smoke. "That is good. Take this away. I'm going to kill the baby."

"Our grandmothers smoked during pregnancy," Lauren says.

"We kissed, once, Tim and me," she says. "It was friendly, then more, and then nothing. A slip of the tongue. That's it."

"He was gorgeous, wasn't he? Whatever happened to him?"

Sarah shrugs. "No idea."

Lauren looks past Sarah, over her shoulder, over the backyard, at the roofs of the houses on the block behind theirs, at the skyline beyond that, at the pale blue gray of the sky. She'd hooked up with Tim Alhadef, once, a party at his parents' place, in what was then, to her, the wilds of Brooklyn but was probably, she realizes now, somewhere near where she lives. She can't remember where Sarah was that night, but knows she wasn't there as she took the subway alone, spent the night at her friend Michelle's apartment, though she told her parents she was at Sarah's. Tim stripped out of his sweatshirt, which was heavy with the smell of him, armpits and cologne, pulling her nearer and nearer. He was strong, he was hairy, and he was persistent, working a hand down the front of her jeans, working a finger up and inside of her, the first time a finger not her own had been there. She kissed him for a while, felt guilty, pushed him away, made some excuses.

Lauren stubs the cigarette out, shreds of tobacco, a black streak on the table. Sarah fiddles. "Shit, is my hair going to smell like smoke?"

"Let's sit out here for a minute in the fresh air," Lauren says. "No one will ever know."

————·————

The makeup artist, Ines, makes less of an impression than Danielle. She's quiet, has a vaguely Eastern European quality, reminds Sarah of a spy, or a flight attendant. Her hands are soft, her touch tentative, and her work requires her to be so close, so intimately involved with Sarah's face. Sarah's just giving into it, though. She feels like a piece of poultry, being trussed, dressed, prepared. Ines's breath smells of spearmint gum and, beneath that, but discernible given the four inches that separate their heads, coffee.

"Look up, now," Ines says, almost whispers.

She means for Sarah to aim her eyes to the ceiling without moving her head or neck, which will have some kind of effect on the skin under her eyes, something Ines needs to mask, or perhaps capitalize on. Her approach is complex, almost pointillist. Sarah's own application of makeup on a daily basis is, well, cosmetic. Color on the parts of the face we've decided need more color, working within the palette she learned decades ago best suited her. This is a thing you learn young, via quizzes in magazines, experiments with friends, the sage advice of older sisters, the occasional visit to a persuasive woman on the ground floor of Saks.

Sarah knows that this matters, on a daily basis, and that it matters more, on a day like today, a day photographs will be taken, the sort of photographs you're supposed to treasure for decades. She's interested in looking her best, but she can't quite forget that her best looks the way it does. Her best is realistic, which is complicated by the fact that best, for her mother, is movie star.

At some point, all those "She looks just like her father!" must have started to sound a great deal less enthusiastic to Huck and Lulu, or less like cause for celebration, anyway. Lulu's never implied to Sarah that she's anything less than beautiful, but most of her parents' positive reinforcement had to do with brains, with achieving high, for which Sarah is grateful. Isn't that more important? She's had moments of envy, but they are genuinely fleeting. Lauren's hair, for example, wouldn't she love hair like that, so long but so thoughtless, so full and lovely—genuinely effortless, Sarah knows Lauren well enough to know that: inexpensive shampoo, the occasional, desultory brushing. Sarah's own hair almost a meteorological instrument. Danielle has done her work, and it looks wonderful, and she'll touch it up in a bit, bring it back to life, once Ines has had her turn. Sarah feels apologetic, though there's little she can do about the fraught relationship between her hair and the day's relative humidity.

She looks at Lauren, seated before the mirror, postcards tucked into the frame at its perimeter. Sarah is far from the vanity, a mercy that she doesn't have to study her own face, reflected back at her over Ines's shoulder. She is pretty, Lauren, always has been. A mystery, how the alignment of your features determines so much. It's an accident. Her brothers are not handsome; they're unremarkable. Lauren has always been otherwise.

When you are pretty, people notice it the first time they see you, so Sarah had seen it, been drawn to it, known immediately that she wanted to claim it, claim her friendship, and she had. She remembers it quite clearly. That the friendship endured turns out to be one of those things: unplanned for, but welcome. She needs her. She understands Lauren. She relishes knowing her, and if there have been times, times when they were younger, mostly, when she envied her—though, no, there haven't been. It wasn't envy so much as magic Sarah wished; she wanted to be Lauren, once, though she doesn't any longer. Her prettiness hasn't faded, has in fact grown, and Sarah takes a strange pride in this. She's chosen wisely.

"Look at me, please," Ines whispers, her voice intent yet somehow far away.

"Sorry," Sarah says, shifting eyes forward.

"How are you doing over there?" Lauren asks.

"Holding up," Sarah says. She hasn't snapped at anyone or thrown a tantrum about anything, but still, everyone's using a gentle, encouraging tone with her. She's trying not to let it irritate her. They're acting like she needs to be placated, which is making her want to act like a monster.

"Almost done," Ines says.

"You look amazing!" Lauren's stood, slipped away from Danielle, and is standing behind Ines.

Sarah opens her eyes. The two of them, Ines and Lauren, beaming down at her, like a child they're proud of. "Do I?" She wants to know, she realizes as soon as she's said it.

"You do," Lauren says. Her smile takes over her face. She smiles with her mouth, but also her eyes, her voice, her being.

Danielle comes over to inspect Sarah. "Gorgeous," she says.

"You guys are miracle workers," Sarah says.

"Shhh," Lauren says. "You always look great. You look like yourself. Your best self. Isn't that what the magazines say you're supposed to be?"

Sarah goes into the bathroom, brushes her teeth in one of the matching sinks—the left, she's always preferred the left-hand one. Ines has brought a toothbrush, bright orange, still in its plastic package, and a miniature tube of toothpaste. Sarah hadn't expected these women to be so thorough, but she's grateful. She feels bad that she's going to have to brush her teeth, muss her face, but whatever—Ines works for her, after all.

She finishes, tries and fails to dry her mouth without smudging the lips, stains the towel, even, but she doesn't care. She cups nose and mouth with her palm, exhales, tries to breathe in her breath, gauge the smell, but of course, she can't; this never works, though everyone tries it. There's smoke in her hair, across her shoulders, a whisper of it, a suggestion, she's sure of it. Does it matter? Downstairs, it'll be warm—all those tuxedoed bodies, dancing, waiters weaving through the crowd with trays bearing a crisp white wine, which she thought would make it seem more like summer, a dark, heavy red, and waters, still and sparkling, the latter with pretty twists of lemon and lime. The room will smell like sweat and bodies, like flowers, like food—little shots of a creamy tomato soup in tiny glasses, mushrooms stuffed and topped with a sprinkling of bright green chive, a sweet little concoction of beet, salty goat cheese, and a single, candied pecan. No one will notice the touch of smoke lingering about Sarah's body, certainly not her parents, who seemed never to notice the smoke or beer on her breath those years she and Lauren—and it was always with Lauren that she got up to such things—came back to this house stinking of both.

Of course, there's Dan. He notices everything. No matter; he's too logical to care. Even when it's something that annoys him, he never gets impatient. To those things—not refilling the ice trays, say—he proposes a logical response—buying a new refrigerator, say, one with an icemaker built in. That's Dan. On television and in movies, people who are getting married talk about wanting to spend the rest of their lives with someone. That doesn't seem like something a normal person would say in reality. Sarah doesn't think people are designed to think about the rest of their lives. If we had to grapple with that, we'd never get anything done.

She's not marrying Dan because he's the man she wants to spend the rest of her life with, though she will, and that's great, that's fine, but in a way, it's the added bonus. The reason she's marrying him is because he, exasperated about her not refilling the ice cube trays, suggested that they buy a new fridge. This somehow seems to explain everything. Does she love him? Of course, what a stupid question. What do you do with that love but get married, and maintain it?

Sometimes Sarah thinks: What if this is something only the two of them have discovered, that only the two of them know about, and what if everyone else really is unhappily married? She's glad they're getting married. She can't imagine her life without Dan, because this life they've started on is so good, and she believes it will only get better. She and Dan have never discussed this, not in these terms, this question of their love, their reasons for getting married, their expectations for that hopefully long arc of the rest of their lives. She assumes that it's a condition of their being so well suited to each other that it's redundant to even discuss it. She knows they share the same expectations, believe the same things. She knows because it's always been this way.

Lauren knows this house so well. She may know it better than she knows her own family home, because at home, she was never paying attention, whereas here—there was always a lesson to be learned here. She can scoff at Lulu now, but Lauren was once in her thrall. She's long since grown out of that. As any child, with any mother, she now regards Lulu as something less complex than what she once seemed: just another person, making another set of mistakes.

Lulu's crammed the house so full of things that you're forever noticing details previously unremarked upon. In the powder room on the second floor, Lauren recalls the wallpaper—chinoiserie in blue and white, panoramas of pagodas and flying creatures, but she doesn't remember the ornamental shelf over the toilet, with its chubby soapstone Buddha, all flopping tits and squinting eyes, a tiny, round box, malachite, swirling, an impossible green. She opens the box. A lone earring, a pearl, missing its back; a half-spent book of matches from a restaurant in midtown; two Italian lire.

She lifts the seat of the toilet, pushes down her pants, sits, confronts a little wrought-iron table, the kind you'd leave in your garden, painted orange, piled high with copies of the *New York Review of Books*. It would never have occurred to her parents that some guests might like to read while they shit. What happened in her parents' bathrooms was a matter wholly unrelated to the rest of life; thus, soaps in the shapes of seashells, clustered together in a little porcelain dish, tiny towels with silken flowers on them that were useless for drying your hands, an apple cinnamon–scented candle flickering decorously throughout the evening.

Lauren selects the issue from the top of the pile. It's from 1997. That year, they were fifteen. She can remember herself at fifteen, there's a particular feeling around fifteen, the way synesthesists perceive in numbers a color, or a scent. Her friendship with Sarah has always been about nostalgia. At fifteen, it was about them at eleven; in college, it was about the tough-talking girls of fifteen they'd once been; in that shitty apartment in the East Village, it had been about the eager little undergraduate selves they'd sloughed off, the ones who flirted with socialism, or performance art. Now, what is it they see when they see each other? Old selves, old periodicals, a currency no longer in circulation. This house, it's a museum.

She pees, flushes the toilet. Her body feels lean, empty, hard, and the thought of the fried and salted things that will certainly appear the second the I Dos have been uttered renews her. She wasn't lying about Sarah's makeup; it's good, so having seen that, Lauren's less scared about having Ines minister to her face. Willa is in Sarah's room, steaming the dresses. Sarah will wait while guests arrive, kiss hellos, sip their spritzers, take their seats, gossip and anticipate. The more Lauren thinks about it, the less sense it makes, all this pageantry and pretend. Why the implication that Sarah exists on some celestial plane, but will be made flesh at the appointed hour and descend, literally, to the garden, to be wed? She remembers something she'd genuinely forgotten all about— the spring dance, their junior year of high school. Theirs was a progressive and serious institution, uninterested in the rites of limousines and corsages, rented tuxedos and photographs before some backdrop meant to communicate an evening in Paris. Still, the party was planned and they were not so cool they didn't want to get dressed up and go to a ballroom at a hotel and dance. They didn't go with dates, much to Lulu's dismay: Lulu, clutching the camera at the foot of the stairs, as she must have seen some mother on some sitcom do, the pantomime of parenthood. They wore dresses found at a thrift store in Connecticut, a simple column for Sarah, pale pink but not princessy, a black flappery thing for her, though they did go to Bloomingdale's and buy new shoes. They felt so beautiful, even if they felt embarrassed, or uninterested in feeling beautiful, as they flew down the stairs, hammed for Lulu's camera, tottered out into the night, awkward as foals but relishing the echo of their heels, the spring air on bared flesh, the appreciative grins of strangers on the street. They were beautiful, in that moment, and there's a picture, proof of it, tucked into the corner of a larger collage of pictures outside Sarah's door. She's got to remind Sarah of that, that night. Taking the subway uptown to the hotel, because it seemed hilarious to take the subway so dressed up, then arriving, evaluating how pretty the girls looked, admiring how cute the boys looked, dancing, first with a knowing smile, later, with real abandon, in some cases fueled by the flasks, surreptitiously sipped, that some boys had snuck in interior jacket pockets, pretending to be James Bond. Cheeks flushed red, ties undone, and she thinks, but isn't sure, that Sarah made out with Patrick Alden, the same boy she'd once overheard dismiss Sarah, or maybe he was just summarizing her. After, piling into taxis, calling for car services, some of the boys unbuttoning shirts, other boys slipping on jackets and fixing pocket squares. They reconvened at a diner in the East Village, where the boys ate scrambled eggs and hash browns and the girls smoked cigarettes and laughed. Lauren remembers it all, compressed into a few seconds of thinking. She thinks about that girl, quiet, dark eyed, in the old-fashioned dress that didn't flatter—her breasts too big; she should have opted for postwar abundance rather than Roaring Twenties privation. You're supposed to remember your previous self and imagine the advice you'd give to you then. If she could go back in time, back to that night, what would she say to that girl? She'd tell her to put the cigarettes out and order some food. At this moment, she'd kill for those hash browns, crispy, oily, salty. The Odessa Diner itself is long gone; it's now a nail salon.

Lauren walks down the steps, toe then heel, toe then heel, the report of shoe on wood exactly like hammer on nail, or an impatient judge's gavel, announcing *look at me, look at me* with every step. She keeps a hand on the railing, because the steps are slippery.

The house is transformed. A few chairs and tables and knickknacks have been banished, for the time being, to the front rooms of the basement, where, long ago, the nanny had lived, a part of the house forbidden when she was in residence and forgotten over the years since. There are flowers, everywhere, arrangements in innocuous glass vases, white peonies the size of fists, roses a pale, limey green. There are tea lights in glass votive holders in clusters: on the mantel, the coffee table, on each step, on that little ledge of step peeking out past the railing, which seems unsafe. Later, it'll be someone's task to move through the house as quickly as possible, lighting them. A couple of rugs have been taken up, and the dining table repurposed as a bar, where a pretty redhead is lining up glasses and taking stock of the bottles. There's something else: a thrum, an energy, distant voices, nearby whispers, footfalls, anticipation. The guests will arrive soon. Sarah has sent her downstairs to see what's what.

"Just come see for yourself," she'd told her.

Sarah shook her head. "I can't."

"You're going to just sit up here and wait like . . . like what, like a prize in a piñata?"

Lauren gives up out of her own curiosity and a desire to get away from Sarah, who is not speaking, because there's nothing left to speak about. She's promised to report back on what she finds. So far, so good. Willa and Lulu have done an impressive job, reorganizing the elements of the house to show it to its best advantage, to make the most of the house's charm, but also its expanse, the fact that it continues to unfold all around you, that beyond the living room there's another sitting room you wouldn't have anticipated, that off the dining room there's a powder room, that there are so many places in the house to sit and catch up, or congregate and laugh. It's a good house for a party and the obvious choice for the wedding, even though she knows it wasn't Sarah's first choice. She knows just why, too—that air of inevitability. Sarah hates doing what is expected of her, even though that's just what she ends up doing most of the time.

Lauren does the circuit: through the living room, into the library, back into the hallway, peeks in the dining room, takes the stairs down. Here, too, an impressive job, the kitchen table and chairs banished, the room open and light, and beyond, the garden, tented, in case of rain, though there's none threatening, after all. There's not enough room for many seats, just a few for the older guests, but standing, everyone should be able to see the ceremony, lit by paper lanterns overhead. It's pretty. Dan is here, in his tuxedo, with his parents.

"Lauren!" Dan waves her over. She walks through the kitchen and he walks through the yard and they meet just at the threshold. He touches her arm affectionately. "You look beautiful."

"Wait until you see your almost-wife," she says.

"You remember my parents." Dan gestures toward his distinguished-looking parents, his silver-haired mother, Ruth, in a sensible but still chic dress, not baggy but certainly forgiving, his father, Andrew, his tuxedoed twin, the very image of Dan's own future: thick neck, puffy hands, intensely focused eyes.

"Hi, again," Lauren says. "Did you have fun last night?"

"It was wonderful," Ruth says. "I ate so much. Sarah told us the whole evening was your idea, and I have to say, you really put together an incredible party."

"That's so sweet, thank you," Lauren says. She's being sincere but a false note always creeps into her voice when she's talking to other people's parents.

"A great time," his father agrees. "How's everyone holding up here?"

"I think we're basically ready," she says. "I'm down here on reconnaissance."

Huck ambles over to them, draping an arm over the shoulders of father and son. "The inner circle," he says. "What are we talking about?"

"I'm just saying I snuck down here to check things out," Lauren says. "We're all ready and waiting up there, but I wanted to be where the action is."

"I'd say it's upstairs, no? The lady of the hour." Huck grins.

"Sure," she says. Huck has to have his say.

"Just tell Sarah to come downstairs," Dan says, impatient.

Ruth looks scandalized. "Daniel! It's terrible luck."

"Mom." Dan rolls his eyes. We're all teenagers again, when our parents are involved.

"I tried, believe me," Lauren says. "Propriety, though."

"It's not 1951," Dan says.

"Have a little respect for tradition, Dan," Andrew says. "You've only an hour or so to go."

"That's assuming that everyone will arrive on time, which I think we all know to be unlikely." Huck laughs. "My poor daughter. Should I go up to visit, help pass the time?"

"Pass along some fatherly words of wisdom?" Ruth might, possibly, be teasing Huck, but it's so gentle no one notices.

"I have some of that," Huck says.

"I'm sure she'd love some company," Lauren says. "She's just sitting up there waiting for her life to begin."

"Now, now," Huck says, as though it's the beginning of a thought, then trails off, says nothing more.

"Has Sarah eaten?" Sarah's mother-in-law-to-be: concerned.

"She's eaten," Lauren says. "I made her two boiled eggs. Protein."

"You're a good friend." Doctor Ruth Burton squeezes Lauren's forearm gently. "I remember when we got married, I was starving, no one told me I had to eat anything, and then I could barely focus through the whole damn thing, and to this day when I look at our wedding pictures I look so angry, because I'm hungry."

"Well, this will all be over soon enough," Dan says.

"What kind of a thing is that to say?" Dan's mother shakes her head disapprovingly. "Maybe you need something to eat, Daniel."

"I'm just saying I wish Sarah was down here at the party instead of shut up upstairs like a woman in purdah," he says.

"I'll go," Huck says. "I'll sneak up a glass of champagne and we'll while away the hour."

Huck is so present that he doesn't even seem to walk away; rather, the rest of the space around him seems to move past him, like the background in a cartoon. He is gone, into the kitchen, where they can hear him barking at one of the polo-wearing waitstaff to find some champagne, cold.

"So, you ready?" Lauren feels a strange urge to punch Dan on the shoulder. She's never sure how to relate to him, so finds herself acting like one of the guys in his presence.

"I'm more than ready, to tell you the truth," Dan says, glancing at his wristwatch. "I'd like to get this show on the road."

"All in due time," Dan's father says, one of those perfectly meaningless things fathers specialize in saying.

"Someone's ready for the honeymoon," she says, and immediately regrets it. The words sound unmistakably sexual coming out of her mouth, the implication disgusting. A misstep: She's usually good with parents, adept at keeping the conversation moving and G-rated.

"You and Sarah have been friends forever, I hear," Dan's mother says.

An out. She's so grateful. "We've known each other for . . ." She does some math. "Gosh, since we were eleven. Two-thirds of our lives. Crazy, right?"

"So wonderful, really." She squeezes Lauren's arm again. "It's wonderful to have an old friend."

"I'm actually her something old," Lauren says. "I'm working on new, borrowed, and blue."

"Guys, excuse us for a second, would you?" Dan places his hand gingerly on Lauren's back, but only barely touching her. She must look immaculate. She lets him push her back into the house, floats away at his touch, happy, for the moment, to cede control to him. She doesn't know what to do with herself anyway.

"You want a drink?" His tone is less formal, but still not quite intimate. Dan's always respected the distance between them.

"Maybe I do want a drink," she says.

Dan nods at a girl who's standing at the kitchen island, measuring out piles of paper cocktail napkins.

"Where do you think we could get a whiskey?"

The girl smiles a smile that says she's helped many a nervous groom. "I've got some ice right here," she says. She stops what she's doing, fills tumblers with ice in one fluid motion. "There's whiskey upstairs or"—voice dropping to conspiratorial whisper—"there's the good stuff, from their regular bar. You want the good stuff, right?"

"We want the good stuff," Lauren says.

She points down the hallway. "It's in the apartment. Do you want me to go grab it?"

"We'll get it," Lauren says. "You're busy." She takes the tumblers from the girl. "Thanks."

Lauren's never actually seen the apartment, and in her imagination, the place was amazing, impressive. A teenage daydream: that Sarah, at sixteen, could have relocated down there, come and gone as she pleased, though in fact, she enjoyed plenty of liberty, not to mention more square footage. The place is disappointing—sealed up, a relic of another time, like those underground bunkers where families once imagined they'd while away the hours, post-apocalypse. The bottles that usually crowd on the kitchen counter have been transplanted to a table here. Lauren chooses the Oban, a splash in each glass then, upon reflection, another splash. She's not the one who's pregnant.

"Cheers," she says. She lifts the glass in salute.

"Thanks." Dan touches his glass to hers, sniffs the whiskey, takes a tentative sip. "I needed that."

She sits on the one corner of the bed not covered by plant stands, coffee-table books, magazines, vases, and other accessories temporarily moved from the upstairs rooms. The mattress groans, but nothing falls over. She's not sure she's ever been alone with Dan before.

"How's she doing up there, really?"

"Great," Lauren says. "She looks amazing, we're all good to go."

"She always does. Is everyone driving her crazy?" Dan smiles. "Sarah doesn't like to be fussed over, you know."

"I think she's taking it in stride," Lauren says. It's sweet, how the first thing he says, in response to being told of Sarah's beauty, is a reflexive "of course." "But, you know, I think she wants it to be over."

"We're pregnant, I know she told you."

"Another thing to say congratulations for," she says.

"Thanks. I'm excited."

"You should be."

"The next chapter, or something." Dan pauses. "I'm glad Sarah has you, had you to talk to, about the baby. You were the first person to know."

"As well I should have been," Lauren says.

"She's lucky, to have you, to know you." Dan looks embarrassed. He takes a long sip of his drink. "I'm nervous. Is that stupid?"

"Drink up," she says. "You're going to need it. The madness hasn't even begun."

"That's what I'm afraid of," he says. "This wedding thing got a little out of hand. Almost two hundred guests? This ridiculous menu?"

"It's fun! Your parents look thrilled. Everyone will be so excited to see you both. Just let it go." Lauren finishes her drink, but sits, looking up at him.

"You understand, though," Dan says, talking to her, but also not to her, almost like he's delivering a monologue. "You're not like this, we're not like this, the big wedding type. The first dance, the bad hors d'oeuvres."

"First of all, those hors d'oeuvres look amazing." Lauren pauses. "Anyway, who cares? It's a wedding."

"That it is," he says. "Pomp and circumstance. Pageantry. How many people here do you think will count backwards when we send the birth announcements and be scandalized?"

"No one," she says. "It's not 1951, as you yourself just said ten minutes ago."

"I feel like you're the only sane person at this wedding. Where's Rob?"

"Oh, he'll be here, eventually," she says. "He was sleeping it off. Last night got a little crazy."

"I amend my previous statement. You and Rob are the only sane people at this wedding, except for Sarah and me. I have to tell you—I wish we could ditch everyone and go have ice cream or something."

"Like something out of an independent film."

"Something like that," Dan agrees.

Lauren needs to eat something herself. One drink and it's in her head: that warmth, that swim. "Our moment is over, groom-to-be." She stands. "Willa is going to be looking for you. They're going to want to do your picture with your parents, to move things along later."

"Willa." Dan snorts.

"She who must be obeyed." Lauren takes his empty glass. "I'll ditch these. You go find the folks, put on your big smile, and then go greet the guests. We'll talk later."

"We'll talk later," he says, taking her by the wrist, because her hands are full. "When I'm a married man, I guess."

"I guess," she says.

———·———

"It's time to get dressed." Willa speaks in a firm, quiet voice; every sentence ends with some emphasis, like she's clapped her hands, though she wouldn't do that. Willa's talents are wasted coordinating weddings; she should work for the president.

For the occasion, Willa has had a large standing mirror moved upstairs from Lulu's dressing room. Sarah looks at herself. She's wearing a tank top, gray, something she'd wear to the gym, and sweatpants, green, the sort of thing she'd never wear out of the house, or in front of anyone but Dan. The mirror is so big, the ceilings so high, that somehow she looks small, in the mirror, like a child. Fitting: Getting dressed had once been play. She's read that play is actually work, that children need to do it to understand the world. So they pantomime fetching cakes from ovens, when really they're conjuring plates of sand from thin air. Or they pack imaginary bags, head off to the office, cannily echoing daddy's unconscious, put-upon sigh. This is genius: rehearsal for our unremarkable lives. She herself did this many times, wrapping Lulu's scarf around her waist like a skirt, announcing she was leaving for "lunch with Kissinger," as one favorite and probably apocryphal family story has it.

She can hear, downstairs, the bustle—chairs being set up, trays being arranged, flowers propped up and back to life. But she's been forgotten. She feels, for a moment, like stamping her feet, like demanding attention. This is her game they're supposed to be playing. The feeling passes. The dress, strapless but somehow modest, is on a hanger, the hanger hooked over the top of the closet door.

"You look beautiful." Lulu charges into the room, hair pulled back tight against her face, showing, to best advantage, the shape of that face, its flat planes, its soft beauty. She looks at once older and younger. "They did a wonderful job."

Sarah's about to respond when Danielle steps in, and then Ines, and Lulu redirects the compliments directly toward them, and again, Sarah's forgotten. The three of them talk, their voices excited; even Ines, who was so subdued before, seems to come alive near Lulu, a not uncommon phenomenon.

Lauren comes in, carrying a can of soda. "I stole this from the bar," she says.

The can is very cold, and wet. Sarah takes it. Relief. She needed something, she didn't know this is what it is.

"Let me get you a straw," Ines says, digging in her things.

"Oh, don't drink that now, honey, it's time to get dressed!" Lulu clucks her tongue.

"You get dressed first. I'll drink this."

Lulu makes a disapproving face—she's always thought soda trashy—but steps into the bathroom, where her own dress awaits.

The soda tastes odd, because her mouth is so clean, but the cold and the sugar penetrate some part of her brain, rouse her just enough. "Thank you," she says.

Lauren shrugs. "I just knew." She gives her a knowing look, follows Lulu into the bathroom. After a few minutes, the two emerge, transformed. It's amazing, the extent to which a garment can change every aspect of your being. When she disappeared into the bathroom, she was Lauren; emerging, she's—something else. Yes, she's made up, that's part of it, but it's the dress. The way it reveals parts of her body, highlighting the parts of the body that remain hidden; the way Lauren seems to understand, somehow, that she has to move her body differently, and then does, expertly, almost automatically. She looks like she wears dresses like this all the time. She looks—it's not pretty, it's more than that. It's that old Lauren: the person Sarah loves so much that sometimes she wants to be her.

Lulu steps out of the bathroom. Her dress is navy, cut close, showing her body, its softness, its curves. She's fiddling with an earring, looks like herself: a star. She smiles at Sarah, smiles at all of them, the practiced smile of a woman greeting her public.

"Your turn, my love," she says.

Sarah looks at the dress, the white billow of it, like a cloud, almost sacred.

"My turn," she says, to no one in particular.

She listens to the sounds of celebration: clicks and clacks on the parquet, the tinkle of glasses, hellos and kisses, the occasional shout of excitement. Danielle smooths her hair. Ines examines her makeup. Sarah can't sit, because of the dress.

Her father comes upstairs, full of chuckles, but is distracted by the arrivals. Her mother comes back upstairs, still glowing from all the compliments. Lauren comes back upstairs, brings a glass of iced water. Willa comes upstairs, tells her it's almost time. The photographer comes upstairs, snaps pictures of her with Lulu, her with Lauren, her alone, the three of them lined up at the top of the staircase, waiting for the signal from the string quintet that will be playing them in.

It feels like a surprise party that they are in on. This silly en- actment of a ritual makes Sarah want to laugh, and she does, and Lauren laughs, too, and Lulu hushes them, and they stop laughing, and the music begins. Willa has to signal them; they can barely hear it.

Dan looks handsome. Dan is smiling. Sarah feels ridiculous. Everyone stands. She walks slowly, just like Willa urged her to. Slow, slow, counting down in her head. Huck relinquishes her arm, takes his seat. She looks out at the crowd. Sees aunts, uncles, cousins, friends, her parents' friends, her friends' parents. Everyone looks back at her.

She looks at Dan, looks up at him, because he's taller than her. His face is broad, a little chubby at the chin. His skin gleams. He shaved that morning. His cheek looks soft. He smells like soap. His hair looks different, a layer of product holding it in place. She remembers not the first time she saw him—that memory is lost to her, a remarkable moment only in retrospect—but another time, years later, years ago now, at the wedding of Ben, Meredith's brother, Dan, in a black suit, leaning against the window of the Princeton Club, candlelit, so himself, so handsome, that she'd known right then that she'd marry him, and in fact, here they are.

———— · ————

Rob kisses Lauren hello. It begins as a kiss on the cheek, turns into a kiss on the lips, becomes another kiss, when no one is watching, his tongue grazing hers.

"You've been drinking," he says, not accusatorily.

Then she goes back upstairs, takes her place in line, parades in and stands by the couple as they wed, an ally. She scans the crowd as they're saying their vows, finds Rob, tall, standing with hands folded behind his back like someone examining a painting in a museum. She wants to signal to him, somehow, a raised eyebrow, a grin, a mouthed word, but she can't, because everyone is looking, everyone will see. That he is hers feels like a wonderful secret.

They say a few words, then more words, then there's a cry of delight, and applause, and the guests who are seated stand, and Dan kisses Sarah.

Everyone practically chases the couple as they attempt to retreat down the aisle. They stop, abandon the plan, giving hugs and kisses, accepting compliments, wiping tears. Every cell phone comes out, photographs are taken.

Rob worms through the crowd toward her. Lulu has vanished. The recessional will not continue. Lauren puts her bouquet of green roses on a seat, takes Rob by the hand. "Let's get a drink," she says, loudly, to be heard over the chatter.

The day is cool, but the garden is so crowded that even the outside air feels warm. Food appears, and drinks. Dan and Sarah disappear to have their photograph taken on the front steps. Huck and Lulu disappear, too, then reappear. Huck tells stories in his booming voice, drowning out even the string quintet.

The musicians pack it in and leave. The DJ arrives. There are more appetizers, then more drinks, and finally the servers come through, collecting empty glasses and encouraging everyone to go inside, upstairs, to dinner, a buffet laid in the living room.

Lauren takes a plate—salmon, red potatoes, asparagus—and she and Rob sit on the steps, eating, watching the sky grow darker. It is night. They take their plates inside, deposit them back near the buffet. A girl in a black polo shirt whisks them away.

There are speeches and toasts, back in the garden. The chairs are gone, the lanterns are lit. The photographer moves through the crowd. He pauses before them, and Rob drapes an arm around her shoulder, pulls her nearer, and they smile. Huck makes a speech about the first time he held Sarah, and how a parent never stops holding his child. It's a good speech, but that's what he does for a living.

There are cupcakes filled with strawberry jam. They drink more whiskey. Lulu sings a song, then another, and there is applause, raucous, excited. She beams. The DJ begins to play music. The kids dance. Some of the older guests dance. Most of them go inside, to drink, tell stories, listen to Huck. She and Rob dance, then sit, and watch the dancing, watch the faces, and then, a couple of hours later, it is over.

Sarah's hunch is wrong. It's a boy. Called Henry, for her dad, and then Andrew, for Dan's. He's small, a surprise given how big she got. The labor, which she's been privately terrified of for weeks, is simple. There is pain, yes, and it's a pain that is beyond any definition of pain she's previously accepted or understood, but it's brief, and in the end, there's the baby, and the pain diffuses, floats away like a cloud, and there's a dull, general atmosphere of fatigue, a warmth at the hips, an ache in the back, but there's also him, furious mouth pulling at her nipple, leaving her a little bit ecstatic, and even more spent. It's so animal it's almost like incest. She sleeps, and the baby is taken away, and then he is returned to her, and Dan is there, and she pulls on a gown, ties it up, her nipples sore and leaky against the thin cotton. When she is decent, Lulu comes, fragrant with perfume, then Huck, then Andrew and Ruth. Everyone wants to hold and kiss Henry, so they do, in turn, then they leave, and she sleeps and nurses and drinks cup after cup of iced water. A day later, Dan pushes her and Henry in the state-mandated wheelchair to the curb, and they wrangle with the six-point harness on the as-yet-unfamiliar car seat, then drive home, very slowly.

She had steadfastly declined, those months, the opportunity to be showered with gifts, as is the custom. Lulu was horrified.

"This is just what people do," she'd said.

"I just made everyone come and watch me get married. I'm not going to make them celebrate me again so soon."

And here's the thing: Pregnancy gives you authority. No one wants to anger you, and if they do, you can display that anger without fear of seeming irrational. Pregnancy makes every emotion into a force of nature, something to be respected, honored, even. There was no shower: no white cotton onesies, strung on a line, no party games, no baby bottles filled with prosecco.

So, détente: an afternoon meet and greet, at her own apartment, not her parents' house, so Hank can nap in his own bed, or anyway, the little upholstered box in which he sleeps. Just a few snacks, most ordered in from the same service that brings the groceries: a plate of baby carrots and celery sticks with a bowl of garlicky hummus at its center, an arrangement of suspiciously perfect-looking strawberries and orange arcs of cantaloupe. She's put on a pot of coffee.

Meredith is first to arrive. A baby blue gift bag in hand, visage of a stuffed, soft monkey just visible between the twine handles. Meredith kisses her on one cheek, then the other, barely brushing up against her body like she's afraid of hurting her. *I just pushed seven pounds of arms and legs out of my vagina,* Sarah feels like telling her. *I can take anything.*

"You look beautiful," Meredith says.

"So glad you came," Sarah says.

"I can't wait to meet the little man!" She grins. "Should I take my shoes off?"

Sarah shakes her head, guides Meredith into the apartment. The baby is snoozing happily, noisily, in the seat. His snore is surprisingly loud.

Meredith considers the baby. He's so small, but so much bigger than he'd been only weeks ago. She pantomimes her excitement, lest she wake him, clasped hands, open mouth, a gasp. Mouths: *He's gorgeous!* The exclamation mark is implicit. She perches on the edge of the sofa, looks up at Sarah. "Tell me everything," she says.

"Everything is good." Sarah sits. The air-conditioning whirs to life. "I mean, you know."

"I don't, but I can imagine." Still whispering. "Just look at that face!" Meredith seems almost overcome.

"Thank you." It has occurred to Sarah since giving birth that it might be easier to accept compliments relating to her offspring had she adopted. Thanking someone who praises his beauty seems to be tacitly endorsing that she and Dan are themselves beautiful and somehow responsible for this. She just says thank you but doesn't entirely mean it. Henry, young as he is, is an entity independent of her. "How are you?"

"Oh, you know." Meredith waves this question away.

Sarah does know: She knows that her matchmaking has been successful, and since the wedding Meredith and Jamie have been seeing each other constantly. She'll marry him, Sarah's sure of it. Meredith will ask Sarah to be her matron of honor. The couple will probably be very happy.

"You look good," Sarah says. She's not sure what else to say. She's not interested in talking about the baby: Almost every conversation ends up being about the baby, and they're not interesting. She's been hungry, starving, actually, for a real conversation, one about a book, about someone's experience at work, a bitter complaint about a relationship, plans for a vacation—anything. But now, confronted with Meredith and the opportunity to have such a conversation, she can't think what to say. She needs Lauren. Profane, honest Lauren. They will have a real conversation.

The buzzer rings once more, and she realizes that of course she won't have to make conversation today, after all—when playing hostess, you never get to speak to anyone in any satisfying detail. They're not there to talk to her anyway; they're there to coo, to give presents, to pay respects.

It's Fiona, who's taken the elevator up with Lulu and Lulu's friend Sharon, Auntie Sharon, a silver-haired, soft-spoken woman, a photographer of great renown, one of Lulu's closer friends. Sharon is carrying a big tote bag—Lulu has no doubt prevailed upon her for some photographs of the new mother, or, more likely, one of herself and grandson. Sarah's eye falls first though, on Fiona, the swollen tautness of her belly. As etiquette decrees, a warm hug for Sharon, whom she's not seen since the wedding, then a quick hello to her mother, then an embrace, the first she means, with Fiona, so tall and expansive, pulling her nearer to her body, its leaking nipples.

"You didn't tell me," she says. "Congratulations."

Fiona brushes this aside. "It's your party," she says. "But yes, now you see."

"Playdates! We'll have playdates." Sarah finds this genuinely exciting. She closes the door.

———·———

The right gift eluded Lauren. Her initial thought had been a blanket. Then she had a drink, one night, with Jill, poor Jill, eager for some female companionship. Jill had e-mailed, Jill had called, Jill had kept the nanny on late one Wednesday evening and Jill had met her at an annoying Cuban-cum-French place that had always driven Lauren crazy but Jill chose, and Jill paid, so she went. She drank rosé, listened to stories about Jill's nanny, who seemed to be the only connection to reality in Jill's life. Jill's nanny was a painter, and her boyfriend was a photographer whom Jill described, more than once, as sexy, which was an intriguing admission. Lauren used the opportunity to do some focus grouping.

"Whatever you do, don't get her a blanket," the first thing Jill said, upon being asked the best baby gift, without knowing that's just what Lauren had planned on.

She didn't protest, didn't counter that it was Missoni. Jill knew, Jill must be heeded. So, no blanket. Lauren spent a few days in the stacks at various bookstores, putting together a list of the least-boring children's board books, the ones with the best pictures, the ones with the least-sexist stories, but then she remembered that she worked in books, and such a gift would seem like something plucked from the free table at work. The big-ticket items were a possibility—a stroller, a crib, a high chair—but there was nothing special in those, the presents a wealthy aunt would send.

"A Tiffany rattle?" she tried.

"Very WASP," Jill said. "Perfectly good taste, perfectly useless."

Uselessness was the point, but it did have the feeling of anonymity; a silver rattle is what your husband's employer's human resources department would send by way of congratulations.

Lauren assumes the doorman at Sarah's building knows her, but he doesn't. He looks at her, looks at the box in her hands, understands, and says, "Burton?" The doorman rings the apartment without asking her name, waves her along.

The package is unwieldy, but not heavy. She's settled on some ridiculous clothes, the sort no reasonable mother would buy for her own child: a tiny, cashmere cardigan; a gingham button-down shirt with faux mother-of-pearl buttons; a pair of velvety corduroy pants, bright green; a very small fedora; an honest-to-God sailor suit, with navy blue shorts, crisp white smock, and neckerchief printed with tiny anchors and cartoon whales, all meant to be worn when he's a much bigger boy—she's even accounted for season and his relative age, buying the sailor's suit in size 12 months, so Henry can wear it at some point next summer. She's also bought a photo album, or a blank book anyway, bound in green leather, and plans a lecture about how no one gets actual printed photographs anymore, but there's something about flipping through the pages of an album that scrolling around on a telephone cannot replicate.

Sarah answers the door. She looks very different, at first, and it's because Lauren's mental image of Sarah is Sarah on her wedding day. Sarah looks, now, nothing like that. Her hair looks thinner, somehow, or flatter, which is odd, given the day's humidity. Summertime Sarah's hair is usually so voluminous. There's a hardness, too, to her face—she's lost weight, that's what it is.

There's that residual glow, of pregnancy, which has mellowed into the satisfaction of the parent. Lauren wasn't sure what she expected—dark circles under the eyes, maybe, a general harried air—but she knows that Henry's a decent sleeper, actually, eats his fill like clockwork, then dozes and mews in his little sleeper, attached to their bed. It makes a certain kind of sense that Sarah would have a perfect baby; it's of a piece with the general expectation, in her life, of perfection. She looks good. She looks like her younger self, and it's a look that seems better, more beautiful, now than it did then.

"Hi!" As she kisses Sarah, Lauren spies the small crowd in the apartment. She wills herself into party mode.

"You're here." Sarah pulls her into the apartment, closes the door.

It is cold inside, almost like a refrigerator. The apartment smells, as it always does, of nothing at all. It's like a hotel, she's always thought, Sarah and Dan's apartment, anonymous, incongruous, well ordered and maintained, like a model home.

"Is he awake?" She's seen the baby already, of course, but only the once, at the hospital, Sarah sleepy and crazed-looking, Dan sweaty and pleased. Newborns are never all that cute unless you have a genetic stake; Henry looked like a red alien, or how she imagined a turtle might look, without its shell. Lauren oohed over him, left them with some flowers, then, the next day, had some groceries delivered to their apartment, including many ready-made dinners you needed only heat in the microwave. She's wanted to give the new family their space; this has been her gift to them. She thinks she knows what new parenthood entails: sleepless stupor, casual nudity, marital bickering, forgetfulness, anxiety about in-

251

oculations and insurance. A new parent needs time to process this, doesn't need to spend her days making chitchat with gawkers.

"He's dozing, but he'll be up soon." Sarah leads her into the living room, where Meredith, Amina, and two older women she doesn't recognize are stabbing baby carrots into a bowl and having a conversation in an exaggerated whisper speak that's frankly every bit as loud as normal conversations. Lulu and Fiona, who is clearly pregnant herself, her long, elegant body somehow made longer and more elegant by the rise of her stomach, are just offstage, in the kitchen, where Lulu is doing nothing to keep her voice down.

The baby is in his seat, amid all this general hubbub, a blank expression on his face, lips set in a perfect little pucker, his cheeks moving, almost imperceptibly, as he snores. The hair on his skull looks almost drawn on, like the lines of a pencil. He's sweet; babies are designed to seem sweet.

"You know everyone," Sarah says, her tone carrying a clue. "You remember my aunt Sharon? And my colleague Carol?"

"Of course! How are you?" Lauren offers a hand to both the women, unsure which is Sharon and which is Carol. It doesn't matter. She hasn't seen Amina or Meredith since the brunch, the Sunday after the wedding, an understated, hungover occasion. She and Rob sat with Sarah and Dan and the four of them ate quiche and pastries and mostly ignored the rest of the guests. The three of them exchange half hugs and half kisses, as is the custom. Their trip together—bathing suits and bangles, sunscreen and that pristine water—seems like something that happened to someone else.

"Can you believe this kid? I'm dying to wake him up," Meredith says. "I can't wait to get my hands on him."

Sarah disappears into the kitchen.

"You better not," Amina says. "My sister says the one rule is never wake a sleeping baby."

"How are you supposed to resist, though?" Meredith stares longingly at the baby.

Sarah has kept Lauren abreast of things. She knows that Meredith and the blind date who was arranged to escort her to Sarah's wedding are now an item. Judging by the rapacity with which Meredith is studying the baby, the poor guy stands no chance.

Fiona joins them, porcelain teacup cradled in her hands like a bird settled into a nest. "Hi, Lauren," she says. Some special note of friendliness there: She and Rob spent an hour at the wedding with Fiona and her husband, Sam. They sat on the stoop, the four of them, balancing plates on laps and eating dinner, then smoking Sam's cigarettes, talking. Lauren likes Fiona, though she's also a bit afraid of her, has always had a healthy fear of women who are too beautiful. Much as pregnancy has amplified the effect of her remarkable body, it's accentuated the impact of her beauty. She has it—the glow. And she's cut her hair short, like a boy's, so all you can do is take in the planes of her face, the evenness of her skin, the sweet peak of her nose, the luxurious green of her eyes.

"Congratulations," Lauren says, which is what you must say in these situations, when it's impossible, indeed uncomfortable, to deny the fact of another person's pregnancy. "When are you due?"

"November," Fiona says. "Not long now. How have you been? How's Rob?"

"He's good, thanks," she says. "He's good. I'm good. We're good."

Rob is good. That may be the easiest way to sum him up: good. Things between them have been much the same—dinner here, or a movie then a drink, a stroll around Chelsea to look at the second-rate summer group shows, an hour in the park, on a blanket, with the newspaper. The first weekend of August, their first time away together. She'd felt guilty, like they'd ditched the third wheel that had accompanied them wherever they went: the city itself.

Rob's idea: a vacation rental in the Hudson Valley, though they never caught sight of the river. They stopped at a big, clean grocery store, bought a rotisserie chicken and some dry pasta, the makings for hamburgers, a bottle of vodka and a twelve-pack of beer, a package of Oreos and every idiotic magazine in the checkout line. The house had a hot tub, and they sat in the quiet night, naked, until the heat had completely soaked into their bodies. They dried off and fell asleep, woke up and fucked. There was no computer, no television, even their phones didn't work all that well. She spread a sheet on the patchy lawn and lay there in the summer sun, reading tabloids. Rob fell asleep on the sofa and snored, then woke up and grilled hamburgers. They sat naked in the tub again, again fell asleep, and woke early the next morning, too early, because they hadn't done anything and therefore weren't tired. They packed their things, drove to a nearby town, looked at some terrible art galleries, ignored the antiques shops, ate bagels and drank iced coffee. Rob drove them back to her place, and then Rob went to return the rental car on his own, and she was surprised to find that she was relieved to be alone again.

She has been impatient for September, and now here it is: three books launching, related parties and events scheduled, that back-to-school feeling in the air and even if you're the sort to sing "no more pencils, no more books," there's something comforting in the sense that the world is getting back to business. Lauren's ready, ready to shake the hands and soothe the egos, to demonstrate efficiency, to reach for excellence. She's ready for more. Sarah has a baby, for Christ's sake. What the fuck does she have?

"Lauren, come sit and talk to me," Lulu says, beckoning from the sofa. "Come, come."

Lauren makes an apologetic face to the younger women—Lulu must be obeyed—accepting before she goes, from Meredith, a glass of white wine.

"How are you, then? So beautiful, look Sharon, this is Sarah's oldest friend, isn't she beautiful?" Lulu's friend nods in agreement, or benediction.

Lulu has this quality, sometimes, of seeming very drunk, when in fact she isn't. Lauren has never understood what brings this on in her. "How are you, Grandma?"

"Ah." Lulu clasps her hands. "I've decided on Mamina—Henry's going to call me his mamina, isn't that lovely? I am, in my old age, you see, getting more interested in my roots. Mamina. That's how I called my mother's mother, so it's got a history to it. And of course, we'll have to raise him with Spanish."

Lauren nods. "They say it's easy, when you start from birth."

"It is, well, of course it is, we were raised in English, Spanish, French, we never knew any different, we just answered in whatever language we were spoken to, this is how it should be. This country, the way people insist on English, it's so small, don't you think?"

Lauren agrees. It's easier, with Lulu, to agree.

———·———

The thing Sarah wants least, now, is to open the presents, in front of everyone, but it is clear that's what people expect, or at least Meredith and Lulu, the most vocal among them. So she does. Amina is holding the baby, who isn't doing anything because babies can't do anything, and Sarah perches on the leather pouf from that Moroccan shop in the West Village and unwraps. There is: a sterling silver rattle in telltale blue box, plus a stuffed monkey, very soft, from Meredith; a blanket, off-white cotton, hand-embroidered with a motif of small giraffes, and the very practical package of onesies, from Carol; a dozen little board books, from the black-and-white ones that are meant to be the only thing a small baby's eyes can discern, to actual storybooks, the sort she'll read aloud at some impossible-to-imagine point in the future, from Sharon.

"Mine next!" Amina, arms full of Henry, nods at a box wrapped in yellow.

Lauren hands it to Sarah, and she sits with it on her lap, for a second, looking at all of them, looking at her. She has a baby. This realization has come a couple of times now, each of them surprising. She knew she was going to have a baby, she was there when the baby emerged from her very body, but still, in moments, it's possible to forget, or be so preoccupied with remembering things like which side of the diaper goes in back, quickly, before his little penis dribbles out yet more of his perfectly clear urine, that the very fact of it is lost, or buried. This is probably by design; the baby keeps you busy so you don't have time to reflect on the fact that you have a baby. She doesn't want to think too much, because she's terrified of postpartum depression and has come somehow to equate the two. Sometimes, thinking too deeply is a mistake, is a trap. Sometimes it's best just to do.

It's a sound machine, Amina's gift, buried inside a plush sheep. Sarah's read good things about this. "Thank you!"

She's not making a list but feels like she'll be able to remember who gave her what; the gift reflects its giver's personality, somehow. She'll know that the hand-crocheted mobile in the shape of an antique bird's cage was from Fiona, because only Fiona would give a present nominally suitable for baby and yet so stylish. She's glad that Fiona is pregnant—is happy, of course, as you would be, for a friend, but selfishly, too. There are no mothers in Sarah's close circle, and even though she's only a couple of weeks into it, she feels alone, or like she'd benefit from some peer support. She supposes, now that she considers it, that maybe she's always imagined doing this with Lauren, getting married, vacationing together with their husbands, who would, of course, be friends, or friendly enough. Then having babies, passing hand-me-downs back and forth between them until they could no longer remember who had originally bought those Old Navy overalls. Foolish, she guesses; she thinks, or knows, that Lauren will probably never have a baby, and even if she did, Lauren wouldn't approach it the way Sarah's going to approach it. She still remembers, though, the things she once thought, even if nothing has happened quite as she imagined it would.

There's only Lauren's gift now, a bounty of clothes, ridiculous every one—outfits for a man, scaled down for a baby, and a sailor's suit like a baby in a Shirley Temple movie might have worn. She laughs. She understands, immediately, that this is both a joke and not.

"These are ridiculous," she says.

"I couldn't resist," Lauren says, also laughing.

There's also a blank book, in a pretty jeweled color.

"For photos," Lauren says. "Real pictures. Not just data on your cell phone. Old school. You'll be glad you have it later."

"Wonderful!" Lulu snatches the book from her hands. "I've been saying the same thing. All the pictures, we have all those pictures in the house, and they're so wonderful to have. The way things are done nowadays . . ."

"You're sounding old, Mom," Sarah says. "But you're right. There's something nice about real photos. Thanks for this. And that's enough gifts."

The afternoon trickles away, and the women trickle away, kissing the baby, kissing her. Fiona is left, legs curled beneath her on the sofa; Lauren is left, picking up used napkins and little bits of ribbon and tossing them into the garbage can under the sink.

"You don't have to," she says.

"I do," Lauren says. "Just sit."

Sarah does as she's told, sitting with Henry in her arms, his eyes wide, which will last for a few minutes, but then they'll grow smaller, and she'll feed him, and put him down on his back and let him sleep, hopefully for a couple of hours. She's not tired, exactly, but she could sleep. So, too, could she get up and clean the living room. But she can tell it makes Lauren feel good to help, so she doesn't.

"What are you thinking for a name?" Sarah asks.

"We're torn," Fiona says. "Sam is keeping a list, but I keep vetoing everything on it. Declan? Theo? Quinn? None of those seems exactly right to me."

"I like Declan," Sarah says.

"It's a big responsibility, a name," Fiona says. "The first act of parenting, and your first chance to fuck up."

Henry's name was a foregone conclusion, once they discovered he was a boy. She's not sure why her parents hadn't named her brother after their dad but is glad they didn't—naming the baby for his dead uncle would have been too fraught. Henry should be nothing but cause for joy. Sarah wonders, though, if there isn't, in Lulu and Huck, some muscle memory associated with cradling a brand-new little boy. She's always known it intellectually, but now she's a parent and knows it in a different way: There can't be a worse horror than losing a child. The baby has given her a new view into Lulu, a new empathy for her. A new bride in a foreign land when she wasn't much more than a girl; a mother at an age when she still could have used some mothering herself. And then: for him to die? It seems impossible. It's no wonder they've never discussed it.

Sarah feeds the baby, draping one of the big muslin blankets over his head because she doesn't feel like sharing her chapped and swollen nipple with Fiona and Lauren. Fiona fills a napkin with carrots, then when she's eaten them all, she leaves. Lauren finishes tidying, brings Sarah a glass of iced water, and stays. The baby goes down, snoring steadily. She transfers him to the bedroom, switches on the monitor, leaves him there, and she and Lauren are alone.

"So how is it?" Lauren is on the floor, her back against the sofa, looking up at her. She's cradling a cup of coffee. "You're a mother."

"I know," she says. "It's . . . I don't know yet, is that a weird answer?"

"Not especially," Lauren says.

"One day I was myself, then one day I had a baby, and now I'm still myself, but I'm also not. It's not like something magical happened. I mean, sure it was magical and chemical and blah blah, but mostly, I still feel like the same person with a whole new set of things I have to think about during the day. Every day. For the rest of my life."

"That seems like a pretty succinct description of parenthood," Lauren says. "Of course, it's all another country to me, so to speak."

"Maybe not forever," Sarah says.

"Maybe forever," Lauren says. "What do I know?"

"What do you know? Tell me about Rob."

"Nothing to tell," she says.

"Nothing at all?"

"He's good, I don't know. Would you like his number?"

"Don't be an asshole." Sarah sighs. "We're making conversation."

"I'm not being an asshole, I'm just saying. Rob's Rob. It's good, it's fine, it's the same, it's not important. We're here together for the first time since you had a baby, I don't want to talk about some guy."

Some guy—this is a telling turn of phrase. Sarah sees it immediately, that Rob will not last the year. Something has changed, Lauren's mind has changed. Sarah's disappointed, maybe not as disappointed as she'd have been a few months ago, before a baby monopolized her every emotion. She likes Lauren and Rob together but is somehow not surprised. "What should we discuss? South Sudan? The election? I can conference in Papa if you'd like."

"I don't know, your baby?"

"Yes, he's very important," Sarah says. "But he's very boring. He sleeps, he nurses, the doctor says he's healthy. You're not going to turn me into one of those women who only talks about the consistency of their baby's poop."

Lauren frowns. "The dignity of motherhood."

"Do you ever think about it, having a baby?"

"The last time I thought about it was because I was going to and had to take care of it."

Sarah remembers Lauren's abortion, of course—the year after college, for all those years of expensive education, it was the first year they actually learned anything. Lauren didn't have a doctor, as she'd been seeing student health clinicians the previous four years, so Sarah had found the place, out in a part of Queens that was otherwise all tile distributors and malls that catered to Chinese people. They took a car service there, Sarah sat in the waiting room, which was trying so hard to be tasteful, with its plants, its upholstered seats, unobtrusive classical music, its general, genial air. Before, and after, despite not wanting to interfere, despite wanting to simply let Lauren heal, she'd urged her to discuss the thing with Gabe. He had a right to know, didn't he?

"Shit." Sarah thinks for a minute. "This isn't hard for you, now, is it, this baby stuff, because of that?"

Lauren shakes her head. "Ancient history."

Sarah doesn't know if Lauren ever actually told Gabe about it. She's almost sure she didn't. "Not so ancient."

"Ten years, basically. A decade. A lot has happened in ten years. Look at you. You're a wife and a mother."

"I am a wife, and a mother." Sarah doesn't want to think about it—what a ten-year-old boy or girl would look like next to her own baby. Still, she can't help it.

"Don't say it like it's a bad thing. It's your thing. It's the thing you were meant to do."

Sarah is quiet. Everyone's been tiptoeing around it, concerned words, delivered in hushed voices. This is a surprise. "Thanks a lot," she says. She's mad in that way that only Lauren can make her.

"What thanks a lot? It's not an insult. It's a good thing. You've got a good thing." Lauren finishes her coffee, sets it on the glass table.

"Do you think that this is all I am, is that it? When people say someone is a wife and mother, what they mean is that she's *merely* a wife and a mother. *Only* a wife and a mother. There's this implicit *poor thing*."

"You're hearing things," Lauren says.

"I am? Maybe what I'm hearing is the collective voices of every woman of the last two generations ready to throttle the first person who brings up having it all. Please, Lauren, I know you well enough. Don't condescend and tell me it's a compliment."

"You're hearing italics where there are no italics," Lauren says. "You're wonderful; why are you getting mad at me for pointing out how wonderful you are?"

"It just feels like you're emphasizing the difference between us for some reason. Like I've made some choice that you would never make. Because. I don't know. Because I'm stupid, or old-fashioned, or something."

"Yeah. You've never thought that I've made any mistakes," Lauren says. "You've never acted like my being me is totally insane and not the way to do things." She stands. "I should finish cleaning up."

"Just leave it, I can clean up later," Sarah says. They can do this, switch from annoyance with ease. They don't need to have a big let's-clear-the-air. All this time, all these years, the same conversation: It shifts, it evolves, but remains essentially the same.

Lauren sits on the sofa. "Okay." She's quiet. "Lulu seems to be taking grandmotherhood in stride."

"Mamina, did she tell you?" Sarah snickers.

"She mentioned."

"It's hilarious. My whole life the only times I've heard her speak Spanish is to hotel maids. Suddenly, she's an abuela."

"You're forgetting the super, on Eleventh Street. Ramon? She talked to him *en español*."

"The super?" Sarah can only barely recall him.

"When we moved in, or right after, she came over, with a bunch of crap for the apartment, then she saw Ramon and gave him a long lecture in Spanish about how he had to look after us or something, I couldn't follow it, but actually, I could tell what she meant."

"I never knew that," Sarah says. She remembers that day, though—Lulu, with lamps, a rug, some framed photos, a coffee table, a plant, a plant stand, a huge number of things for their ridiculously small apartment. The rug had covered almost every inch of the living room. "That seems like a long time ago, somehow, Eleventh Street. It seems like longer ago than college. It seems like longer ago than actually being eleven."

"It does. I wonder why?"

"I remember all that other stuff so well, you know. Being eleven. With you. Being with you is mostly what I remember. Weekends in Connecticut, the horse, stealing Papa's cigarettes."

"I remember that stuff, too," Lauren says. "Drinking wine with dinner on Sunday, that was the first time I ever had wine. Your mom, pouring me a glass, like it was totally normal. I never saw anything like that."

"Mom's always been a social drinker."

"Lulu is a social everything. I can just picture it now, can't you, ten-year-old Henry getting a little shot glass of cabernet so he can join in the toast?"

Sarah can see it, with such clarity, such certainty. Lauren truly knows her family. "I never knew that," she says, "your first glass of wine."

"My first so many things, Sarah. You've been around for so many of my first things. My first trip to the state of Connecticut, I'm pretty sure. The first horse I ever rode on. My first kiss, the first time I touched a penis, you've been there for all that. We are old."

"We're not," Sarah says. "We're good. We're happy. We're just getting started."

"That's what I meant," Lauren says. She laughs.

"It's still possible," Sarah says. This is what she most wants to tell Lauren, what she most can't tell Lauren, because it will make Lauren mad, and maybe she's right to be mad, maybe it's condescending to hear this from someone who's only three months and nine days your elder. Lauren, beautiful Lauren, smart in a way Sarah will never be, of the world in a way Sarah will never be, powerful in a way Sarah will never be. She can do anything, and seems not to know it.

"What is?" Lauren's stood, is tidying up, despite being admonished not to.

"Anything," Sarah says. She means it. "Anything."

"Maybe," Lauren says.

———— · ————

After a while, the baby starts crying. It begins as a snuffle, what sounds like a sneeze, something involuntary, then it turns out to be voluntary, then it turns out to be loud. Lauren slips on her shoes, slips out the door, Sarah, on the sofa, her nipple elongated and purple, vanishing into the baby's mouth. Lauren remembers, when the elevator reaches the lobby, that she meant to get Sarah another glass of water before she left. She's heard that breastfeeding mothers need lots of water.

It's near October, but still, the heat is a palpable thing. The air is a soup. The city smells. It's getting darker but only marginally cooler—one of those nights when there's lots of crime, and it's too hot to touch anyone. She's not hungry, it's impossible to

be hungry in this kind of weather, and she's not interested in anything. Even watching television at home sounds unpleasant. She
could take the train from right near here, but she decides to walk.
She can walk in a straight line, but walking down those stairs and
going underground is another thing she doesn't want to do. She's
read somewhere the temperature on the subway platform rises
from the heat of the arriving trains.

She rarely thinks much about the apartment on Eleventh
Street, and Sarah's right—it seems more remote than things that
happened a decade before they lived there. Memory is odd, in
that respect. It was small, that apartment, but it had its charms.
The bathroom had a pretty view, over an adjacent backyard, to a
community garden, one very well tended. The window was in the
shower, the windowsill where they kept their bottles of shampoo
and shaving cream. She could shower and look down at all that
green and feel something.

Her mother had said nothing, or very little, when she explained that Sarah was having a baby.

"That was fast, they just got married . . . when?"

Lauren had been able to picture her mother, doing the mental calculations. Her mother had not brought them anything to
that apartment on Eleventh Street, not even a plate of cupcakes,
though she had taken them out to the Japanese restaurant around
the corner one night, her, Sarah, Gabe. She remembers the look
on her mother's face when she realized that Gabe was probably
going back to the apartment with them, that there was absolutely
nothing—no sense of propriety—to stop him from doing so.
They'd fucked once, Lauren remembers, in that shower, Gabe be-

hind her, their hands braced on that windowsill, the two of them looking down at that community garden.

Her mother would do the math, of course, that is the sort of woman she is.

"She was pregnant before the wedding," Lauren explained. "Nothing planned. It just happened. So we kept it quiet."

Her mother offers only an *I see*. What Bella Brooks sees, what she has to say, it's all a mystery to Lauren. She feels implicated in this, that she scares her own mother, that her mother is so careful when they speak, so fearful of saying the wrong thing, being the wrong kind of person. Worse still, that she's not wrong. She loves her mother, but her mother's responses to things drive her crazy. She knew every thought going through her mother's mind as she told her about Sarah and her baby: disapproval—sex before marriage, a baby barely inside wedlock, the tacit lie to all those wedding guests. It's classless.

Then, maybe more to the point, what about her, Bella? Will she be a grandmother, will Lauren ever marry, have a baby? The one without the other might, might be forgivable. It's a shame to deny someone who'd be so gifted a grandmother the opportunity to be one.

Bella's disapproval would vanish, though, if she ever came to the city, saw Henry, saw Sarah's cool and charmless apartment, the nice sofa, the prettily wrapped presents. Certainly Sarah's the daughter she always dreamed of, the daughter she thought she'd be getting. Lauren's annoyed by her mother, yes, but always feels appropriately guilty about the fact that her mother annoys her.

Lauren is supposed to call Rob. She'd told him she would, that morning, but now she doesn't want to. Has no interest in it, in hearing his voice, in talking to him, in trying to communicate to him what she wants or doesn't want to do, in hearing what he wants or doesn't want to do. What she wants is to walk, through the city, and think about nothing in particular. When she first lived here, in that apartment on Eleventh Street, sometimes she'd just walk for hours. She felt so proprietary about the city then, the city in which she'd previously always been just a visitor. In for the day, for school; in for the weekend, with Sarah. Then, at twenty-one, in for real, in this city, her city. It feels like a long time since she just walked around, not going anywhere in particular, making her way in the general direction of home, but free to stop if something—a slice of pizza, a folding table covered with used paperbacks—catches her eye.

Sarah thinks that long-ago abortion is causing her pain, after these many years. It's touching, and telling, very Sarah. For all her money, all her sophistication, all her worldliness, there's something so naive about her. For Lauren's second abortion, which she's never told Sarah about, she went with Gabe; the same clinic, where she'd had a nice experience, or a nonhorrible experience. It was at the end of things, Gabe asking her to marry him, trying to convince her to do this with him, have a baby, make a life, that it would work, that it would be wonderful. She couldn't make him understand: that she knew it never would.

"I'm not supposed to pressure you, or question your choices." Gabe had a huge, very prominent Adam's apple. He was so much taller than her it was right at her eye level. "But Lauren."

That second time was harder, she admits that. Gabe, tears in the corners of his eyes. A good man, a great man for someone else. He'd gone out to get maxi pads, sorbet. He still asked her about getting married, even after, but with less optimism, with something like heartbreak. If it wouldn't have worked before that day, it certainly wouldn't have worked after. From that moment on, nothing between them was the same. Sarah doesn't know any of this, no one does—a secret you keep from your closest friend is one you share with no one. And she is that, after all this time, isn't she, Sarah, her closest friend?

It's the sort of evening that makes you feel very small in the world. Maybe she will give up the apartment and sell the cute little vintage sofa and go to Portland, maybe she'll buy a dog, and learn to drive stick, and become a vegan. Maybe she'll stay here and marry Rob and have a baby and time it to the birth of Sarah's next baby and their children will be best friends just as they are best friends and every Sunday they'll get together for a big, communal dinner, a roast chicken, on colorful porcelain plates. Sarah thinks anything is possible, but of course, for Sarah, anything is possible. Lauren has never quite believed that.

Lauren is not Sarah, and Rob is not Dan. There's not going to be a fairy-tale wedding at a mansion; there's not going to be a happy, healthy heir to the throne, or the family fortune, anyway. She's a different person, they are different people. She knows what she wants to do, after all. There's a movie theater on Sixty-Sixth Street, an artsy one, but there's a stupid-enough movie playing, so she goes inside, takes her seat, turns her phone off, and watches the movie.

The baby eats, dozes, complains, burps, a little of the milk, un-digested, spilling out of his soft, gummy mouth and onto Sarah's shirt. There's a washcloth somewhere around, but she ignores the wet spit-up, hushes him, calms him, and he's asleep. She places him in the bassinet, carefully, then sighs with relief. The apart-ment is mostly tidy. She dumps the cold coffee from Lauren's mug, runs the dishwasher. The steady thrum of the dishwasher is so reassuring. She takes a shower, stripping out of her milk-scented clothes, running the water lukewarm, gingerly soaping her tits, which were bloody only a week ago, horrifyingly. Women are raised to be comfortable with blood, but you never expect to see the stuff on your breasts.

Sarah considers her naked body in the mirror, after the shower. One of the disadvantages of this particular bathroom, a note she'd pass on to the developers if ever she met them: Few people want a huge mirror to confront them as they step out of the shower. Her breasts are enormous, even though Henry's only just done the hard work of depleting the supply of milk therein. Her hips are wider than they were before, than they were a year ago, and what she knows but doesn't quite want to admit is that they're this way forever; she can stick to whole grains and lean meat for the next ten years but nothing will make her very bones shift. At least her vagina looks less swollen, less purple, and the discharge has stopped altogether. Her physician recommended some exer-cises, starting to urinate, then stopping; it's meant to forestall fu-ture incontinence. She's horrified but also mystified; did Lulu go through this? She can never ask her, of course.

Her hair looks good. It's always been thick, but the pregnancy seems to have tamed it somehow, and of course, it's always looked its best right out of the shower, or while in the pool, wet, as one mass, tucked demurely behind her ears. She's always felt her ears were nice, and overlooked. Not everyone has nice ears. This body. This body Dan wanted to possess, and together they made a baby, asleep right now in the very next room. She tells herself that he's alive, that he's well, though some instinct in her tells her, every so often, that the baby is dead, that she needs to rush to his side. Either this will pass, or it never will. This is motherhood.

Dan is home. She steps out of the bathroom, her body hidden in the robe, her hair hidden in the towel. This always makes her feel terribly old, when her hair is wrapped up in terrycloth; she hates for Dan to see her this way.

"Hi there." Dan's mouth is full of baby carrots.

"Hi yourself." She kisses him on the lips, gently. "How was work?"

"Work was work," he says. "How were the festivities?"

"Festive."

"I see you had a good haul there. Presents galore."

"I should write the thank-you notes tonight, while I'm thinking about it." She has some, stashed in the desk drawer. It won't take too long.

"Society won't collapse if you wait a night," Dan says. "How's the little man?"

"He's good." She smiles, an involuntary response at even the thought of Henry. "He was the hit of the party."

"Naturally. Those good looks. How could he not be?"

"You should have seen it, though." She tries to paint the picture for him, but knows she's failing. "Amina held him, Mom held him, and he was just so chill and happy. He's a people person."

"Your dad, I think." Dan pops another baby carrot into his mouth. "It's in his blood."

"Still, he's the best, right? Our baby is the best."

"Our baby is the best. Can I go look at him?" Dan knows to ask permission.

"As long as you tiptoe. Seriously, wake him and I'm sending you to the pharmacist for estrogen shots. You can feed him yourself." She unwinds the towel from her hair, which flops down unhappily. The hummus is drying and cracking like mud in the blue enameled bowl. There's a stack of napkins, unused, and a bowl of chocolates, wrapped in gold foil, from a box sent by the staff at the store, a box of chocolates to celebrate a new baby, how incongruous, though it's the thought that counts. She should clean up. She should dry her hair, put on some comfortable clothes, make them something for dinner, nothing elaborate; there's a box of baby spinach that could easily become a salad, there's half of a rotisserie chicken inside the fridge that could easily become two sandwiches. Dinner, on plates, with napkins, at the table, or on the coffee table, a glass of water for her, a glass of wine for Dan, this should be easy. She has the wherewithal. He worked all day, he works every day; this is her work.

Dan creeps back into the living room, leaving the bedroom door open the barest crack. "That is one good-looking kid," he says.

"It can't be denied." She's in the kitchen. She'll dress later. She pulls the spinach from the box, using her hands; it's been rinsed, right? She drops it into a big wooden bowl, douses it with olive oil, looks for the half lemon she knows is around there somewhere. She's forever cutting new lemons when there's already a cut half rolling around in the fridge. She unearths one, from behind the jar of mustard; gets both, and the mayonnaise, and the chicken. She rips the skin from the carcass, tosses it into the sink, pulls off fistfuls of the flesh.

"How was Lulu?"

"She's herself. A very pleased grandmother. I'm not sure I would have predicted that."

"You wouldn't have?" Dan's typing on his phone.

She slides a bottle of wine across the counter toward Dan, then the wine key, then a glass, one of the set they received as a wedding gift, from her cousin Tatiana, she thinks. They're massive, these glasses, you could keep goldfish in them, and though they're quite expensive, Sarah believes in using their best things in their everyday life. It makes things seem more special.

"Thanks." Dan pries the foil off the top of the bottle. "I think doting grandmother—excuse me, Mamina—is the role Lulu was born to play, frankly." He sits on the stool on the other side of the counter, sighing as he does.

"Tired?"

"We're prepping Topoforimax for the final round of tests. We've been back and forth about a million times with the ethicists about the test, and of course, we're getting a lot of pressure to rush this one."

"This one is diabetes?" She can barely remember.

"Topical insulin." Dan pours the wine into the glass, peers down into the bowl of it suspiciously.

"The patch." She nods. She runs the knife roughly over the chicken, dumps it into a bowl, scoops in mayonnaise, studies it, tosses in more. A few flakes of sea salt, some pepper, some mustard, a stir. There's dill, she remembers, pulls some of the fragrant fluff from the stalk, doesn't bother chopping, just drops it into the mix. There's two-thirds of a baguette, and she finds the serrated knife, slices a segment of the bread, halves that, then splits it. She spoons the chicken salad into the bread, replaces the top on the bottom half, pushes down on it, forcing out the air. It's still resilient, the bread, so she takes a clean kitchen towel from the drawer by the stove, drapes it over the two sandwiches, balances the heaviest cast-iron casserole on top of it.

"I have some news, though," Dan says.

"Oh?"

"I have to go to Minneapolis for the final phase of the test," he says. "It won't be until November, but Doctor Inglis had to drop out, and there's no one else."

"Well, if you have to go, you have to go." She squeezes the half lemon into the palm of her hand, catching the seeds in the crevices between fingers, tossing the sticky pips in the general direction of the sink. Since Henry, Botswana has been forgotten. Even Minneapolis now sounds to her as far away as the moon. She dips her lemony hands into the spinach, tosses it, working her fingers over the oily leaves. She shakes them clean, washes them quickly, pauses, listening: Is that the baby? No, nothing.

"I'll fly back, weekends, of course."

"So much flying," she says. "Back and forth. If you need to stay, you should. You should get some downtime. Find a nice hotel, order room service, the whole thing. You don't want to spend every weekend at the airport."

"We'll see. November in Minneapolis." Dan yawns. "I'm not exactly thrilled about it."

Pecans. She remembers there are pecans. She breaks the seal on the airtight canister, snaps pecans in half and tosses them on top of the spinach. "What about Thanksgiving? Mom mentioned maybe doing it in the country this year."

"In the country?"

"A new tradition," she says. "Grandchild playing in the leaves while Huck bastes."

"I'm all for new traditions," he says. "Though I don't know that he'll be up for frolicking in the leaves this year. We'll be lucky if he can hold his head up by then."

Sarah loosens and then reties the sash around the robe. She doesn't want to go into the bedroom, wake Henry, so she'll dress later, or just slip into bed naked, the sheets cool against her skin, and she'll pull Henry close to her when he cries; it'll be easier for his little mouth to find her breast. She won't even need to wake up. It's weirdly second nature already, and she knows she's lucky that it hasn't been too hard, or too painful. She lifts the dish off the sandwich. It needs a good forty minutes to really compress, but never mind. There's a traditional sandwich made this way, tuna, lots of olives, oil, and bread—something she had in France, once, as a child, on vacation with her parents. She's forgotten it until now. You wrap the sandwich in plastic, compress it for hours, eat it at the seaside. She'll do that, before the summer's out—they can pack a picnic, drive to Long Island; Amina's mother has a place in

Quogue. Sarah puts the sandwiches on plates, divides the salad in half. Forks; no need for knives. She should have put capers in the chicken, but never mind. She carries the plates out of the kitchen and into the living room, places them on the coffee table, a twinge as she bends, still some soreness there, right at the hip.

"Dinner and a movie," Dan says. He stands, picks up the glass, walks to the sofa. "Thanks, babe."

She shrugs. "It's nothing special." Salt, pepper. She goes back to the kitchen for the saltbox, the pepper mill—a matching set, a wedding gift from Dan's aunt and uncle. She brings these to the coffee table.

Dan's switched on the television, volume turned low. "Stupid sitcom, reality show about cake, reality show about hairdressing, reality show about singing?"

"I think that's dancing, actually, that one. I vote for cake."

"Cake it is, then." Dan flicks the volume up, just a bit, brings the sandwich to his mouth. "Delicious, babe. Thank you."

She plucks one of the pecans off the salad. Are they a superfood? She can never remember what the superfoods are, or what they promise. Her hips do not want her to sit on the floor, as she normally would. She perches on the edge of the chair across from the sofa. It's leather, midcentury, and she's recently decided it's not her taste. She should send it to the store, it's the kind of thing that always finds a buyer quickly. She takes a bite of the sandwich. It would have been better with capers. Through the open bedroom door, she hears the snuffle, the tiny wail with which Henry announces he's awake. He'll be wet, and he'll be hungry, too.

"Be right back," she says.

Trucks—Sarah said he likes trucks. But a truck T-shirt? A book about trucks? A puzzle depicting trucks? A realistic, German-made plastic scale model of a truck, or a handcrafted hunk of wood that somehow communicates the essence of a truck? A little plastic package with five metal trucks inside or a set of pajamas emblazoned with trucks or a toothbrush that comes with truck toothpaste or a box of markers that's shaped like a truck or a bouncy red rubber ball with a picture of a fire truck on it or a green plastic truck that's meant to go in the sandbox or to the beach and comes with a little shovel and a tiny rake? Lauren doesn't know what a five-year-old boy likes, or thinks about, or cares about. And she doesn't know it for certain, but it's reasonable to guess that this particular five-year-old boy has a fairly significant arsenal of toy trucks, truck books, truck clothes, truck ephemera, at home.

She settles on a truck made of wood, a jaunty green semi, pulling a simple wood car trailer, bearing four little wooden cars, but as this is fairly inexpensive, she also buys a pair of books, texts, taxonomies, really: photographs and jargon (what child needs to know about a goose-neck trailer truck?) but the girl at the book-store swears they're very popular. She wraps them in paper that's bright blue with white polka dots, and taken in sum the three packages look alluring and bountiful, particularly when stuffed into a little paper bag, tied, for good measure, with a single, bob-bing balloon. Henry will probably be diverted by the balloon and bag, mostly, in accordance with the law that deems the packaging more interesting than the contents.

The party is at their house. All that space—why wouldn't it be? And that backyard, a simple rectangular lot, but excavated and carved and contoured and polished by the previous owners (landscape architects both). An arbor wrapped in vines bridges the kitchen and the yard. She's sat there with Sarah and Dan, din-ner, candlelit, a charmed summer evening, and looked down into the spill of all that yard, the stone terrace, planted with herbs, that runs the length of the garden, the single pine at the very back, making it possible to pretend their neighbor's house doesn't exist. She's been there for dinner with Matt; she's been there for dinner with Thom. Sarah liked Matt; Sarah did not like Thom. In the end, Lauren liked neither of them, and now they're both mostly forgot-ten, footnotes, background in different, more important memories: dropping by with Christmas presents for Henry, bringing over a bagful of cookbooks for no particular reason, eating spatchcocked chicken Dan grilled under two aluminum foil-wrapped bricks, even the very first time she saw the house. Matt had driven her over. It was March, and the trees were naked, and the house was empty, so the windows were bare; thus, the rooms were drenched in pale light, and the place seemed holy, blessed, massive beyond reason. Matt, anyway, had been impressed.

The toy store is not far from their place, so she walks. It is sticky—New York in August, the air dense and swampy, what little breeze there is hot and ineffectual. The asphalt looks shiny, like it's melting, and the garbage cans on the corners, overflowing with discarded Popsicle wrappers and other effluvia, smell terrible. The tote bag weighs heavily on her shoulder—she's brought her most recent book, for Sarah, a monograph on creative spaces for children: playrooms with chalkboard walls, an old ballroom fitted out with a trampoline and basketball court, bunk beds carved to look like a pirate ship. Silly, but it had been fun to work on.

Lauren rings the bell, waits, then, hearing nothing, knocks, loudly but hopefully not insistently. She's thirsty.

She can see Dan's sweaty face through the door, distorted by the warp of the glass. He gives an impatient wave before pulling the door open. "Lauren," he says. "Hey!"

He sounds mildly out of breath. He's gained weight, Dan, a gradual process, over the years, but heavier, now, he looks more like himself, like the person he's always been in the process of becoming. Sweating has made his hair a little unkempt. He's wearing a blue polo shirt, so faded at the collar, it must be a well-loved one, and khaki shorts, swollen with pockets. "Hi!"

"We were wondering where you were," he says. "Hot, right? Come in."

"August," she says. The house is cool; the previous owners installed central air-conditioning, a rarity in these century-old brownstones. It's very quiet inside.

"August," he says, closing the door behind her forcefully, shutting the month of August outside where it belongs. "Sarah's just tidying up."

"Tidying up?" She follows him down the stairs to the basement. The steps lead directly to the kitchen, mostly white, very bright.

Sarah is standing at the island. "You made it!" she says. "Sorry, this is disgusting." She's scraping some sort of brown goop into the sink. She grimaces, rinses her hands, dries them. She walks toward her, waddles really, hugs her, as much as is possible, given her incredible girth.

"Wow," Lauren says without thinking. "You look—great." She does though; Sarah, hair pulled back, pregnant and fat, like a lady of the canyon, like a painting from Northern Europe's Renaissance, all creamy skin and sly smiles.

"I look massive, you mean," Sarah says. "I know. Six weeks left, too. I think he's going to be a basketball player."

"Where's Henry?" She looks around—the kitchen, too, is quiet. There are no sounds from the playroom, behind them.

"Henry's asleep," Sarah says. "The party ended at twelve."

"Shit," she says. "I thought it was at two."

Sarah shrugs. "He'll probably sleep another hour. It's fine. This way we can talk."

"I missed the whole party?" She feels foolish.

"A kid's party," Sarah says. "You didn't miss anything. Henry's worn-out, from all that running around, all that sugar. Plus all the stupid presents."

"Sugar?" Lauren drops the parcels onto the kitchen counter.

"Cake's in the fridge. It's so hot outside it was melting. And there's ice cream. A ridiculous amount, actually. Help yourself."

"I'm going to finish up those e-mails," Dan says. "Lauren, say good-bye before you go." He trots back up the stairs.

"I can wash those," Lauren says.

"I won't even argue." Sarah perches precariously on a stool. "Just rinse. We'll run the dishwasher."

"I'll load," Lauren says. "After cake." There's still more than half the cake left, a sprawling chocolate thing in the shape of a fire truck. She takes it from the fridge, sets it on the kitchen island, opens the freezer door, takes out the chocolate ice cream. "Do you want some?"

"Why the fuck not," Sarah says. "I can't possibly get any bigger."

"You're eating for two, enjoy it," she says. She serves: modest slices of cake, massive mounds of ice cream. She scrapes the paper carton clean, tosses the container in the garbage. The spoons are silver, incredibly shiny. She tastes it. It tastes exactly how she wants it to taste. It's so good she leans into the island. Standing across from Sarah, as though they were bartender and patron: This feels confessional, or therapeutic. She's moved to ask Sarah to tell her all her problems, though here, in this beautifully cold kitchen, with cake, with shining silver spoons, she seems not to have any. "Sorry I missed the party."

"You don't have kids," Sarah says. "You're on human time."

"I just thought you said two," she says.

"It's better this way, we can talk. I haven't seen you in forever."

"So another boy, huh?" Sarah had mentioned it before; Lauren can't remember when. "Is Henry excited?"

"He is," she says. "Baby brother. He talks about him constantly. We'll see how he feels about sharing a room, though."

"Sharing a room?" Lauren gestures at the ceiling, at the many square feet that unfold overhead. "You must have plenty of space."

"The baby will be in our room for a while, but Dan's moving his office down a floor, and we're getting an au pair, so she'll have the top floor to herself. I felt guilty about putting the baby so far away, up there with her like a servant, so we're going to make that other room a guest room."

"I see," Lauren says.

"I didn't want him to get that younger kid complex, you know? You made me sleep upstairs with the help, that sort of thing."

"Au pair? Sounds sort of sexy."

"She better not be," Sarah says. "I'm hoping for someone moody and bespectacled, who likes to read poetry and go to the museum every weekend. We'll see."

Lauren tries and fails to imagine Dan seducing a French adolescent. "Are you ready?"

"Ready as I'll ever be, I suppose. Henry's starting school, so I'll be able to devote some attention to this one. It won't be the same as with Henry but it never is, I think. It's just not possible."

"Right. I'm the oldest, remember, so I got the bulk of my parents' nurturing." Lauren licks her spoon clean.

"And look how you turned out!"

"So the au pair will au pair—and you'll . . ." Lauren pauses. She doesn't know how Sarah does it, how Sarah hasn't lost her mind. Primed for a career doing whatever it is she does and then—to spend years just wiping bottoms. Lauren knows that's how it's done, she just can't believe it.

"It's enough work for three, let alone two," Sarah says. "In my fantasy, she'll do the drop-off with Henry in the morning, so I can deal here. Sleep. Cook. Maybe go to the gym, can you imagine? Then I'll do the pickup while she gets the baby to nap. I thought maybe Henry and I could start a mother-son date tradition or something? Afternoons at the bakery or the playground. I want to make sure both the boys get their alone time with me. I've read that can be a problem when you have the second."

"It'll be fine," Lauren says. "You'll find a way. You always do." She pauses. "Something's different in here."

"We redid the playroom," she says. "And new floors there and in here."

"New floors. I knew there was something. Are these reclaimed?" Lauren's been at the design imprint long enough to recognize reclaimed wood. The floors feel very solid underfoot.

"They are reclaimed," Sarah says. "A barn in Pennsylvania. I don't know anything about them. Devin, our architect, he insisted there's a big difference."

"They're strong," Lauren says. "But they have that patina, that spirit—it makes the house look less new, more like it's been around forever. It's nice."

"He promised that two kids wouldn't be able to destroy them, anyway." Sarah pushes her empty bowl away. "You want to see the playroom?"

"Sure," Lauren says. She puts her bowl on top of Sarah's and places them in the sink. She follows the mass of Sarah's body, moving slowly across the floor, which is clean and toy-free. There's a big dining table, rustic, simple, set with benches, between the island and the pocket doors, which are set into the sort of elaborately carved walls common in houses of this era. The doors move open effortlessly, and quietly, on their casters.

The playroom is bright; though they're in the basement, they're not so far below street level, and the windows are big.

One wall is floor-to-ceiling shelves: toys, books, framed photos, even a miniature library ladder that reaches to the uppermost shelf. There's a sofa, large and low-slung, off white, inviting a stain but surprisingly clean. There's a small child-size desk and chair, and a child-size easel, and a child-size guitar and a child-size drum set. There are paintings on construction paper, framed in simple white frames, dozens of them, hung on the facing wall. On each, Sarah's written Henry's name, and the date the artist completed the work. The room is quiet, cool, beautiful. There are many trucks, but Lauren does not see the truck she has brought. The room is perfect, of course. She feels sheepish about the book she's brought with her. This room could have been in there.

"Let's sit." Sarah eases herself onto the sofa. "I can't handle the stairs right now. Maybe I should start sleeping down here."

The sofa is firm, but comfortable. Lauren thinks it must be stuffed with actual horsehair, a rarity in this day and age.

"So, how's work?"

"It's good, actually." This is true but still feels like a surprise. "I'm producing a book with this queeny old designer who's about a hundred, you should see his rooms. Gold andirons, hand-painted wallpaper, murals on the ceilings, that kind of thing."

"Do you miss cookbooks?"

"I don't," Lauren says. "I think I was ready for this change. Enough of the best turkey burgers ever. The one-hour dinner party. I was done. Now, I'm developing titles, reaching out to new writers and soliciting designers. And we're doing well. Actually making money, in books, which is nice."

Sarah yawns. "I'm sorry. I'm not yawning because you're boring, I'm yawning because my brain is very tired."

"Not offended," Lauren says. "You're pregnant."

"So any other news?" Sarah gives her a knowing look. "Come on."

Lauren considers telling her about David, has considered telling her for weeks now—fine, it's months—but hasn't. David is still secret. David is still hers. If she does talk about him now, she's worried the real truth will come spilling out of her. There's been Gabe, there's been Rob, there's been Matt, there's been Thom; all good, all fine, all happy enough memories, if she overlooks the worse parts, which is easier as time goes by. The worse parts slip away, with her knowledge of algebra and the world capitals.

It's not that David is different, though he is that, it's that her feeling about the thing is different. She can see what she could never see before: the future. Marriage can't be musical chairs; grab a mate when the music stops. The music stops, for most of the women she's known, somewhere around thirty-three, and the marriages begin. And six years from then, right about now, in fact, as the cycle dictates: the divorces. She tried to see this—with Gabe, with Rob, with Matt: the future. It never came into focus. It never seemed possible, as much as they, and Sarah, and her mother, and her father, might have wanted it to. She still hasn't introduced her parents to David, but curiously enough, she wants to.

"I'm ready for a vacation," she says. "I'm over this summer."

"We're going away on Monday. We're renting a house in East Hampton with Fiona and her kids. Family vacation. I even convinced Dan to take three days off, but only three, because he's worried about the paternity leave coming up. But we'll all be together those three days, and actually Henry and I are going for ten. You should come out."

"Fiona. She's got kids plural, then?"

Sarah nods. "Owen's just a little younger than Henry, Eliza is almost two now."

"So cute," Lauren says. "You guys should have synced up your second borns, too, you could have had family vacations together forever."

Sarah is quiet. "We did, actually. Not by design, but it happened." She pauses. "I lost the baby."

Lauren looks at her. Sarah looks calm, her posture, her demeanor bearing no real relationship to the words she's just said. "Oh God, I'm sorry. I had no idea. When was this?"

"I never told you." Sarah exhales deeply. "I don't know why, to be honest. I just. It was so bad, Lolo."

Lauren pulls her feet up under herself, pivots in the sofa so she's almost sitting on Sarah's lap. She touches her arm, tentatively. Sarah, so fat, so solid, seems fragile. "Were you far along?"

She'd been sixteen weeks. It was old hat, pregnancy. She threw herself into it, and it felt as if it had been longer because she'd gotten so big, so quickly. In utero, Henry had cooperated, blossoming after she walked down the aisle, but the second one had made her presence known early. Sarah had dug out some of the less offensive pregnancy clothes, stored in a plastic box in the basement. She'd bought books for Henry, books about being a big brother, about how love isn't diminished, but rather amplified, when you add another person into the mix.

She'd told her parents, she'd told Fiona, she'd told the nanny. She'd been on the verge of calling Lauren, actually—it was on her to-do list—when, one otherwise unremarkable Tuesday, she woke up feeling different, somehow. The baby hadn't really started moving, but Sarah felt a stillness there, inside her taut belly. The doctor asked her to come in, but it was the radiologist, whom she didn't even know, who gently placed a hand on Sarah's knee and confirmed that there was no heartbeat.

One of those things. They had to dilate her. They used seaweed, of all insane things. The twenty-first century and that's how it's done. She went home, came back, and it was all a terrible mockery of what had happened four years earlier, with Henry: the room hushed, the pain nonexistent, the final moment not an anticlimax even. Dan held her hand, and she cried. She declined to look at the baby, declined the offer of an autopsy. She went home and, two days later, took the big brother books out of the pile by Henry's bedside.

"Four months. Showing and everything. Then, one morning, spontaneous."

Lauren's mind races, trying to latch on to the right thing to say, trying to give voice to all the questions that come up. "But why didn't you tell me? This is terrible. I could have——. I don't know what I could have done. But I could have done something. I could have tried."

"I know." Sarah squeezes Lauren's forearm. "It's not you. I wanted it to be over. I wanted to come home, and just be here, with Henry, and Dan, and be quiet. I thought I was pushing it, with the universe. I thought I was asking too much. I just wanted to . . . to never think about it again."

Lauren thinks, immediately, of Christopher. Ghost brother, the lost boy Lulu never talks about.

"Hey, we got through it," Sarah says. Another squeeze of the arm. "I should have called, I'm sorry."

"I should have been there," Lauren says. "I'm a terrible friend."

"You're not. You're my best friend. It's fine. Here I am. Look at me." She spreads her arms open wide to indicate the bulk of her body. "He's fine in there. It's all okay."

"I'm so sorry, though." Lauren reaches up to take Sarah's hand, which is cool, and soft. "I don't know what to say. You're so. Fine. But I know you. I know that you must not have been fine. I wish you'd told me."

"Just one of those things, that's what the doctor kept saying. *Sarah, it's just one of those things.*"

"One of those fucking horrible things."

Sarah is quiet. "I didn't know, Lolo. I didn't know if I could call you. With that. I didn't know if you'd . . . if you'd understand. No. I knew you'd understand. I just didn't . . ."

Lauren gets it. She does. She's offended, but it washes away quickly. She understands why Sarah would keep this from her, would keep this to herself. And she understands now that she can't be mad, that she can't shift the focus, from Sarah to herself. This is one of those moments: real life happening. She has to take it for what it is. She looks around the room. The books on the shelves are arranged by height and by color. "You could have told me," she says, as gently as she can. "But you're telling me now."

Sarah looks away. "I didn't want to bother you."

"You say you're done being sad about this," Lauren says. "So let's be happy. You're going to have a baby. It's a happy ending."

"It is a happy ending," Sarah says.

Lauren smiles. "I brought a present," she says. "Trucks."

"Henry will love it, I'm sure. But I apologize in advance if he's not thankful enough. He got so many presents. It was like a religious experience for him, ripping open all that paper."

"As long as he remembers me," Lauren says. "He'll remember me, right?"

"Auntie Lauren? Yes. He'll remember you." Sarah pauses. "But, if being remembered is a big concern, well, the surest way to deal with that is to come around more. You should. Actually. Come around more. I don't know why you don't."

"I'm here," Lauren says. Then, admitting: "You're right."

"I moved to fucking Brooklyn, Lauren," she says. "I'm right here, twenty minutes away."

"You got married and had a kid and now you're having another one and it's life, Sarah." They'll have this conversation forever. "Twenty-six years, I've known you. Here I am."

Sarah shrugs. "So, a year from now, at Henry's sixth birthday, you'll come over with Legos, or whatever six-year-old boys like, and we'll talk. But we could do it sooner."

"I know. I get wrapped up in being me," Lauren says. "You're not missing anything." Now she can't tell Sarah about David. It'll just confirm Sarah's suspicion that something is being kept from her, even if that's not what's happening, or not what Lauren means to happen. She smiles, at the thought of David, his bright eyes, his fidgety hands. Sarah will like him, Sarah will love him, when they meet.

"You're sure it's not because you're so busy with hot guys and amazing nights out that the last thing you want to do is come to Park Slope and drink white wine in my backyard?"

"Come to your mansion and sit in your beautiful garden and drink white wine? Are you joking? I will do that, anytime. I'll remember. That we should do that."

"I am lucky," Sarah says, looking around the beautiful, quiet room. "I know it. Let me ask you a question."

"Shoot."

"Do you want a glass of wine?"

"I'd have a glass of wine," Lauren says.

"Good," Sarah says. "Because I want two sips of your glass of wine. Two. Maybe three."

———·———

July was rainy, August sunny, so the vines draped across the arbor are full, green, alive. There's lots of shade, but still, sliding the door open, there's a blast of heat, as might accompany the opening of an oven. Sarah wiggles back into a chair, tries to ignore the weather. There's no point talking about it, anyway.

Ten little children, eight boys and two girls, red-faced, damp-haired, have ridden their little metal scooters home, gift bags (temporary tattoos, bottles of bubbles) in tow, and presumably ten other sets of parents are right now enjoying the respite of their child's unexpected afternoon nap. After all that exertion, that running and screaming, Henry, compliant, had stripped out of his shirt, wiggled into his sheets, his room cool and quiet, and started to snore. They have, maybe, another twenty minutes.

Lauren has the glass and the bottle, only a third empty, as few of the parents drank at the party. She tips some of the yellowish wine into the glass, sips it.

"Mmm," she says, approvingly. "Here." Lauren hands the glass to her.

Sarah takes a tiny sip. It's fruity, sweet, like biting into an apple that's been soaking in alcohol. She shouldn't, after what she's been through—losing the pregnancy, which is how she thinks of it, a pregnancy, not a child. It was the darkest time in her life and made her realize how light the rest of it has been. She knew that, of course, would never have described it as anything else, her life, but still.

Without Henry, she'd have given into it: the grief, the darkness, the sadness. The memory is both distant and fresh, in the past and right there with her. Sarah feels better that she's told Lauren. She hadn't told her, because she thought that would make it easier to get through. But not telling Lauren made it worse. Now, though, she does feel—if not better, lighter, a sense that things are right between them.

Something about being around Lauren makes her want to indulge in vice. She's dying for a cigarette, which she can't quite believe. She can't think of the last time she's had a cigarette.

"Well, that's fucking great," she says. She hands the wineglass back. "Take it away." It's very big in Lauren's hands, very big near her face, which is small, delicate, lovely. Her eyes look darker than Sarah remembers. She seems good, Lauren. She seems happy.

"This yard is incredible," Lauren says.

"It was the real reason we bought the house," Sarah says. "It's so thoughtful, the way they did it. I guess it makes a difference, when you're an expert. You just see things in a different way. It would never in a million years have occurred to me to do this." It's true. The asymmetry of the yard, the way it's all chopped up into zones, runs counter to what she'd have thought would make the small garden feel bigger, but it's brilliant, and the place feels like it just goes on forever. And here, in the middle of it, the big birthday present: a swing set. Custom made, to save them the trek to the playground a few blocks over, good for just running out and getting a quick bit of play in. It's very simple and slender, as not to take up too much space: a pair of swings, one for a baby, one for a big kid, though the bucket seat for baby can be replaced. The woodworker who built it showed her how easy it will be, when the time comes. The frame of the swing doubles as a ladder, which Henry had been more delighted about than the swing, actually, climbing, reaching up toward the sky, grabbing at nothing, lost in his own, fluid reality.

"It's wonderful," Lauren says. "When you go on vacation to the Hamptons, I should come here to stay. Central air, this backyard, I can't ask for more from a trip."

"You should come out to see us," Sarah says. "The house is huge. And without the husbands there it's going to be so empty. Take the train out. There's a pool." She's looking forward to the ten days on Long Island, the sweet coolness of the evening breeze, the silence of the afternoons. She's booked some time with a real estate agent while they're out there, just in case. She always has a good time with Fiona, but loves the idea of Lauren there with them.

"I should," Lauren says. "It's not easy, this time of year. It's summer and a lot of people are out, but there's still a demanding production schedule in place. September is a huge month for us."

"Of course," Sarah says. Maybe it's for the best. She's not entirely certain, but she thinks it may be the case that Fiona is not that fond of Lauren. But Fiona is excellent at pretending.

"Say, how are Huck and Lulu? I was sort of looking forward to seeing them at this party."

"You just missed them. Huck likes to make a big fuss about commuting out here from the city. They're the same."

"Of course they are," Lauren says. "Tell them I said hi, though. I'll send your mom my new book, when it's out. She'll get a kick out of it."

"How's your family?"

"The same," Lauren says. "They're fine. Ben and Alexis are having a baby."

"Your parents must be psyched." Sarah doesn't say what she thinks, which is that Lauren must be relieved that her brother is taking the pressure off her. She's never fully understood the complexities of Lauren's relationship with her parents. She's met them. She remembers them as perfectly pleasant. She can't understand, but then, unhappy families, et cetera.

"Oh, they are," Lauren says. "They're planning a baby shower that's only slightly less complicated than a royal wedding." She takes another sip of the wine.

The door to the kitchen slides open, and Henry emerges from the house, face still flush with sleep, skin marked with lines from his bedding. His hair, thick, so like his father's, stands on end. He frowns. "Mommy," he says, his voice hoarse.

"Hi, baby," she says. She opens her arms and Henry, aware that she can't leap up to embrace him, wiggles over toward her. His body is hot, and soft. He smells wonderful. "How was your nap?"

"Good." He yawns. An automatic response; good manners. "Mommy, can I swing?"

How she lives for it, this *Mommy*. Soon, too soon, it will be *Mom*, then, impatient, angry even. *Mom!* Doors slamming. Hard to imagine, though maybe it won't be that way. She wasn't that way, was she, as a teenager? Sarah can barely remember. It seems unimportant, now, what she was like; the only thing that matters, anymore, is what he will be like, him and his brother. The baby startles, kicks. She has a theory he does that at the sound of his big brother's voice.

"It's so hot," she says. "We should get you a cup of water." He looks up at her, his eyes dark, bottomless, under those eyelashes. He's beautiful in the way she never has been. And it's his birthday. Let him swing.

"Let's swing," she says. She heaves herself up, bracing palms against the iron table, a hand-me-down from Lulu, the one that sat poolside in Connecticut throughout her youth. She wonders if Lauren recognizes it. The table scrapes against the concrete. "Lauren, you coming?"

"Right behind you," she says. She refills the glass, and they follow Henry, racing, awake now, down toward the swing set.

He leaps onto the seat, face pure joy. "Push me," he says. "Push, push."

And she does. The grass beneath her bare feet, swollen and fat, she pushes, back and forth, back and forth, stepping aside slightly, to keep the swing from banging into her belly. Henry laughs, such a sweet sound, and she keeps pushing, back and forth, up and down.

Thanks to Julie Barer and her colleagues at the Book Group, and to Megan Lynch and Kate Cassaday and their colleagues at Ecco and Harper Canada. Thanks to Dan Chaon, Alexander Chee, Mira Jacob, Edan Lepucki, and Emma Straub. Thank you to Vern Yip and Craig Koch, for their generous hospitality. Thank you to Dr. Bhoomi Brahmbhatt, for her expert insight. Thank you to Jennifer Romolini (for "groupthink"), Kristina Dechter (my first reader), Emily Hsieh (for the think tank), Samantha Turner (for the mascara), Lauren Whitehouse (for the ice), and Amanda Guttman and David Tamarkin (for everything else). Thank you to the weirdos on Twitter who kept me company while I worked.

I wrote this book mostly between the hours of 8:00 P.M. and 3:00 A.M.; this would have been unthinkable but for David Land, who shouldered the responsibilities (financial, parental, you name it) that I shirked for many months. All people should have a partner so generous; all children should have a parent so devoted. How I got so lucky, I will never know.